Praise for Mickey Clement's
The Irish Princess . . .

"A pleasingly told tale that touches the heart."
—*Kirkus Reviews*

"The sorrows and disappointments that come their way never overwhelm the underlying sense that we learn and grow from everything life brings us, good or bad."
—*Washington Post Book World*

"It is innocent without being naive; gentle without being sentimental; real without being harsh . . . a novel that celebrates life."
—*Troy (NY) Record*

"A love story set against the backdrop of a strong extended family."
—*The New York Times*

"I declare myself captivated. The Malloy family is brought to life so vividly . . . And they are so likeable. I wanted another hundred pages at least. This is a charming, moving, just plain wonderful book."
—Richard Selzer

THE IRISH PRINCESS

Mickey Clement

Aug 10/95

To Ann,
all my best.
Mickey Clement

BERKLEY BOOKS, NEW YORK

This is a work of fiction. Any references to historical events, to real people, living or dead, or to real locales are intended only to give the fiction a sense of reality and authenticity.

THE IRISH PRINCESS

A Berkley Book/published by arrangement with
G. P. Putnam's Sons

PRINTING HISTORY
G. P. Putnam's Sons edition/March 1994
Berkley edition/July 1995

ISBN: 0-425-14830-0

BERKLEY®
Berkley Books are published by The Berkley Publishing Group,
200 Madison Avenue, New York, New York 10016.
BERKLEY and the "B" design
are trademarks belonging to Berkley
Publishing Corporation.

PRINTED IN THE UNITED STATES OF AMERICA

10 9 8 7 6 5 4 3 2 1

For my parents,
Marjorie McDonough Flynn
and Charles F. Flynn

ACKNOWLEDGMENTS

I'd like to thank Ann Birstein and my fellow writers at the Writers on Writing Program at Barnard College for their suggestions and help when this work was taking shape, Dr. Michael Byrne of Long Island University for his technical expertise, Dr. Richard Selzer for his generous encouragement, and my family, John, Nell, Amy, and Johnny Clement, for their continuous love and support.

THE MALLOY FAMILY

John Malloy *m.* Bridget Hannaway

Pat *m.* Meg	Jim *m.* Mary	Dan *m.* Hildy	John *m.* Anna	Bridey *m.* Paul	**MIKE** *m.* **CLARE**
Gracie Raymond		Peter Gretchen	Jody Kathleen	Paulie Susan Colleen Erin Shannon Brian	**MAUREEN (Mo)** **MARGIE**

THE IRISH PRINCESS

Micky Clement

1

Uncle Pat

March 1964

❦

Meg

I lay awake, waiting for Pat's key to turn in the lock.
You would think after all these years of marriage I could
sleep without him by my side. Without his snoring, his
sometimes beery breath, his heat. You would think I'd
welcome the aloneness of the cold sheets. No, it wasn't
like that for me. I'm used to people, lots of people,
sometimes too many people, crowded into rooms that
are too small, drinking, eating, telling jokes, some off-
color, some about Jews, or Polacks, or coloreds, or telling stories about the old country, stories that their
grandparents had told to them.

When the call came, I was ready for it. I suppose
I'd been ready my whole life. Pat lived so hard, played
so hard. It was almost a relief, the knowing. What I'd
dreaded and knew would happen finally did.

I remembered that Raymond was sleeping over at
Peter's so I had to take Gracie with me. Jesus, I thought,
what am I going to tell the child? I grabbed her out of

1

bed and wrapped her in her Sunday coat. I didn't choose it for any reason. It was just there, the first thing I found in her tiny closet. I carried her out to the car. She made little noises. "Beary," she said, and I ran back in to find the toy. Imagine running back on a night like that for a toy. But I had to. I tossed Beary into the backseat and that kept Gracie quiet and then I drove like a madwoman through the empty streets of Troy, up Hoosick and then over Fifteenth. It was cold, so cold that even the street corners outside the bars were empty. The streetlights at the intersections were swaying in the wind and changing for no one except me.

I met them at the hospital, St. Mary's, thank the good Lord. I was happy for that. The sisters were kind, holding my hand, praying with me. And the priest had given Pat the Last Rites.

"He was already gone 'fore he got here, Margaret," Father O'Brien had said. I'd wished he hadn't called me Margaret. Mrs. Malloy would have been more respectful, or if not that, Meg. But Margaret, my saint's name. No one thinks of me as Margaret. Mike must have given them that name when they brought Pat in.

"We gave him the Last Rites, anyways, in hopes that his soul is lingerin'." The priest spoke with a tinge of the brogue and I thought, Pat would like to be ushered out with the sweet sound of the mother country. I pictured Pat's pure white soul floating nearby, as white as the bib that the sisters wear to hide their chests. Pat's soul, stainless because of confession, waiting over his tired body for that last blessing, and then flying up to

Jesus. I'd hoped that Father O'Brien was right.

The young man with the curly hair and big nose and thick glasses came over to me and took my right hand away from the sisters. He had a strange voice, deep and strong, for such a skinny body. He spoke in a downstate accent, probably Brooklyn, I thought. He must be the new Jewish doctor Bridey had told me about. Imagine a Jew happy to work at St. Mary's, surrounded by the flutterings of the sisters and the priests in their purple vestments giving the Last Rites. He took my other hand.

"Your husband froze to death, Mrs. Malloy."

"Jesus, Mary, and Joseph." My feet slipped away and I could feel hot vomit coming up from my stomach. Then black mud spilled into my eyeballs and that's all I remember about that terrible night.

Gracie

Before Daddy froze he used to make me popcorn every night and then we'd sit in his big green chair with the poofy pillows and he tole me stories.

The best story was how he used to jump on iceberks to ride down the Hudson River to Albany. His brothers and him used to wait by the shore till a big one with thick ice floated by and then they'd jump! He tole how they pushed with sticks or sometimes my grandma's broom to get away from shore.

My grandma's dead, too.

Then he'd say to me, Boy did I ever get a lickin', Gracie. When my ma found out about the iceberks she took our pants right down and spanked us with a strap! Gracie, don't you ever do anything so foolish as ridin' iceberks or you'll get a lickin', too, from me, my daddy said.

My daddy's family was so poor when they were kids that they had to share one egg for breakfast for six kids and no orange juice. At Christmas they got an orange in their stocking and that was all! On Christmas Santa brung me a Cathy Doll with yellow hair that grows. You pull real hard and then brush it and then it grows just like real persons hairs. I wonder if Daddy's hair will grow. I heard Peter, my big cousin, whispering to my brother, Raymond. His hair will grow, ya know, and his fingernails and toenails, too, and my brother said **SHUT UP** you big jerk you or I'll punch your stupid face in.

My Aunt Mary whispered to my momma. Meg, he looks just like he's sleepin'. I thought I could open his eyes when she said that. I thought if I could open his eyes he would wake up and not be dead anymore.

Daddy worked on the railroad and Momma tole us we would get penshun now. I think that's like penuns you get before First Holy Communion. Next year in second grade my sister will be Sister John Mary. I make First Communion in second grade and penuns, too. I get to wear a bride veil and a little bride dress just like the Barbies have with white fluffy lace. I wish my big girl cousins would get married so I could go to a real wedding. I could maybe be the flower girl and throw flowers all over the church. There might be as many flowers as here. The second-grade girls get flowers for their Communion from daddies. My momma says don't worry even if we are on railroad penshun she'll make sure I get flowers, too.

When I was really little I had bad dreams about Daddy falling off the train and down between the cars. They weren't really dreams because I was not sleeping. I would have them when I was alone in my bed. Momma said they were daymares not nightmares. I'd see Daddy falling under the big black wheels and then the train just sliding over him and *squish* and his head would come rolling at me and smiling and he says be a good girl for your momma, Gracie. I had those bad thoughts and I needed to smell my blankey and hold my Beary to make them go away.

When Momma woke me that night I knew something bad had happened. She made me put on my good dress coat over my jammies and carried me out to the car. When we got to that place I heard police cars and it was dark. Momma wouldn't let me go in with her. I sat out in the dark a long time. I was scared. I remembered that Frank Stein movie that Raymond took me to when Momma tole him he couldn't take me and I promised not ever to tell and so I couldn't say Momma I'm scared to stay here alone because of Frank Stein. I kept thinking the monster would come and get me and take me outta the car and up the hill and into the woods and then I'd get crushed, too. I wanted my daddy and I called DADDY DADDY and if only he could come and hold me on his lap with his big arms I would be safe from Frank Stein.

I sat in that car a long time before anyone got me. It was Uncle Mike.

He picked me up and he held me. He smelled like Daddy, too.

Gracie honey, there, there, I didn't know you was out here or I'da got you sooner Uncle Mike said and he wrapped his plaid coat around me, too. Everything's gonna be all right darlin', he said.

But it wasn't.

Mike

Finding Pat like that, I can't tell you what it did to me. It would break your heart. We'd been playing cards, our regular Thursday night game with all the Malloy brothers: Jim, Johnny, Danny, Pat, and me. I'd had a run of luck, a straight flush one hand and three queens the next. I was feeling pretty good. It was late and my brother Danny had passed around the last of the corned beef sandwiches. The beer was gone, too. We'd laid a lot of money on the table that night, probably a couple hundred. God, this is my lucky night, I thought. Clear winnings and maybe, if I was careful and tucked it away, we could spend a few extra nights at Lake George this summer. Pat got up about one o'clock and threw his cards on the table. "Callin' it quits," he said. "Not a lucky night for me." No, Patty, it wasn't, God rest your soul.

I was the first to leave Danny's house after Pat, but that was at three in the morning. I knew I'd catch hell from my wife, Clare, but I didn't really mind because I was on a winning streak and I hadn't had one for a long time. I picked up my money and helped Danny carry some of the bottles out to the back porch. It was then we found him lying there. The Jewish doctor at St. Mary's says he must have fallen on the icy step and hit his head. Being unconscious, he couldn't call for help so he just lay there and froze to death. Mother of God, my poor brother Pat.

Danny cried like a baby at the wake, saying it was his fault his big brother was gone. "I shoulda put salt on the steps, I shoulda broken the game up earlier, I shoulda cut off the beer," he said. All those "shouldas" like they would have made a difference.

I told him, "Danny boy, it was God's will." But Danny just sat there, his head in his hands, his face so flushed from crying that it almost matched the red of his wavy hair, and kept blaming himself, and I don't think that was much of a comfort to Meg or the children.

Gracie took it really bad. She was Pat's baby and she'd been left all alone in the car that night. Meg was so out of her mind, she'd forgotten the little girl. When I found her, she was shivering and crying, making a noise almost like a little sick cat. At the wake she stayed right by Pat's coffin and once, when no one else was looking, I caught her trying to open his eyes. "Jesus, child, what are you doin'?" I asked her.

"Why won't Daddy wake up, Uncle Mike?" she'd said.

Who could blame the child? Pat did look like he was sleeping. Such a fine figure of a man, lying there in his best dark suit, his black hair parted neatly on the side. Almost looked like he might sit up and call the kids to go to Sunday mass.

My own little girl, Margie, came over and sat on my lap. She's almost too old to do that anymore. At the wake, though, she didn't seem to care what her teen-aged sister, Mo, or her older cousins thought. She sat on my lap and put her head on my shoulder. It was a comfort, I'll tell you.

"Ah, my little Irish Princess," I said. "You'll be missin' your Uncle Pat, I'm sure."

"You, too, Daddy."

The words just about broke my heart and I, too, cried like a baby.

Margie

It was spring when Uncle Pat died. Cold enough for snow, below freezing, of course, that night. If it wasn't, Uncle Pat would still be alive. Here in Troy we can call

8

it spring in March, but sometimes we get bad snow-storms and days off from school right into May. Still, I love spring here. Even though now I'll always remember that Gracie's daddy died in the spring.

I guess I like it so much because it means new things. We always get new clothes in the spring. We get to put away those old wool coats, that smell so bad when they're wet and itch if they touch your neck. Each year Mommy puts mothballs in the pockets and says, "I hope we can get another year out of them, girls," and then she hangs them in the way back of her long, dark closet. Then we go to Stanley's and pick out wind-breakers, new jackets that are yellow or light blue, and new shoes, saddle shoes, that we can wear to church and to school. This year Mo refused to get saddle shoes and I was surprised that Mommy didn't get mad. Instead, she just smiled and said, "Okay, honey, now that you're in high school," and then she let Mo buy black flats for school and church. I loved those black flats, but Mommy said not till I was older. What's really funny is that Mo wants to try out for cheerleading and the cheer-leaders have to wear saddle shoes, so if she makes it, she'll have to get them anyways.

We wore our brand-new shoes and our last year's navy blue Easter coats with the lace collars to Uncle Pat's wake. It was funny having it in O'Sullivan's Funeral Parlor, which was really just a house that had been changed into a funeral home by the undertaker, Harry O'Sullivan, my Aunt Bridey's brother-in-law. I didn't like Harry O'Sullivan; his skin was greasy and reddish and he kept calling Uncle Pat "the dearly departed." I don't think Mommy liked him much, either, because she really didn't talk to him. She just shook his hand and walked in. When Mommy likes people, she brightens up and talks and smiles and they feel really special, but she just kind of ignored Harry O'Sullivan. Later, she told me that all the Malloy wakes and funerals would be at O'Sullivan's from now on, since he was Aunt Bridey's brother-in-law, and he was family. Not my family, I thought, and I was glad that I wasn't blood-related to any of those scrawny O'Sullivans.

I didn't like the funeral parlor and I wondered why here in the city they didn't wake people from the house like they did up-country in Granville, where Mommy's family lives. Grampie McDonald's wake was at the house on Potter Street where Mommy grew up. His coffin was right in the living room, between the two maroon sofas. I remember the great-aunts sitting wedged together on those sofas, all of them crying and saying their beads, while in the kitchen the cousins and uncles and aunts drank beer and laughed. That bothered me and I told Mommy it wasn't right. "Don't judge people so harshly, Margie," she'd said and then explained that this was the way her family, the McDonalds, knew how to deal with the dying.

I didn't like having to sleep upstairs in that house, either, with a dead body right down below me in the living room. At Uncle Pat's wake I thought about Aunt Meg leaving Uncle Pat at O'Sullivan's, his body all alone, surrounded by flocked wallpaper and too sweet-smelling flowers. It was all so un-Pat-like that I thought he'd probably rather be like Grampie, lying in his own front room, with the bay window that looked out over Second Avenue, his friends coming and going on the busy street below.

I saw Gracie when she tried to climb up and open Uncle Pat's eyes. I wouldn't want to touch a dead body, even if it was my own father's. I remember when Mommy told me to kiss Grampie good-bye, right before they closed the lid on the coffin. I wouldn't and Daddy had said in a really mean voice, "Do what your mother tells you, Margie." But Mommy said, "It's okay, Mike, she's frightened," and I went over and kissed my mother for knowing how I felt.

Daddy saw Gracie, too, and he lifted her down really gentle-like and he held her on his lap, whispering things in her ear. I watched while he talked to her and then I felt a little jealous, her sitting on my father's lap and all. But then I thought, and I felt really bad about this thought, that I was glad it was Gracie's daddy lying in that coffin and not mine. When Gracie got down, I went over and sat on my father's lap.

"I guess you'll be missin' your Uncle Pat, Margie," my father said and his voice sounded sad. I nodded, but in my mind, I thought, well, not really. It wasn't like he was Grampie and used to live with us. It wasn't like our everyday life was going to change. We only saw Uncle Pat and Aunt Meg and the cousins, Raymond and Gracie, after church on Sundays and on holidays. It wasn't like when Grampie died and no one read us stories anymore or would walk us to the drugstore to buy us Three Musketeers. I really missed Grampie.

"Bein' he was your godfather and all," my father continued.

I put my head on Daddy's shoulder and closed my eyes and pictured my godfather, lying stiff, frozen like an ice cube and see-through like an ice cube, too. How did frozen work? Did your blood stop moving and become like a hard red pencil in your body? Was ice inside of you? The morning after it happened, when Mommy told me, I pictured my Uncle Pat in a pond, lying under the ice and people skating in circles above him. His eyes were open and he was watching them from below. I was disappointed to find out it all happened on my Uncle Danny's back porch.

Who would be my godfather now? I wondered. We make such a big deal about godparents in our family. Everyone has them, you get them when you're baptized. They're supposed to watch out for you and take care of you if your parents die. They're supposed to make sure you grow up in the Faith and see that your parents bring you to church and confession and all. Now that Uncle Pat was dead, who would take care of me if my parents were killed by robbers or in a fiery car crash? My godmother, my mother's sister Nora, lives far away in Saratoga. Would I have to go live there if my parents died? And what about the birthday presents? Would I still get birthday presents and Christmas presents and big chocolate eggs with pink icing at Easter?

Did your godfather's family stop sending those things if your godfather was dead?

I always knew that Aunt Meg picked out the presents anyways, because they were always girl things. My favorite was a rhinestone bracelet that opened and closed like an accordion. Mo wanted to wear it to the prom last year, but Mommy said it was my choice and I said no. I don't have too many things that Mo can't have. I wondered if I would ever again get such a nice present from my godfather's family. I thought about my birthday next year, a big one, because I'll be thirteen. Besides Mommy and Daddy's gifts, Uncle Pat's was the only birthday present I could really count on. Aunt Nora sometimes remembers to send a card with five dollars in it and sometimes she doesn't. I started to feel sorry for myself and my eyes got teary.

"It's okay, darlin'," my father said. "Don't be afraid to cry."

I started to explain about the presents when I noticed that Daddy was crying, too. I stopped. I'd never seen him cry before. Since then, I've seen him cry again, mostly at wakes and really bad when the baby died. But that was the first time I ever saw my father cry. The second time was for Uncle Johnny.

2

Uncle Johnny's
Rope Tow

Johnny

That March, after Pat died, I couldn't find enough to do. It seemed that winter would never be over; every day was gray and windy. When I was off my shift at the firehouse, I used to wander around the kitchen like a sleepwalker, hoping to find something to do, thinking all the time of my brother Pat, six feet under the frozen ground. Christ, these Northern winters are a curse! I wondered why we all didn't pick up and move to California like the Kelleys did. Jim Kelley just sold his house and left, dragging his wife and three kids with him. He's gotten a job as a mailman out in Torrance and Frannie Kelley is pregnant again, with their fourth. I've heard he's never had one day of regret and they don't worry one iota about the earthquakes.

The morning after the blizzard—it must have been late March because it was a few weeks after Pat died—Anna looked at me over coffee and said, "Why don't you build the kids a rope tow, Johnny?"

Anna's from Sweden. When I first saw her, I thought she was the most beautiful girl in the world. I still do. She has bright blue eyes and white skin stretched fine over high cheekbones, but unlike her Scandinavian family, her hair is jet black. She'd grown up on skis and skates and that's why, I suppose, winters don't bother her as much as they do me.

Our hill, below the house, was perfect for a rope tow and I liked my wife's idea, so I set to work right away. It gave me something to do.

We were lucky getting this house, even if it only has two bedrooms. We really don't need more than that, anyways. After Anna's last pregnancy, Dr. Moriarty cautioned me about her having any more babies, so we just have the two girls. It's hard, the abstaining and all. Sometimes I look at my beautiful wife and I know it's the wrong time of month and I wish to God we could just ignore the Church teachings. Anna says God doesn't give you a cross you can't bear. I suppose she's right.

I would have liked a son. John, we would have named him. After me. When the last little girl was born, Anna must have known her body couldn't take another, because she insisted we name the baby Johanna. Anyways, Jody—that's what we call her—and her older sister, Kathleen, are in one room and Anna and I have ours, so our little two-bedroom house with its big hill works out just fine.

Getting back to my hill, my brothers and their wives hate it. They say it's impossible to get up the driveway in icy weather, and it is. But the hill is what I like best about the house. When the kids were little, I taught them to roll down it, holding their arms tight to their little bodies and keeping their legs straight. So many summer nights, Anna and I would sit on the porch, sharing a cold beer and watching our little girls go up and down the hill. "We're blessed, Johnny," Anna would say to me. And she was right; we are.

Anna was right about the rope tow, too. Our hill is perfect as a ski slope and it was easy to make the tow. I used a simple motor that one of the lieutenants at the firehouse had in his basement. When I called to ask him if I could borrow it and told him about the rope tow, he laughed. "You'll never grow up, Johnny," he said. "You're just a big kid at heart. I'll bring it right over."

"I'll save you a trip, Jake," I said. "I have to go out, anyways, to the hardware store for rope." I'd decided that docking line, the ropes that rich people from New York use on those big yachts you see going up and down the Hudson in the summer, would be just right for the tow.

I worked all morning on that rope tow, climbing up and slipping down my hill with the line, putting down stakes, setting the motor up. It was hard work. I was even sweating. But it took my mind off things. When I'd finished around noon, the morning winter grayness had burnt away to a sunny day with a bright blue sky. It was cold, but perfect for skiing.

My rope tow was a hit! Soon all the neighborhood kids were out with their skis and I called my brothers and said, "Bring all your kids on over. Anna will make hot cocoa and sugar cookies and they can spend the day." Somehow they all managed to get up the hill that day.

Even Kathleen's friends from the community college came and you should have seen those kids. Did they have fun! They were good skiers, too. One of the boys, who was about my size, called out to me, "Mr. Malloy, why don't you try it? You can use my skis." Well, I thought, hell, you only live once, and I got right up on those skis. Pretty soon, I found myself lying in a snowbank, covered with snow, laughing like a fool. I can't tell you the last time I had so much fun. And I surprised myself: I didn't think about my brother Pat once that afternoon.

Mo

I couldn't believe it when my cousin Kathleen called the morning after the blizzard and said that her dad had made a rope tow in the front yard. "He's never gonna grow up," she said and she tried to make her voice sound cool, but I could tell she was excited about the tow and proud of her father.

My Uncle Johnny isn't the youngest of all my father's brothers; my Uncle Danny is, but Uncle Johnny acts it. Last summer, when we were all bored and just hanging out, he got a whole group of the older cousins together and took us camping at Lake George. He had a few days off from his firehouse shift, so he just packed up his big truck with sleeping bags and tents and away we went. He even borrowed a boat from a friend at the firehouse and hitched it up to his truck like there was nothing to it. He said we'd all try waterskiing. And we did! It was so much fun. We put all the stuff in the boat and went out to a campsite on Turtle Island. We stayed there for two days, cooking out hot dogs on real fires and roasting marshmallows at night and telling ghost stories, and Uncle Johnny was the only grown-up. "I don't know why Johnny bothers, Clare," my dad had said to my mom when he'd heard about the boat and the camping trip. "It's just fun for him, Mike," Mom answered.

When I heard about the rope tow, I got Daddy to drive Margie and me over. We both have hand-me-down skis, but I certainly wasn't going to be embarrassed by that old equipment on my own uncle's hill. When Daddy finally got up the driveway, he got out and looked at all the kids going up and down the hill—there must have been thirty of them—and he put his hands on his hips and just shook his head and smiled.

Was I ever surprised to see Teddy Greaves and Donnie Melius there. They must have known Uncle Johnny is just too good-natured to hold a grudge. They were the boys Kathleen and I were out with the night that Uncle Johnny crashed the fraternity party. Well, "crashed" is what Kathleen called it. It wasn't like he just pounded his way into Sigma Chi. He was real polite. He just knocked on the door and asked to speak to his daughter. If it were my father that did that, I would have died of shame, but Kathleen never batted an eyelash. She just walked up to her dad and said, "What's a grown man like you doing at a fraternity party?" Uncle Johnny didn't take any nonsense from her, though, even if he is good-natured. "What's a seventeen-year-old college freshman doin' out at three in the morning?" he said, and then he made us get into his car and go home. Aunt Anna was waiting up for us and you could tell she must have been really worried. She said she thought we were both dead in a car crash. I suppose she made Uncle Johnny come looking for us. I always wondered why he didn't tell my parents, but the more I think about it, that was just like Uncle Johnny, too. He was on the side of kids.

Margie

Winter came back after Uncle Pat died. We had a bad blizzard and got a day off from school because the roads were so bad. The storm killed the purple crocuses that had just peeked through in our backyard garden. Mommy had to get the winter things out of the closet. She said she'd jinxed us by putting them away so early and she'll never do that again.

After that bad blizzard my Uncle Johnny made a rope tow. It is my most favorite memory of him. I can just picture him flying down that hill on that college boy's skis and landing in a snowbank at the bottom. We thought he was dead, because he didn't move for a long time. Jody and I ran down the hill to dig him out and my Aunt Anna said, "Oh my God." But when we got there, we could hear him laughing and we knew he was fine.

We skied all that day on the hill. I must have gone up that rope tow a hundred times. I had on Mo's purple-and-gold stocking cap that Mommy made for her last Christmas. It's her school colors. One of the college boys said, "Do you go to Troy High, honey?" I was so embarrassed that he called me "honey" that I could hardly answer. My sister, Mo, said, "She's only in seventh grade, so stop trying to rob the cradle, Donnie." Everyone laughed except for me. I just got red. I wish I didn't blush so easily. It gives all my secrets away. If I like a boy in school but I never tell anyone and people start talking about him, I blush. Then everyone laughs and says, "Margie likes him," and I get even redder.

When I went in to have hot cocoa that day, the rope tow day, my mother was sitting at the kitchen table with my Aunt Anna. "Take your cocoa and go in and sit by the fire, Margie," Mommy said. And I knew that they were talking about things they didn't want me to hear, so I listened.

"Johnny needs to see a good doctor, a specialist, Anna," my mother said. Mommy is the only one of the Malloys that has a college education and so everyone listens to what she says. "I know you think Dr. Moriarty is good, but he just hasn't been able to find the cause of the pains, and you know something is wrong. Don't you?" There was no answer. "Don't you, Anna?" she repeated.

I thought of Uncle Johnny at the comedy film festival at the Ritz last month, right before Uncle Pat died. "Don't sit next to him," my cousin Jody had whispered to me. "He'll embarrass you. He always laughs too loud." I really didn't care about Uncle Johnny laughing too loud, because he wasn't my father, anyways, and I wanted to share his big box of Good & Plentys, so I sat right next to him. After a really funny part where Tony Curtis was dressed up like a woman and climbed into Marilyn Monroe's bed on the train, my Uncle Johnny had tears in his eyes from laughing so hard. He was holding his side. "What's wrong?" I asked. "Just en-joyin' this too much, Margie. Must have strained some-thin'."

I thought of my Uncle Johnny with his hand on his side after mass last Sunday. "Just that old ache again," he'd explained to Daddy.

"How long before you get that taken care of, John?" my father had asked and his voice sounded somewhere between angry and sad. My Uncle Johnny shrugged and blessed himself with the holy water at the back of the church and walked out.

Was that pain what they were talking about in quiet voices in the kitchen? After I finished my cocoa, I tried to go back into the kitchen to hear more, but my mother just shooed me out. "This wonderful day won't last forever," she said and she was right.

Later that spring, when Uncle Johnny was all hooked up to tubes and machines and so little and skinny in that bed that he looked like a sad little boy, I tried to remember him flying down his hill, yelling and laughing. The doctors tried to get volunteers from the brothers for some special experiment to save him, and Uncle Johnny and Aunt Anna went all the way to Boston to see a doctor there. Daddy and Mommy were talking about that late one night when they thought I was sleeping.

"It's not without risk, Clare. They take the blood out of me and mix it with Johnny's blood and then put it back in me, and perhaps my body can fight Johnny's disease better than his can. There's a pretty good chance it can work," my father said.

"Oh, and is there a pretty good chance you could be infected with Johnny's blood disease, Mike?" My mother's voice sounded funny, almost disrespectful, like she was mocking my father's plan to help his brother.

There was a long silence and then my mother said, "No, absolutely not. I won't stand for it, Mike. I love Johnny, too, but I can't lose you. I won't let you risk it. What about your own children? You'd leave them orphans, too?"

"Orphans"? I thought of that terrible, red brick building called Vanderheyden Hall where all those noisy, rude children that ride our school bus live. I might have to live there if Daddy got Uncle Johnny's disease?

"Johnny's not your brother, Clare, and it's not your call."

I heard a chair move and then the door slammed. My dad had left the house. Then I heard my mother crying.

My dad volunteered. He was the only brother who did. But his blood wasn't a match. When we found that out, I was happy because it meant I didn't have to think about Vanderheyden Hall anymore. But I was sad, too, because that meant there was no one left to save Uncle Johnny.

At Uncle Johnny's funeral mass, Father Mullen talked about what a brave fire captain he was, how he had saved many lives, and how he'd been such a good brother, and husband, and father to his children. I felt gypped that Father Mullen didn't say what a good uncle he was to his nieces and nephews. He was the best.

When the funeral mass was over and we walked out of the church, all of us Malloys around my Aunt Anna and Jody and Kathleen, we saw that firemen from all over the county were standing at attention. They were lined up as far as you could see, wearing their dress-white hats and navy blue suits and white gloves. They all wore green carnations in honor of Uncle Johnny being Irish, the same kind of green carnations they wear in the St. Paddy's Day parade. The Emerald Society Bagpipe Band was playing "Danny Boy" and some of the firemen were crying and trying not to show it. In the crowd I saw Donnie Melius, the boy from the rope tow who had called me "honey." He looked different in his jacket and tie and he looked like he was trying not to cry, too. Aunt Anna was all dressed in black and had a veil over her face, so I couldn't see if she was crying, but I'm sure she was. My cousins Jody and Kathleen were bawling all over the place.

Seeing all those people so sad and missing Uncle Johnny so much made me so angry. I had just received communion, but I felt like yelling up at God.

"Why couldn't you make the blood match? Why couldn't you let the experiment work?" I guess I had forgotten all my fears about the orphan asylum by then. "Why does Uncle Johnny have to be dead instead of building us rope tows or taking us to the movies?"

I got into the big black car with dark tinted windows that was bringing us to the cemetery and I remembered my Uncle Johnny laughing and yelling and flying down his hill. When I think of him now, I picture him laughing in that snowbank forever. I wish he could have lived long enough to see Aunt Bridey's babies. How he would have laughed at the sight of them!

3

Aunt Bridey's Babies

July

❧

Clare

I love sleeping here at the camp. I wake up feeling so rested and well and God knows I have to watch my health now. At home when I wake in the morning, I'm already exhausted, half from listening to Mike snore all night and half from thinking of all the chores we have to do or the papers I have to finish grading before we all go off to school. I wonder why Mike doesn't snore here. It must be the fresh mountain air, or maybe the cold nights.

In the morning here, I often wake up before dawn and lie under the thick, wool blankets listening to the birds chirping in the pines that surround the cabin. Just last night I invited the girls to get up early with me to see the sun rise over the lake. Of course, Mo thought it was a terrible idea; I believe "dreadful" was the word she used. But Margie liked my idea, so this morning when it was still dark, we put on our long pants and sweatshirts and our new, yellow life jackets and took the rowboat out to Sweet Briar Island. Mike wanted to sleep, so we left him with Mo. I made a special picnic breakfast of bacon sandwiches and thermoses of orange juice and hot chocolate for Margie, and one just plain coffee for me. I know I should eat better now, but just the thought of any food in the morning makes me feel like I'm going to start throwing up again.

Margie is so excited about Bridey's unborn baby, she can hardly talk about anything else. She jiggled so much this morning when she started to talk again about this new cousin-to-be that I thought she'd tip us over.

"Margie, settle down," I said, "or you'll be swimming with the perch."

"Will it be a boy or a girl? What do you think? Can I babysit? Will she or he be as big as my baby doll Henrietta?" She fired questions at me.

"Maybe," I answered the last, thinking of Margie's large doll with the chopped-off brown hair and the big, staring eyes. "Your Aunt Bridey is awfully big." I thought of my sister-in-law Bridey, her short, stocky frame bloated with the extra weight of pregnancy, her fair skin, red and blotchy from the hormonal changes. Even her lovely blond hair, her main vanity, was now drab and stringy.

"Why is she so big, Mommy?" Margie asked me and I knew then that the boat ride was going to turn into a "twenty questions" on babies until Margie had found out everything she wanted to know.

I explained about the water that surrounds the baby and keeps the baby cushioned and how the women in the Malloy family sometimes have big babies that weigh as much as ten pounds. I explained how Dr. Moriarty thought that Bridey was having a very, very big baby.

"Did you get really big before I was born, Mommy?" Margie asked me.

I remembered myself in the ninth month of my last pregnancy, weighing almost 160 pounds. Everything swollen—my ankles, my wrists, my face. . . . With each of the girls, I'd gained over forty pounds. I thought about how hard it was to lose all that weight after the deliveries. I thought about how fat and clumsy I was. I thought about not being able to work because of the tiredness and the throwing up. I thought about all these things and I started to cry.

"What's wrong, Mommy? What's wrong?" Margie's voice was shaky like she, too, was about to cry. I could tell I was scaring her. She reached over for my hand so suddenly that the boat lurched to the left. I wondered what would happen if we capsized. What effect would the early-morning, frigid lake water have on this new life I was carrying? For just a second I was tempted, but then I said, "Sit still," and Margie obeyed me and the rocking stopped.

I looked around at the lake and I lied. "All this beauty," I pointed my hand at the sun rising over Buck Mountain. "It's just so overwhelming."

Margie accepted my simple explanation. Yes, it was so overwhelming. I wondered how I would tell Mike about the baby, about having to leave my teaching job when we need the money from my salary. I wondered how Mo would feel about having a new sister or brother when she was turning seventeen. There I sat with my baby, Margie, who was hardly a baby anymore to anyone but me, in the stillness of morning on the lake, pretending to cry about the overwhelming beauty of the sunrise instead of the overwhelming burden of this unwanted pregnancy.

Mike

Mother of God! When we heard the news about my sister, Bridey, on Monday—on the radio, no less, because it was such a big event for the local hospital—I thought I'd just bust with excitement. We were sitting on the couch with the Indian blanket cover, playing cards and listening to *Mystery Theatre*. We don't have a TV here at the cabin, and though I miss the Friday night fights, it's almost a relief not to have that blue eye on us all the time.

Anyways, we'd just come back from a speedboat ride. Art, the owner of the cabin, had taken us out in the *Indian Runner*. That's his fastest boat. We sped up the lake to Diamond Point and then over to Paradise Bay. I asked him if he'd mind spinning us by Huletts Landing. He said, "Hell no, Mike. That's no problem at all, but what's so special about Huletts Landing? It's just a ramshackle old hotel and a beat-up wharf." I explained about it being the place where Clare and I met twenty years ago, when she was just about Mo's age. Art gave me that funny grin of his and said, "A place with a lot of good memories for you then, Mike."

I nodded my head and smiled back and we took off toward Huletts and I remembered the night I first saw Clare. We both were waiting tables in the big lodge dining room. She was just out of her freshman year at Albany State, and so fresh-looking and perky that all the waiters had their eyes on her. She hung out with a big, red-headed guy by the name of Chad, a friend from her college. I'd heard she'd set her sights on being a teacher and marrying well. The other guys said she'd only date college men, so I lied and told her I went to R.P.I. I was afraid if I told her that college was out for me, that I had to help support Ma, that I was fresh out of the army and looking for any good job I could get . . . I was afraid if I told her all that, she wouldn't give me the time of day. All that summer I pretended to be an engineering student. By late August, when it was time to exchange addresses and return to our campuses, I had to tell her the truth. Funny, by then it made no difference to her. She just shrugged it off and said something about me getting my degree later, when she would be teaching. It was then I knew I was into a long-term thing and I've never regretted it from day one.

Getting back to my sister, Bridey. Lord knows how she and Paul are going to manage with all those kids and those big hospital bills. Paul makes good money at the Arsenal, but three babies on top of three kids are a lot of mouths to feed and they say the babies are going to be in the hospital for a few months, till they're strong enough to leave.

After we heard the news on the radio, I went down to the Algonquin Inn on the other side of the bay from our cabin. I dialed the hospital on the pay phone there and I managed to get through to Bridey. She sounded so tired and confused, I offered to drive back down to Troy to help out. "It will only take me a few hours, darlin'," I said.

"That's all right, Mike. I need to get my sleep here in the hospital. When I'll really need your help is when the babies come home. I'm worried about Colleen, too. She's hardly more than a baby and Paul tells me she cries herself to sleep every night for missing me. She's always been a favorite of yours, Mike. Maybe you can help me out with Colleen . . . when you get home."

I thought of my little red-haired niece, Colleen, only three, once the baby in my sister's family, now the middle child in a family of six kids. I thought about all the attention that those little babies were going to get, and the attention they'd take away from Colleen, and I got a great idea.

"Bridey," I said, "why don't you let me come pick her up and bring her up to the lake for the rest of our vacation? The girls will help watch her and I'm sure Clare won't mind and Colleen will have a great time and forget about missing you."

Bridey perked right up. "Are you sure Clare won't mind, Mike? You know she works so hard at the school all year and this is her vacation. She might not want to watch other peoples' kids in the summer, too."

"Shush, Bridey. You're not just 'other people.' You're the only sister I've got." I smiled to myself, happy with my idea.

"I love you, Mike," my younger sister said.

"I love you too, hon," I answered and then we made plans for Colleen's pick-up.

Mo

I got to water-ski all the way up the lake today, from Bolton Landing to Huletts Landing. Dad asked Mr. Paget to take us there in the *Indian Runner* so he could show us Huletts, because that's the place where he first met Mom. He said she was just about my age when they met. That's pretty weird when you think about it. I can't imagine meeting anyone this year that I would want to marry.

Anyways, when we got to Huletts Landing, I climbed back in the boat because my arms were really tired from skiing so far. Daddy had his arm around Mom and they were holding hands and looking at that bro-ken-down hotel like it was a palace. Mom looked so pretty, almost like a young girl. Her light brown hair was curly and loose from the boat ride and freckles were popping up all over her face. Her eyes were the same dark blue as the deep lake water. She was just staring at that old hotel and smiling. She was in a good mood then!

Later, when we got back to the cabin and heard about Aunt Bridey on the radio, I thought Daddy was going to jump through the roof, he was so excited. "Imagine that, Clare," he said to Mom, "three babies at one time! That's quite an accomplishment." My mother raised her eyebrows when he said that. "I'm gonna run down to the Algonquin Inn to try to call for more news," Dad said and he grabbed his jacket and took off down the path that leads to the bay.

He was gone a long time. After he left, Mom was really quiet, even though Margie kept pestering her with baby questions, like "How can three babies fit inside you?" and "How does that happen that you get three babies instead of one?"

When Margie started in on her questions, I thought for sure we'd get the birds-and-the-bees lecture. Mom hardly ever misses an opportunity for that one. And it was about time she clued Margie in on that kind of stuff. But she didn't. She didn't seem to want to talk about babies at all. Margie went on about three playpens, and three cribs, and three high chairs, and what were their names, until I got sick of hearing about those babies and Mom did, too.

"Margie, PLEASE be quiet for a little," Mom snapped.

Margie looked surprised when Mom said that because that's not like our mother at all, not to answer our questions. She's usually interested in everything we have to say.

After she yelled at Margie, Mom walked out to the little deck that's in the front of the cabin. It was cold, but she stayed out there a long time, just staring at the lake and watching for my father. By the time he got back, my mother was not in a good mood!

Margie

The thing I remember most about Lake George is the way we found out Mommy was going to have another baby. I learned a lot of things about my mother that day. I learned that she swore, I learned that there were some things about my father's family that she didn't always like, and I learned that she wasn't really happy about having another baby. That made me think a lot about things.

It all started when my father told my mother about his big plan to get Colleen. We had just come back from riding in Mr. Paget's boat. Mo had tried water-skiing and she was pretty good, but I couldn't get up at all. "Next year, Margie," Mr. Paget said to me and he explained that my arm muscles weren't strong enough yet. I looked at the muscles in my sister's tanned arms and I made a vow to do chin-ups every day until my skinny, freckled arms were strong. Anyways, after we got back, we were sitting in the cool of the screened-in porch, playing cards and listening to the radio when all of a sudden, my mother jumped up and said, "Did you hear that, Mike?" She pointed to the radio.

My father looked like someone from *The Millionaire* TV show had just given him the big check. "Did they say 'Mr. and Mrs. Paul O'Sullivan'?" he asked and my mother began to fiddle with the dial to get another radio station for the news. She finally found WTRY from Troy and we all gathered around that beat-up, old camp radio. "And the big news from Troy is the birth of triplets in St. Mary's Hospital!" the announcer said. "The lucky and surprised father, Mr. Paul O'Sullivan, has told us that his wife, Bridget, is doing fine and so are the babies. The triplets, two girls and a boy, are in incubators, and although they are very small, doctors expect them to survive. Mrs. O'Sullivan is the former Bridget Malloy, sister to Councilman Daniel Malloy."

Well, my father was so excited he jumped up and down. Then he said he had to go call Aunt Bridey. We all wanted more news. What were the babies' names? How much did they weigh? How long would they have to stay in the hospital?

My father put on his blue windbreaker jacket and said he'd walk down to the Algonquin pay phone. We watched him leave and then Mo and I got up and jumped on the sleeping couches. We were so excited. My mother went out on the porch and just sat there really quiet-like, watching the lake, and we couldn't tell what she was thinking.

When Daddy got back from the Algonquin, you

could tell he'd had a few beers too many. He had that big smile he gets when he's been drinking and he was talking really slow and particular. My mother asked him why he'd been out so long. "It doesn't take two hours to make a phone call, Mike." Her voice had a cutting sound to it. Hearing her, I knew it meant something unpleasant might happen.

"I was celebrating our new nephew and nieces," my father said.

My mother was quiet and just stared at him, but Mo and I jumped up and started asking all kinds of questions. "What are their names? How much did they weigh? Did they make it to the hospital or were they born in a taxi?" My father laughed when I asked that one.

"You've been watchin' too many TV shows, kiddo," he said and he reached over and tousled my hair. I went to sit close to him. I didn't mind his beery smell.

"Their names are Erin, Shannon, and Brian. Fine Irish names if I ever heard them. And they weighed a total of twelve pounds and five ounces. That's why your Aunt Bridey looked so big," my father explained.

"How long do they have to stay in the hospital, Dad?" Mo asked.

"Well, the little boy, he's a real tiny one. He might be in the hospital for a month or maybe two. But the girl babies could come home in maybe two weeks. That's one of the reasons that your Aunt Bridey needs her rest. When those babies get home, she's gonna be up all night feedin' them." My dad looked at my mother when he was saying about Aunt Bridey needing rest. "I hope you don't mind, Clare, but when I had Bridey on the phone I took it upon myself to offer to have Colleen up for the rest of the vacation."

"Colleen's coming up?" I said. "Great!" I was excited that my little cousin was going to stay with us. She's fun, almost like a real live doll, and I wanted to practice up on babysitting so that my aunt would trust me with those new babies. "We can teach her to swim, and take her to the beach, and out in the rowboat. And when we go to Bolton Landing we can take her for ice cream and show her the little museum there." I'd always wanted a little sister, one that would think of me as the "big sister." I was going on so about all the things that we'd do for Colleen, it took me a minute to notice that everyone else in the room was silent and my mother held her head in her hands and was quietly crying.

"Why, Clare, darlin', what's wrong?" My father went to my mother's side and knelt down, trying gently to pull her hands from her face.

"Don't you touch me, Michael Malloy. Don't you damn well come near me," my mother said and she lunged out of her chair and pushed my father aside. "All you can think of is that precious family of yours, all you Malloys, thick as thieves with one another. Danny, Jim, Bridey, and Johnny and Pat before they were gone, God rest their souls."

At the mention of my Uncle Johnny's and my Uncle Pat's name, my father winced and looked for a moment like he was going to cry again like he did at Uncle Pat's funeral.

"Let's not think about Johnny and Pat tonight, Clare. Let's celebrate the birth of those babies," my father said, and it was almost as if he was talking to himself and not my mother, like he was reminding himself to be happy about the babies.

"You want to celebrate life, Mike? You really want to tie one on and have a big party? You don't need to import Colleen, you're going to have a goddamn baby of your own!" My mother slammed the screen door behind her as she left the cabin. We could hear her walking down the path toward the lake, her feet crunching on the little pinecones.

"Well, I'll be . . . ," my father said to Mo and me as he headed toward the door to follow my mother to the lake. He shook his head and smiled. My mother had left crying, but I could hear my father whistling down the path to the lake, and he almost sounded happy.

Much later, when my parents came back, my mother came in and sat on my bed in the corner of the sleeping porch.

"Margie, I'm sorry for my temper tantrum. A mother shouldn't act like that," she explained. "It's just that your dad surprised me with his plan to bring Colleen up here and I thought he should have discussed it with me first."

I shook my head to show her I understood, but I wasn't going out on a limb. I wasn't asking any questions. I wasn't going to say a thing. I smiled and closed my eyes, pretending to go back to sleep, but my mother wouldn't let me.

"That's not all, Margie. What I said before . . . Daddy and I are going to have another baby."

"What?" I said, sitting up. I hadn't dared to believe it was true, what I'd heard earlier. "Does Mo know yet? How soon? Will it be a boy or a girl?"

My mother shook her head and answered my second question. "In February, close to Valentine's Day. I just told your sister," she added.

"We're going to have our own baby?" I questioned my mother again. I could hardly believe it. For so long I'd wanted a younger sister or brother.

My mother shook her head, but she didn't look happy. "I'll have to give up my teaching job at your school, Margie." Her voice sounded sad. "We'll have to give up a lot of things we've become accustomed to. Like . . . like this vacation."

I didn't care. I'd give up ten vacations to have our own baby. I hugged my mother and I could feel her start to cry.

Later, when Michael was born, I remembered how happy I was that night at Lake George and how sad she was. I also remembered how she'd called Michael "a goddamn baby" to my father. My mother remembered it, too, for when she brought us to see him in the hospital and he was so little and helpless and sick, she said, "I cursed my own baby, I cursed my own baby." And my mother wasn't herself for a long time.

4

The Horse Show

August

❧

Father Mullen

When the parish council came to me with the idea of fund-raising, they wanted to put bingo in.

"Over my dead body," I told them and I explained to them that I couldn't sanction gambling on any terms.

"But other Catholic churches do it," Joe Jablonski said. "St. Peter's and St. Paul's both have it on Friday nights now."

"I don't care what other Catholic churches do. This is St. Jude's and as long as I'm pastor, there will be no gambling."

They all grumbled among themselves, and Ken Felco, the chairman of the finance committee, laid it on the line to me.

"All right, with due respect, Father Mullen, I'll just have to say this plain as day. This church is just not making it financially. We are in need of some kind of a fund-raiser to bail us out. If you won't approve bingo, I suggest you think up something that sits well with you, because if you don't, your good friend Nat Meshstein, our mortgage officer from Union National, is going to foreclose on our loan and we will lose the school."

The finance committee stormed out of the rectory and I was left with the picture of Nat Meshstein, my pal from Rotary Club, putting up a For Sale sign on the door of our school and kicking out the children and the good sisters. Our precious school that we had worked so hard to build.

Was it the words "sit well" that Ken had used that made me think of horses? "You're sittin' well, Brendan lad." I could almost hear my father's voice as he'd watch me take the jumps on our farm back in Ireland. Lord, how I missed the place. I grew up breeding horses, but I haven't ridden a one since the day I entered the seminary in Dublin. No time for horses in my life now. Wait a second, I thought, whoa, slow down. Maybe you've got something here, Brendan, me boy, I told myself. And that's how I first came up with the idea of a horse show.

When I brought my idea of the horse show to the parish council, they were by no means liking it. Joe Jablonski, who was still pushing the idea of bingo, jumped right up. "We're all city boys, Father. We just moved out here to Wynantskill," he said. "We don't know nothin' about horses."

I looked around at the council members and saw the mix of Italian, Irish, and Poles that made up my parish. All of them recently moved from the shabby streets of South Troy, out here to their little Cape Cods in the country. All of them trying to provide a better place for their children. "Not to worry," I said. "I know all about horses and shows. I was raised in the saddle." I was so excited and confident with my idea that I made them believe it, too, and now here we are in our third year, producing good revenues, with entries coming in from all up and down the East Coast and some horse trailers sporting license plates from as far west as Arkansas. We really have done something here at St. Jude's.

Of course, I can't take all the credit. Lord no. What would I do without the hundred volunteers that run the concession stands or the souvenir stands or help organize the different events? Just last night I was talking to Mike Malloy, the fella who's in charge of the food concessions this year. He told me he sold over $500 worth of hot dogs on Thursday and that was the first day of the show, when the crowds weren't even heavy yet. He's got his volunteers all primed for a big weekend. Nice fella, that Mike Malloy. I was sorry I had to bring up that bit about his teenage daughter, but that's my job, too, as much as running the finances of the school and the church. It's more than my job, it's my duty, actually, to be watching out for the morals of the youth of the parish. And that girl, with her long tan legs, her green eyes, and her auburn-red hair is gonna cause trouble.

Mo

Well, Lake George was a drag. I was so glad to get home and see my friends. I wasn't happy about how our house smelled when we got back, though. All our tropical fish died while we were away and that was just one more thing to make Mom cry. I guess Rollie Evans, the neighborhood kid we hired to feed them, got carried away. We found lots of food floating among those slimy fish bodies at the top of the tank. It wasn't like they were real pets or anything. Margie was upset because she thought she was going to breed fish and make money by selling guppies to all her friends. Mom was upset because she didn't want to clean out that smelly tank, so Daddy and Margie did it. I could have cared less. I mean, the fish were pretty to look at, but it wasn't like they were a real pet like our dog, Binky. Now, I would have been really sad if something happened to Binky. Rollie did all right with Binky. I guess everybody knows how to take care of a dog.

Anyways, when we got back it was almost time for the horse show. I was excited about that. After all, I'd just spent every day for the last two weeks with Margie pestering me to do things or to help her watch Colleen. My father caused a big family fight by inviting Colleen up for our vacation. Actually, that part turned out okay, because she's really cute and funny and once she got there, everything was fine. But I'll tell you, the fight they had before she came. Man, it even made *me* nervous.

That's how we found out about the baby. Can you believe! Mom is going to have another baby. I really thought they were too old to do it. I'm almost embarrassed to tell my friends. I mean, after all, I am almost seventeen. By the time this baby is born, I'll be a senior in high school. I hope Mom doesn't think I'm going to babysit all the time, because *I won't!* And I'm not babysitting for those triplets, either, I don't care how tired Aunt Bridey gets. I even think it's kind of weird having a lot of babies like that. But they are cute, I have to admit that. The little girls look just alike. Mom says they are identical twins. They have the same puffy little cheeks, big blue eyes, and blond, tufty hair like Aunt Bridey. They squirm around a lot. They move all over those bassinets. The little boy is darker and longer than his sisters. He looks right at you when you talk to him. The girls scream a lot, but he's more the silent type. I hope we get a baby like him.

I wonder if Mom might have more than one baby. She better not! I can stand one, but more than that and I'll be recruited as chief cook and bottle washer, for sure. This whole thing must have been an accident. Mom and Dad aren't telling, but they couldn't have planned it. Not with me and Margie almost grown. Why would they?

Getting back to the horse show, you'll never believe what happened last night. Daddy came home from his food committee meeting and came into my room really serious-like. "Can we talk, Maureen?" he said. He never calls me Maureen, so I knew I was in for a lecture or something. I thought it was going to be another one of those "let's all pitch in and help Mommy" lectures.

"Father Mullen spoke to me about you tonight, Maureen," my father said.

"So?" I hardly know Father Mullen and I didn't think he knew me at all.

"He asked me to please ask you to dress more modestly, to wear your shorts a little longer and not wear those halter tops to the horse show."

"What!" I said, jumping up from the floor where I'd been listening to my Elvis records. I thought of that cute, black-and-aqua-striped halter that I'd bought with my own money just to wear to the horse show tomorrow. I was going to wear it with my cutoff jeans and a straw-hat. I thought it looked countryish.

"Father Mullen says the way you dress could put a boy into an occasion of sin," my father said and his face got red and he started sweating. He looked embarrassed.

"Well, Father Mullen is just an old fart and I'll wear what I feel like wearing!"

My father looked horrified. "We'll have no talk like that against the Church in this house, Maureen Katherine Malloy!"

"Father Mullen is not the Church! He's just one old man and he doesn't know anything about teenagers," I said and I left my room, slamming the door behind me in my father's face. I knew I'd pay for that later, but I was just so angry I could have spit nickels. Just when I'd gotten a really sharp outfit together, in comes this prissy-ass old priest to tell me how to dress. God! I didn't think he even knew my name. It wasn't like I was one of the parochial-school kids. Mom had taken me out of Catholic school when I was in kindergarten. She said the nuns were filling me full of superstition. It used to make her mad when I wouldn't run up the stairs when she was behind me carrying groceries and Margie. I told her the nuns said if I ran up the stairs, it meant that the devil was nipping at my heels. "That's it, Mike! I'll not have any more of that foolishness being put into her head. She's going to my school!" my mother said. So all through grade school I went to the same public school that my mother taught in.

Maybe that's why! It's probably because I'm a "public schooler." Those priests all think the "public schoolers" don't have any morals. They think they have to save us. Just last year, that new, young priest, Father Tim, tried to get a club together for the kids from Troy High. We had a dance and put on a variety show. After he got to know us better, he invited a few of us who he really liked to go horseback riding with him. He's cute and I liked riding along with him at my side.

When we were alone on the trail, he said, "Maureen, have you ever felt you had a vocation?"

I didn't know what he meant by "vocation," so I asked him to explain.

"A calling from God," he said, "to join the sister-hood."

Why, I laughed right out loud. "I would never live with a bunch of women," I said and I kicked my horse to go faster, to gallop away from him. I liked the way it felt, riding that horse, the rocking warm between my legs. "And I like boys too much!" I yelled back, laughing. I know it was a bold thing to say to a priest, but I wanted to set him straight.

Margie

I hope we get one of those first-day-back-to-school essays on "What I did last summer." I'll be able to fill both sides of the paper. I could write about the triplets, or my mom being pregnant, or Lake George, or the horse show. Well, probably not the horse show, because if I write about that I'd have to tell the exciting part about Mo, and then Mom would be mad. She's already mad enough. She thinks that everyone in town is going to say Mo has a bad reputation. Come to think of it, Mom probably wouldn't want me writing about her having a baby either, although she's already written to the principal to say she has to leave in December. That didn't go over too well, I guess. Dr. Kepner said that if he got another teacher to accept the sixth-grade job before September, he'd have to give them the whole year, and then Mom wouldn't get to work for the first part of the school year.

It will seem funny not having Mommy at school with me. Other kids have to get used to leaving their mothers in kindergarten, but here I am entering eighth grade and Mom has taught in my school since even before I started. I'm glad I go to Wynantskill Elementary and not the Catholic school. We have so much more fun at our school. At St. Jude's they don't have gym, or lunch-fun club. They don't even have lunch! They have to bring their lunch in lunchboxes. I hate lunch-box lunch. It always smells like sour milk and the sandwiches are always warm and sort of floppy-looking by the time you get to eat them. At our school we have May Jones. She's the head lunch lady, in charge of the cafeteria. She even roasts turkeys for us and makes homemade pies. It's a good thing, too, because my own mom never bakes, so at least I won't grow up never tasting homemade apple pies. Maybe if Mom stays home after the baby's born, she can start making pies.

I better not get in trouble in school this year, with my mom not there. Last year when Mrs. Irving sent me to the office for helping Chuckie Brewster paint a bird on Sharon Wetter's arm in art class, my mom stuck up for me and I didn't get the paddle. But I got it from my father when I got home. He was really mad. He said because I am the teacher's child I have to act better than all the other kids. "You embarrass your mother, Margie, when you act out of line. And you put her in a bad position." I wonder if she's in a bad position now with all the stories going around about Mo down under the bleachers. I really don't think it's such a big deal, but Dad sure was mad at Mo. He grounded her for the first month of school and school doesn't even start till next week!

It all started with my sister slamming the door on my father when he was trying to talk with her. For some reason, he didn't want her to wear that cute new top she bought for the horse show. I don't blame her for being mad about that. She worked hard for the money to get it, babysitting those bratty Quinn kids, and The Blouse Bar isn't cheap. I think it cost her $12.99. Mo threw a fit and then she wore it, anyways. She snuck out of the house with it on under another shirt, a black, long-sleeved one with a collar, so Daddy never suspected anything. He didn't realize what she was doing till he saw her across the show grounds, and by then he was stuck behind the food counter with people screaming for hot dogs, so he couldn't do anything about it, anyways.

It wasn't just the halter top that got Mo in trouble. She was one of the kids that got caught smoking and drinking beer under the bleachers. It was during the Lippizaner horses act. Those ladies on the Lippizaners are so beautiful they are the stars of the horse show. I don't even know why Mo would want to miss it. They wear these red, satin gowns with fur collars, even when it's ninety-five degrees. And they make the horses stand up on their back legs and then prance to the music. It's almost like they were dancing with the horse. Everybody fills the bleachers to see their act. Everybody but Mo and her friends, that is. She told me later that she'd met this really cute guy who was a groom for one of the big stables that had sent a whole truckload of horses to compete. I think she said the name was Happy Acres and they came all the way from Kentucky.

Well, anyways, Father Tim, the priest that used to like my sister, caught her down under the bleachers during the Lippizaner horses act smoking cigarettes with that boy from Kentucky. Marcy Marino and Janni Tenyke were there. Mo's friend from Troy High, Michael Gold, was there, too. Daddy doesn't like him, because he's Jewish. I mean he likes him okay. He says he's a nice enough kid and he always has his name on the honor roll. That gets you big points in my father's book. But he's not for Maureen, my father says.

When Father Tim found my father at the concession stand to tell, he also said that the boy from Kentucky had an open can of beer and that he had his hand on Maureen's leg in an improper way. When Mo and my father had it out that night, I really couldn't understand the big deal about the boy's hand. I mean, Mo said he was just leaning against her knee. And she said she wasn't drinking any beer, either. Just smoking. And who can blame her for trying a cigarette? All the teenagers do it.

Mo is ready to kill Tina Glass. She's the one who went blabbing to Father Tim about them all being down under the bleachers. I wonder why she would do that? When she was little, she was one of my sister's best friends. Maybe it's because she's not pretty like Mo and doesn't get to hang out with her much anymore.

Well, anyways, my sister is grounded and my parents are fighting about how long she should be kept in. My father says a whole month. Last night at dinner they had another fight about it. Mom is mad at Mo, but she's sort of on her side, too. "If she's grounded the first four weeks of school, Mike, then she can't try out for cheerleading, and you know how hard she's been practicing for the team," my mother said.

My father put down the chicken leg he'd been gnawing on. Chicken is the only meat we're allowed to use our fingers for. Mom says it's okay etiquette. Anyways, he put down his chicken bone and cleared his throat like he was going to make an important speech. He does that a lot when he and my mother have their "discussions." Discussions are what they call them. I call them "fights." Anyways, Daddy took his time as if he were planning carefully what to say to my mother. You have to do that with Mommy, because she's a teacher and she knows a lot, and if you're not careful, she'll win every argument.

"The girl has to be taught a lesson, Clare. She cannot disobey and I will not have her shamin' the good Malloy name." They were talking about Mo as if she wasn't there, when she was just sitting right in between them, her eyes really big and starting to get teary.

"Oh, for God's sake, Mike. Smoking a cigarette under the bleachers at that silly horse show is hardly something to 'shame the name.' I agree she shouldn't have been with that beer-drinking boy and she's going to have to be more careful about her friends, but don't you think four weeks is a little harsh? After all, we want her to be involved in school activities.''

"I'm not backin' down on this, Clare, and I do not want you underminin' my authority," my father said.

Mo got up and ran from the table. I could tell she was trying not to show my father how much it hurt not to be able to try out for cheerleading. I could tell she was trying hard not to bawl. Mom left the table, too, and followed Mo to her room. She shot my father a real bad look as she left the kitchen. He stood up and started clearing the table. I could tell he was really mad because he was rattling those dishes around like he didn't care if they broke to smithereens. It always makes me nervous when grown-ups do that with silverware and dishes. It makes me afraid the world could just break apart. It makes me worried that things could fall apart just as fast as my fish business did. Just one overfeeding by that stupid Rollie Evans and all my hard work and savings go right down the drain. Down the drain, that's where Daddy and I flushed those dead, silver bodies when we cleaned the fish tank.

Maybe I'll write about the fish on the first day of school.

5

Aunt Lizzie's Last Will and Testament

October

❧

Clare

Driving the sixty miles between Troy and Granville, I could feel myself sinking back down into that familiar sadness that the sight of the smokestack on the old Telescope Furniture Factory, on the outskirts of town, always brings to me. When we drive over that rise and look down on Granville, nestled between those hardscrabble dairy farms and slate quarries, I always have that rush of bittersweet memories.

Mike doesn't really understand. He was raised in the city on hot, dirty streets. He looks at my little farm town as paradise. He pictures me growing up there, rosy-cheeked, covered with freckles, carrying my fishing pole back from the lake, my wicker fishing basket loaded with speckled sunfish. He pictures me picking summer strawberries in the garden in back of the house on Potter Street. He doesn't see me as the little girl crouched behind the big, mahogany dresser as her mother lay gasping for breath in a deathbed. He doesn't see my older brothers lined up in a row, white shirts starched, neckties hurriedly knotted, waiting for my mother's final inspection and final kiss. He doesn't see my father kneeling at the bedside, kissing my mother's hand, saying over and over, "Don't leave me, Margaret, I can't raise these six children alone. I can't. I can't."

And he couldn't, either. He was so consumed with his sorrow after my mother's early death from tuberculosis that he took a job on the railroad, traveling with the trains mostly, between Montreal and New York. He left us for our McDonald maiden aunts to raise. And when they weren't available, a hired housekeeper.

Our life with the aunts wasn't all terrible. They tried to be kind, but they did have their favorites. My Aunt Mame loved my brothers, Jamie, Neil, and Patrick, and my Aunt Kate loved my baby sister, Katherine, who was named after her. My Aunt Mary loved my older sister, Nora, for her red hair. The only one that had a special kindness for me was Aunt Alice, because I looked like her, but she didn't live with us because she was married with a family of her own: my Uncle Jake and their two boys, Joseph and Martin.

Oh, and Nellie loved me best also. And I loved her, too. She was our housekeeper after Mama died. She came on a boat from Ireland and my Uncle Jake had to drive all the way to New York City to pick her up. He was the only one in the family who owned a car back then. Nellie lived with us and I sort of thought of her as a big sister. She had a little room in the back of the attic, but she shared the second-floor bathroom with us kids. I used to sneak into her room at night and she would tell me Irish stories and fairy tales. She taught me to weave a princess crown from clover. None of my aunts would have ever taught me anything like that. Nellie took care of me until she fell down the cellar stairs and hit her head on the concrete floor. She was moving jars of jelly that she'd just made down to the storage cellar, when she slipped on the top step. The doctor that came to the house said she must have died instantly. I'll never forget the noise of her head hitting the floor. It was like someone had dropped a watermelon. I was the only one home when it happened. I had been helping her move the jars. I sat with her body, holding her hand . . . in that dark, cold storage cellar. I didn't even think to call anyone. I guess I must have known she was dead. When my brothers found me, they couldn't pull my hand away from Nellie's. That was two people I lost, in two years.

Now the last of the aunts is gone and we have to go to the reading of the will since all the estate is going to be divided among the nieces and nephews. It's strange how my other aunts predicted that Aunt Lizzie would be the last to go. "She's so mean, she'll outlive us all," they'd often said.

And she did.

She died on my birthday in September. It's really kind of funny in a dark way. Lizzie never really liked me, we never got along, and then she went and died right in the middle of the party for my thirty-ninth birthday, spoiling that for me, too. A parting shot! Well, it wasn't much of a party, just the Malloy brothers and their wives, and Bridey and Paul. But it surely put a damper on the evening. We had to start making arrangements for the funeral. When I got into bed that night, I said to Mike, "Aunt Lizzie zaps me again." I was only kidding, but Mike said, "Have some respect for the dead, Clare," almost like he was reprimanding me.

It's odd, Mike sticking up for Aunt Lizzie that way when she was the most blatant of the aunts in disapproving of him when I first brought him home from Huletts Landing that summer that we met. Lizzie always said she believed in "tellin' it like it is," like she was some sort of soothsayer, who knew more than everyone. "Mike is shanty Irish and no good for you, Clare," she'd said as she took me aside, but she hardly even bothered to whisper and Mike heard and I could tell from his face he was embarrassed and hurt.

In my family, calling someone "shanty Irish" was as insulting as calling them a dago, or a dumb Polack, or worse, a Welshman. The assumption was that because we lived in a nice house and had fine china and crystal from Waterford and took trips to Albany to buy our new spring coats and shoes, we were "lace-curtain Irish." My aunts seemed to forget that my grandfather and his brothers made all their money bootlegging whiskey during Prohibition and not by the sweat of hard, honest labor like Mike's family, in the mills along the Hudson River in Troy.

As we drove along Granary Street and crossed the bridge over the Mettawee River, toward Jack Mc-Killip's law office on Main Street, Mike took my hand. "It will all be over soon, Clare," he said. I think he was afraid that I was upset about the cousins fighting over the house and the silver and crystal. I just smiled back at him. I wasn't going to get into a discussion now about how all those things meant nothing to me, how when I closed the door of Jack McKillip's office this after-noon, I could close the door on the last of the Mc-Donalds and never have to come to this sorry little town with its painful memories again. I wasn't going to go into all that right then, so I just let him think I was feeling a sadness for my family, and the fact that with Aunt Lizzie gone, there were no McDonalds left in Granville.

"She wasn't so bad," Mike said, referring to Lizzie. "Just a little crazy."

I thought of the many insults that Lizzie had thrown Mike's way and I thought of Mike's persistent forgiveness and it suddenly made me angry, at my dead aunt and my too-understanding husband.

"For Christ's sake, Mike, call a spade a spade; Aunt Lizzie was a lot crazy and a lot mean! Just look at the way she took every chance to cut you down, and think of the times she was deliberately mean to Margie and Mo, just because they're our kids." I was really shouting now and the kids, in the backseat, looked scared. The emotions that come rolling out of me since this pregnancy began are so unpredictable, even to me.

"Lizzie had her reasons for being crazy, Clare," Mike said to me.

I ignored him, but the two sets of ears in the backseat didn't.

"What were her reasons for being crazy, Daddy?" Margie asked.

"Oh, your mother will explain," Mike said, expecting me to soften up and tell the girls about their dead great-aunt.

"No, since you now like Aunt Lizzie so much, you tell them about her, Mike." I tried to make my voice sound sarcastic, but I was really just too tired, thinking about the afternoon to come with my cousins.

"Come on, Dad, tell us," Mo said.

Mo is always happy to find out unusual or weird things about the family. I guess it makes her feel unique. I guess I sort of understand that. I just wish she wouldn't concentrate so much on the McDonalds for quaint idiosyncrasies. I wish she'd look to the Malloys.

"Well, your Great-Aunt Lizzie didn't always live in Granville, girls. Unlike Aunt Mary and Aunt Mame, she married and moved away to Rochester for some time."

"Who did she marry, Dad? I never heard Grampie tell of Aunt Lizzie's husband."

Mo wanted to hear more about George, Lizzie's long-dead husband. She was probably hoping he was a dashing gambler who'd abandoned Lizzie for a life on the road, or a highwayman, playing Clyde to Lizzie's Bonnie.

"Her husband, George, had a small dairy farm that never made any money." Mike laughed, as he added, "Your Grandfather McDonald used to tell me that the family would regularly take collections to send money to George and Lizzie in Rochester so they wouldn't come home to live in Granville. I guess George really got a kick out of Lizzie's eccentricities, but the rest of the family didn't."

"Well, living in Rochester was probably pretty boring, but it would hardly drive anyone crazy," Mo said.

"Your Aunt Lizzie became really unbalanced after her baby died," I interjected, and as I said it, I felt the unborn child move in my belly.

"How did her baby die, Mommy?" Margie's voice sounded little and scared, and I knew she was thinking, like I was now, about our baby, not due for another four months.

"He starved to death, Margie," I answered.

"SHE didn't feed her baby? She really was crazy!"

Mo sounded indignant, but excited also, about this new piece of information, her invulnerable teenage attitude distancing her from that long-dead baby, her first cousin, once removed.

"It wasn't like that, Maureen," I said, hoping to chastise her for her excited tone. "Your Aunt Lizzie's baby was born without an esophagus, and in those days the doctors couldn't do anything about it. Aunt Lizzie and her husband, George, just had to stand back and watch as their baby slowly starved, unable to move nourishment from his mouth to his hungry stomach."

"Gee" was all Margie could think to say and Mo was silent.

"I guess that would make anybody crazy, don't you know," Mike said.

No one said any more.

I put my hand on my stomach and said a silent prayer and then fixed my scarf and put on some lipstick to meet my cousins. I thought of Aunt Lizzie's baby, dead now fifty years, as much my cousin as the ones I'd soon be seeing at Jack McKillip's office.

Mo

When Mom said that we'd have to miss a day of school to go to Granville, I got really nervous. I hoped it wouldn't mean that Daddy would find out about the cheerleading. I was supposed to bring a note from my parents, both parents, if I had to miss a practice and if both parents had to sign the note, then my father would know about our conspiracy. That's what I call it, my mother's plan to have me make cheerleading.

After they had their big "discussion" last summer about my grounding, my mother came into my room. "I don't agree with your father's stand, Maureen," she'd said. "And I am going to allow you to try out for the team. But your father must not know until I'm ready to tell him. You must always get the late bus home right after practice and be in your room studying when Dad walks in from work. Do you understand?"

Did I understand! My mother was going to lie to my father for me. This was a first! It's always been the two of them against us kids. I jumped up and kissed my mother. "I promise," I said and then in a fit of enthusiasm, I added, "and I'll be home studying SO HARD every day that you're going to see my name right up there on the top of the honor roll." I don't know what made me say that, but my mother looked very pleased. The teachers at Troy High are always getting her ear about how high my IQ is and how I don't work up to my potential and maybe I'm a late bloomer. So when I told Mom I'd be studying every day after cheerleading, she looked really happy.

"I hate to go against your father, Maureen. But I know this is the best way to handle this situation."

"But how will I explain it if I make the cheerleading squad?" I asked.

I thought of myself in that cute, little, purple skirt and the oversized, gold sweater with the big, purple *T*. I thought about doing cartwheels and how the boys got a look at your panties when you jumped. I wanted to be one of those girls so much, but I was afraid of my father, too.

"I'll think of something if you make the squad," my mother had said.

And now here I was, newly elected captain of the

squad, needing a note from both parents to miss cheer-leading practice.

"I'll sign your father's name and mine, Maureen," my mother said.

Then she added, "But it's time we told your father of your success."

"We"? What's this "we" business? This was her idea. I didn't want to be around when "we" told my father how we'd lied to him.

My mother must have been able to see what I was thinking by the look on my face.

"Don't worry so much, Maureen, I'll find the right time to tell him. And besides," she added, smiling brightly at me, "you are at the top of the first quarter honor roll, and your father will be so proud about that!"

My mother is always pushing me to achieve, so making the honor roll with such high grades and being elected captain of the cheerleaders had made even her unafraid of my father's wrath. Besides, she likes to be right, and her way of handling the whole stupid horse show thing had proved to be the right way. What could my father say?

We all drove up to Granville that day for the read-ing of Aunt Lizzie's Last Will and Testament. Margie and I sat in the back fighting about where to put our feet and who came over the imaginary line down the middle of the backseat. She can be such a brat some-times. I was tired and wanted to stretch out and Margie started to complain to Daddy. When I started to call her names, my mother turned around and silenced me with a look. How could I know that this was the moment she'd pick to tell Dad about cheerleading?

My father must have been in an unusually good mood or something. Maybe he thought we were going to get some money from the will or maybe he was just being kind to my mother because she seemed a little sad to be going back to Granville, with her whole family dead and everything.

Anyways, when she told him, he just sort of looked at her funny and said, "Mo's at the top of the honor roll?"

My mother just nodded her head and smiled proudly.

"Well, I guess you handled it right, Clare" was all he said and we went on driving and talking about my mother's crazy Aunt Lizzie, the one whose baby died because he was born without an esophagus.

When Daddy told me about Aunt Lizzie's dead baby, I thought of Aunt Bridey's babies, how cute and chubby they are, and the nice sucking noises they make when she is feeding them. I thought about those three babies starving and how Aunt Bridey would feel. I never much liked my Aunt Lizzie. I thought she was an old crab, but now I understand things a little better. To have your baby taken from you like that would be the worst . . . it would make you crazy for sure. I leaned forward and touched my mother's shoulder. I wanted to kiss her and hug her and touch her stomach, where our baby was. But all I said was, "Mom, will we be there soon?"

Mike

It was fine seeing all of Clare's cousins at the lawyer's office. They're a good bunch and I wish we could see more of them, but they live all scattered across New York State. Not one of them chose to stay in Granville. Not like us Malloys at all, stuck together in Troy, always in the same place. Afraid to be parted, that's what we are.

When the cousins suggested we all go over to McGarry's Pub for a drink after the reading, I was all for it. But that woman! As long as I live, I will never fully understand that woman. She just flatly refused to go out for a drink with her blood relatives.

"I'm sorry, Martin," she said, "I'd really love to, but we have to get back to Troy by early evening. Mike has his weekly poker game, you know." Clare smiled at me. "He can't miss that," she said, pointing at me and shrugging her shoulders at Martin. "We'll be leaving right after the reading."

I tried to explain that I could miss one poker game, that it wasn't a big deal, but she shushed me up. I got the point. Clare didn't want to stay for a drink.

Then we all went in for the reading of the will and, as Christ is my judge, she surprised me again. She stood up and sold her part of the estate to her cousin Martin for one dollar. *One* dollar! When we could use the money so much with the new baby coming and her losing her job in December. After she signed her rights away to Martin, she announced that we had to be going and then proudly walked out of the room as if she'd accomplished some great thing. As if the McDonald money wasn't good enough for her.

I said some hasty good-byes to the cousins and we all piled into the car and drove toward home. As we crossed over the Mettawee River, I thought about my wife. On the surface she was proper and polite and nor-mal-acting, but down deep, just like the river, there were currents and eddies I just couldn't understand. Or maybe she was really just plain crazy like her dead aunt!

I tried to ask her why. Why had she just given away her inheritance, little as it was? We're in no position to give away money. With the baby coming, we need every dime we can get.

"Tell me why, Clare," I demanded, but she gave me no answer. She just set her jaw in that stony face she can make and there was no talking to her. It was a long ride home.

Margie

When we got home from Granville that night, Mommy and I watched a *Lights Out* rerun together. She doesn't usually let me stay up to watch it because it's too scary, and after that episode last month about the supernatural pearl necklace that kept choking ladies who found it, I thought she'd never let me see the show again. But last night was different.

Daddy had gone out to his poker game. He said he wanted to see his brothers and he left without even kissing Mommy good-bye. Mo was studying. Now that Daddy knows about cheerleading and the honor roll, Mo's not rocking the boat. If I know her, she'll probably end up being valedictorian out of this. That's how she is.

I got Mommy a cup of tea and then I snuggled up with her because she seemed so lonely.

"What does 'shanty Irish' mean, Mommy?" I asked.

"Where on earth did you ever hear that term, Margie?" my mother asked me, and her voice sounded sharp like the needles she was clicking together to make a blue baby sweater. We are hoping for a boy.

"I heard your cousin Lydia use it when she was talking to Martin after you left the lawyer's office today," I answered.

"That bitch!" my mother said, and I was shocked. I haven't heard that word too many times, and certainly not from my mother and certainly not about her own family.

"What did she say, Margie? Tell me everything she said!"

My mother pumped me for information, but I couldn't remember everything Lydia said because I was just walking by her when she said it. It interested me because I thought of the sea shanties we are learning in Miss Emberley's music class and I pictured Irish fishermen singing songs like "Molly Malone."

" 'Shanty Irish' means poor, without a pot to piss in," my mother said and she continued to surprise me by adding "piss" to the list of words that I never thought crossed my mother's lips. "It's what my family sometimes calls your father's family." My mother was mad now and I could tell she might just pick up the phone and tell Lydia a thing or two.

To head off a fight between my mother and her cousin, I tried to ask more questions.

"Aren't we all descendants of the Kings of Tara?" I asked, remembering the fairy tales my father had told me of the Irish royal families in the land of Tara. "That's why Daddy calls me an Irish Princess," I added, flinging out my father's special nickname for me and Mo.

My mother sighed and looked around our living room. The slipcovers were fading and the green rug had a spot where Binky always sleeps.

"There is no such thing as an Irish Princess, Margie. It is a contradiction in terms."

My mother's voice sounded discouraged, like she was tired of fighting or of not having enough money, and I wondered if she was thinking about the dollar that she'd made today. I wondered if she was thinking about the share of the will that Daddy said she was entitled to. They had argued about that one dollar all the way home from Granville.

"Make yourself into an American Princess, Margie.

Grow up and be somebody. Use your potential like your sister, Maureen. She'll probably be winning that scholarship to college."

I thought of my older sister, with her beautiful dark red hair and her cheerleading uniform and her good grades. She was already somebody. I looked at my skinny legs and arms and I thought of my bad penmanship and my daydreaming in class. My hair is too curly and orange and the doctor says I might have to wear glasses. I'm going to have to work hard to get my potential and become an American Princess, whatever that is.

6

Christmas

December

❦

Clare

I couldn't believe when Mike came walking in with that scrawny little tree. He was so pleased with himself for finding it, too. He'd just been to his brother Jim's house and Jim had gotten a little fir tree and put it on a box. Jim and Mary had covered the box with a red tablecloth and thought it looked festive. Mike thought it was a grand idea, too, until he got home, that is. We, the girls and I, were not standing for it.

"Certainly not!" I said as Mike tried to set up that pathetic little tree, all the while explaining how we could put presents out all around it on the box like Jim and Mary did. Mo was making sarcastic comments and Margie was crying and I just had to put my foot down. I know this is the toughest time of the year for Mike, what with two postal deliveries each day and no Saturdays or Sundays off during the Christmas season. I know he's tired from seven days out in the weather. I know I should have been more sympathetic.

Even so, with Mike so tired and all, I just couldn't stand for that tiny tree. In my family, the McDonalds, even if you are having a bad year, you always do Christmas up right. You find the biggest tree you can fit in your house, you buy the most perfect gifts, you cook the best turkey you can find. This year, with the baby coming, I felt it was really important that everything be traditional and right.

"Oh, come on, Mike," I said, "that's a sorry excuse for a Christmas tree. Let's bring it to the Rizzo family up on the hill. They're so poor they'll be happy to have a free tree and we can take the girls out to Miller's Farm in West Sand Lake and cut a tree down."

Mike looked at me as if I had two heads. "For the love of God, Clare. Don't you listen to your own doctor? John Moriarty said you had to take it easy, to keep off your feet as much as possible or your pains might start again. You can't go traipsin' through the woods searchin' for Christmas trees."

"Oh, Doctor Moriarty is an old fuddy-dud," I said, but I knew Mike was right. I belonged on the couch. I sat down, discouraged.

Mike must have taken pity on me, for he said, "Okay, girls, we'll bundle your mother up and take her for a ride, but she's not doin' any work. She's gonna' sit in the car and watch us cut down the biggest tree we can find on Mr. Miller's farm."

We all dressed in warm clothes and drove out to West Sand Lake. It was a beautiful winter day; the sun was shining and the sky was bright blue. I watched my handsome husband, his dark hair poking out from under his green knitted cap, the cap that matched the color of his eyes, lead our skipping daughters across the snow in their search for the perfect tree. Even from where I sat, wrapped in the wool of a stadium blanket, my feet toasting under the car heater, I could see Mike's face, crinkled in his wonderful, crooked smile, and hear the silly jokes he was making for the girls. I crossed myself and said a silent prayer, thanking the good Lord for this wonderful day, for my understanding husband, and my lovely daughters. And yes, even thanking the Lord for this baby growing inside me.

Later that night we decorated the big tree they'd found, covering it with big, colorful lights and red balls and tinsel. It was a sight. Mike made the girls hot cocoa with real whipped cream on top and he fixed hot toddies with rum for us. I had such a wonderful feeling of well-being.

"Let's tell our favorite Christmas stories," Margie suggested.

Margie's idea wasn't original; we do this every Christmas season. It's a family tradition. Everyone gets to tell one story or memory.

"I'll be first," Margie continued. "My favorite story is how Daddy rented a Santa costume and came to the house and knocked on the door and asked to speak to me. Remember, Mo?"

Mo rolled her eyes and nodded. We all remembered. Each year Margie tells the same story of how we got her to stop sucking her thumb.

"Remember how Santa said if I didn't stop sucking my thumb, I wouldn't get that doll that came with all the lipstick and rouge? I really wanted that doll."

"So, that $19.95 rental was worth it," Mike said.

We all laughed at ourselves and the lengths we went to because of Margie's thumb-sucking habit.

"I remember how you hid behind that old blue chair in the living room, you were so scared of Santa Claus," Mo said.

"I was not!" Margie answered. She stuck her lower lip out, ready to defend her twelve-year-old self-esteem.

"Okay, you weren't," Mo gave in, but she winked at me.

"And you don't suck your thumb anymore," Mike added and we all laughed.

"Daddy, tell about how Santa took your toys," Margie demanded.

"Margie, maybe that's not a favorite memory for Daddy," I said, and we all laughed again. Like Margie, Mike tells the same story every year. "The immigrant's version of Santa Claus," he calls it.

"Well, every Christmas Eve, my brothers and I would go to sleep dreaming of new bikes and metal trucks and rocking horses. This was before your Aunt Bridey was born," he explained to the girls.

"Wow, that was a really long time ago," Margie said.

"Yeah, back in the Dark Ages," Mo added.

"Well, anyways, Santa always left the gifts in the front parlor because we usually didn't have a Christmas tree. We couldn't afford one."

"Not even a little, scrawny tree like the one we gave away to the Rizzos?" Margie asked.

"Nope, not even a little, scrawny tree." Mike continued, "We got some grand toys, though: shiny, yellow dump trucks and a spotted horse on runners that rocked back and forth and even made a horse noise, like *neigh. . . .*"

The girls laughed when Mike made the neighing sound.

"We played with those toys all Christmas day. When we woke up the day after Christmas, those toys were gone!" Mike always sounded surprised when he told that part of the story. "My parents, er . . . Santa, that is, had taken the toys away for next year," he explained.

"Boy, I'd hate that if Santa came back for my toys," Margie said, playing along with the story. She hasn't believed in Santa for a few years now.

"Well, when I was about eight, I finally figured it out, because Danny, your Uncle Danny," Mike explained, "got the same shiny yellow truck that I'd gotten the year before. I loved that truck and I remembered it, and there was no way I was standin' for Danny gettin' it, even if a year had passed." Mike shook his head at the memory. "That was the last year Santa took our toys."

"It was really Grandma and Grandpa, because they were so poor, right, Daddy?"

"We were poor in some ways, Margie. Not in others."

"What do you mean, Daddy?" Margie asked.

"Well, we didn't have a lot of things," Mike explained, "but we had each other."

Every year Mike ends this story the same way. Every year it makes me realize how close the Malloys are. Sometimes, even I feel like an outsider with them.

"What's your favorite story, Clare?" Mike asked.

I searched through my memories of past holidays, always focusing on some little story from the time before my mother died. Unlike Mike and Margie, I try to make my stories different each year.

"Well, I remember making gingerbread with my mother when I was really little," I said and as I began to tell my story, I could almost smell the gingerbread spices and feel the warmth of the old-fashioned, black iron oven in our house on Potter Street. I also felt a longing for my own mother, a woman whose face I could barely remember, but whom I still missed, even after thirty-two years. All of a sudden, I had a feeling of nameless dread and I trembled.

"Darlin'," Mike said, "you're shiverin'. And you look like someone just walked over your grave."

He stood up and wrapped an old multicolored afghan that his mother had crocheted for us around my shoulders. "What is it? You're not catchin' cold, I hope."

"I was just thinking of my own mother. I can barely remember her face," I said, just half telling the truth, for what I was also thinking was what would this family do without me if, like my own mother, I died suddenly, leaving my children to be always longing for me? What if I died in childbirth?

Mike put his arms around me and patted my back. "Sometimes holidays bring up all the old memories and it's good to think on them, Clare. You don't want to forget your family."

Our girls watched us for a moment, and then Mo said, "No fair! I didn't get to tell my favorite Christmas story."

"Time out for Mo," Mike announced, making the basketball signal with his hands.

"Well, my favorite story"—Mo smiled coyly at Mike and me—"is about a family that had two daughters and they really wanted a son and so one Christmas, an angel came to visit the family and said to the daughters, 'What would you girls really like for Christmas?' and the daughters said, 'We would like a baby brother, we would!' and the angel said, 'Well, you have to do something to prove it,' and the daughters said, 'What?' and the Christmas angel said, 'Learn to do something difficult,' and the daughters said, 'Like what?' and the angel said, 'Learn to stitch,' and the daughters said, 'UGH!' but they learned to stitch and so . . .'"

Mo jumped up and ran to her room, with Margie following her. Mike looked at me and said, "Learn to stitch?" and we both started laughing, picturing Mo and Margie ever sitting down with a needle and thread and sewing. We laughed till we had tears in our eyes.

Our daughters came back and placed a small package under the big tree.

"Can Mommy open it now, Daddy? Just this one present? Not the Santa presents, just this one from Mo and me?" Margie asked Mike.

"What do you say, Clare? Would you like to open just one present a few days early?" Mike winked at me.

"Well . . . ," I said, playing along with the game, "maybe just one."

"This one, Mommy!" Margie picked up the present that she and Mo had just placed under the tree. It was a small box, wrapped in silver foil with a royal blue bow. Tied to the bow was a blue, plastic baby rattle.

I unwrapped the gift very slowly. I wanted to feel every bit of this, for I knew from the preliminaries that this was a special moment.

I unfurled the white tissue and took out a tiny, white sailor's hat. Embroidered across the brim in bright blue lettering was the name Michael Jr. I held the little hat out in front of me so that Mike could see it, too.

"This is the best Christmas present I've ever gotten," I said and I meant it, truly.

"We just know the baby is going to be a boy," Mo said.

"And if it's a girl, you can name her Michael, too," Margie added. "So all our hard work learning to embroider won't go to waste."

We all laughed and then I said, "I'm sure it will be a boy." And I was sure of that. Somehow I just knew.

Mike

Jesus Christ, but I wanted to tear my hair out, to gouge my eyes out, to bang my head, over and over, against the pale green wall of the waiting room. I wanted to take one of those ugly, orange plastic chairs and throw it through the window. I wanted to take that doctor and smash him to pieces. I know, it wasn't at all his fault, but he was the one that brought me the news. Instead, I just stood there, my brown felt hat in my hands, and said, "It's God's will."

My son was born on Christmas Day, too early for his lungs to work. He lived one day, struggling every minute for his breath, for his life. I spent the day at Clare's bedside, holding her hand, silently praying the Rosary with her. Praying to Mary for a miracle, we were. When the doctors were sure there was no hope for Michael, they asked if we would like to hold him at the last. That was a kindness. They unhooked him from all the tubes and wires and placed him in Clare's arms. I held on to Clare for dear life.

We called for the resident chaplain, a Father Mc-Carthy, on part-time duty at the hospital from the Immaculate Conception Seminary. I didn't think he'd make it in time, so I grabbed my son from Clare's arms and splashed water from her drinking cup on his forehead. "I baptize thee, Michael Patrick, in the name of

the Father, and of the Son, and of the Holy Ghost.''
My son would at least rest with the angels, and not be
condemned to limbo until the Second Coming.

Father McCarthy arrived and baptized our boy
again and then gave him Extreme Unction, rubbing the
oils on his tiny forehead, the same place he had blessed
Michael with the water. I couldn't help thinking that
this was the third time this year I'd stood attendance at
the Last Rites of the Holy Church. First Pat, here at St.
Mary's also, with that old Irish priest chanting the
prayers. Cold as hell, Pat's skin was, for he was dead
and gone by the time we'd brought him into the hospital. And then Johnny, looking at me with those sad
eyes, knowing he was dying and helpless to stop it and
me helpless, too. And now my son, Michael, and what
could I do but to hold his tiny body in my arms and try
to let him feel how much we wanted him, how much
we loved him, although his knowing these things was
still so far beyond him, being such a tiny babe. All before
their time, they were. Way before their time. Then Michael slipped away, so quiet-like, it was as if he'd never
been with us at all.

I held Clare for a long time and then I called my
brother Danny to help me make the funeral arrangements. Clare insisted that she wouldn't allow Harry
O'Sullivan to touch the baby and so we had to go to
Hines Funeral Home out in Albia. I'll catch hell from
Bridey later for not using the O'Sullivans as undertakers,
but right now I have to see to Clare's wishes.

Mo

"I understand and I totally forgive your mother, Maureen. She's not in her right mind now," my Aunt Bridey explained to me. She was referring, of course, to my mother's wish to wake my baby brother from the Hines Funeral Home and not O'Sullivan's.

I really didn't care much whether Aunt Bridey understood or not, so I just nodded my head and took my mother's hand. I hoped she wouldn't notice the front of Bridey's blouse beginning to stain where her milk was leaking through. She's almost like a cow with those three babies. My mother's milk is gone already. Right after the baby died, the doctors gave her some drug to dry up her milk really fast. I wonder if there is a drug for what's wrong with her now.

My father says it will take time. "Time heals all wounds" he keeps telling me and Margie, as if he wants to believe that someday we will all be back to normal. My mother will stop crying, stop staring into space. She will have her teaching job back and everything will be the same.

My father is able to stand at the door and greet the many guests who have come to pay their respects. He shakes their hands and says, "Thank you for coming. Yes, it was God's will." Every time my mother hears him, she tightens her grip on my hand. I don't think she believes it was God's will at all.

My father says my brother looked just like me when I was born. He had little tufts of reddish hair and green eyes like me. I got to see him for only a minute. I never got to hold him. It's weird. He was my brother, as close by birth as Margie is to me, yet I didn't know him. I never will. We have a hole in our family where he should be.

Margie

When I saw my Uncle Danny and my Uncle Jim carrying that tiny white box, I thought of the day at The Waterwheel Park. I guess it was because that little white coffin just looked like a plastic cooler to me. That sounds disrespectful, I know, but I can't help what I think.

Anyways, that day at The Waterwheel so many summers ago, my uncles had carried the beer and soda in coolers to the picnic tables. We were all set up alongside the Poestenkill Creek. Our whole family was there. There must have been fifty cousins, all together. The waterwheel was turning slowly and we were all throwing sticks into the creek and watching them turn through the wheel. I wanted to be like my older cousins, so I gathered a handful of twigs and stood with them at the riverbank. It was a drop to the water, maybe two or three feet and I don't know how I slipped, but I did.

Maybe I was standing too close, or the bank was too soft and muddy to hold me, but my feet went right out from under me and all at once I was in the water.

My cousins were screaming to the aunts and my mother, "Margie's going to go through the waterwheel! Margie's drowning!" I could hear them quite clearly from under the water. I didn't realize I was drowning until I heard them yelling, but it was true. I hadn't learned to swim yet, and my feet couldn't touch, even though I tried.

I seemed to be floating, almost like those tiny princesses in the fairy tales who ride away on lily pads, except I wasn't on top of anything, I was under the water.

I remember looking up through the water and seeing my mother reaching down and screaming. Then I felt my father's strong arms around me, pushing me up to the surface. Later, when I sat on my mother's lap, wrapped in a towel and still spitting out muddy water, I heard Mommy tell my aunts that seeing my eyes staring at her from under the water was the worst thing.

When I think about my brother dying, I think about that day at The Waterwheel, when I almost drowned. How easy it was to breathe in the water. How fast it all happened. I could have just slipped away.

My brother slipped away, just like that, and my father's strong arms and my mother's prayers couldn't stop him. He breathed a little and then he died. The doctors told Daddy and Mommy that his lungs weren't ready yet and they kept filling with water, almost like my lungs did that day at The Waterwheel. I wondered if I would have been buried in a little, white coffin that looked like a picnic cooler if I had drowned that day. I thought about me dying, all through my brother's Mass of the Angels.

7

The Mayor's Wife

February 1965

❧

Bridey

Danny and I lived with Ma till she died, and then Danny
married Hildy Gunderson. Danny was considered quite
a catch for Hildy. All the South Troy girls agreed. Hildy
was pretty, in a big, blonde, coarse sort of way, but
Danny was downright dashing. The best looking of all
my brothers, with his dark red hair and fine, high
cheekbones, and those flashing green eyes. And what a
charmer! He was the darlin' of the Southie girls and they
were heartbroken when Hildy snagged him.

At first Hildy and Danny lived here with me on
Third Street, in Ma's house. But after six months of us
women not getting along all that well, Hildy and Danny
took a place of their own. I liked Hildy, but it was hard
sharing the household duties with her. She's German,
you know, a convert, too, and very set in her ways.
She'd insist that the table be set just so, with starched
cloths and napkins and forks here and knives there, and
sometimes even flowers. It was nice, but it wasn't some-

thing we Malloys were used to. And the meals she tried to serve us when it was her turn to cook. Lord, you could hardly eat the stuff it was so smothered in sauerkraut. Anyways, after six months of us bickering, Danny had saved enough to rent a place over on First Street.

When they left, I was alone in Ma's house, so when Paulie and I married, it was only natural that we live here. That was six years ago and that's how I ended up with Ma's house. My brothers, God bless them, haven't got a stingy bone in their bodies and have never asked for a share of the house that Ma left to all of us. It's a good thing, too, because Paulie and I don't have a dime to spare, and now with the triplets and the extra hospital bills from their stay, things are really tough. I try to be as generous to my brothers as they are to me, though, and that's why I offered to have the family meeting here at my house to discuss Danny's campaign for the special election. When John T. Finnerty, the mayor of the city for twenty years, finally dropped dead of cirrhosis of the liver, my brother got his big chance.

I was not surprised that Hildy refused to join us. There's something strange going on with her and Danny now. My sister-in-law Mary tells me that Danny and Hildy have not spoken a word to each other in three months. I can't imagine them sleeping under the same roof and raising those two kids of theirs and not speaking, but Mary swears on her mother's grave that it's the truth. Anyways, I was not surprised that Hildy didn't show up for the family meeting, but I think she should have.

We sat around Ma's old oak table and tried to calculate the city vote. Jim said he could bring in the police vote. Jim is always a bit of a braggart and Danny raised his eyebrows when Jim was explaining how it would work.

"Don't worry, Danny boy. I'll just tell 'em they got to vote for you, or answer to me. Besides, you're for law and order, right?" Jim had said.

Sure, I thought, Danny's so much for law and order he can't stop his own boy from throwing beer bottles at police cars, or shaking down the smaller kids in that private military school they send him to. That Peter could cost Danny the election. Peter, and his mother, Hildy, if she doesn't pull with the family.

"Yeah, of course I'm for law and order," Danny answered.

"I'm sure you'll get the fire department vote," Anna said. "Everyone knows you're Johnny's brother."

We all stopped talking for a minute and thought of our brother Johnny, how it was really him who should have been running for public office. The sweetest among us, he was. And everyone had loved him.

"God rest his soul," Meg said, and then added, "And the railroad vote, too. People there know you're Pat's brother."

"And, of course, I'll be working for you down at party headquarters," my own Paulie said, "and I can promise you a lot of votes from North Troy."

We all laughed at that. Half the people in North Troy are O'Sullivans and somehow related to Paulie. We have been married six years now, and I still haven't figured them all out yet, the second cousins, the third cousins, the great-aunts. But they all voted for Danny and that's what counts.

Clare and Mike came to the meeting, too. It was their first time out since the baby died. Mike thought it would do Clare some good, and I guess it did, because later she threw herself into campaign work. That night, though, she kind of just sat there, really silent-like. When my babies started crying, which they always seem to be doing, she got up and left the room. I followed her and found her standing over their cribs, looking down. Her face was really sad. I know she must have been thinking about her lost boy.

"Let's go help Danny become Troy's next mayor," I said.

"Yes," Clare answered. "Let's do that. Anything for the Malloys."

Her tone was so funny, I didn't know what to think. It was almost like she didn't mean it. But Clare surprised me. In the end, it turned out that she did more volunteer work at party headquarters than any of us. It gave her something to think about other than that poor little boy of hers. And Danny won the election that spring, hands down, even if his own wife didn't vote for him.

Danny

I'm no stranger to hard work. When I graduated from Catholic Central, I went right to work for the GE over in their turbine division in Schenectady. My brothers were green with envy that I could snag such a high-paying job in a union shop. I'm mechanical, so working with those big machines came pretty easy to me, but it was good timing and the luck of the Irish that got me in the door. Timing, because I had a pool-shooting buddy who was leaving GE and he told me about the job opening; luck, because a lot of guys my age were being drafted for the Big One, but I had flat feet.

I worked for fifteen years in that shop, content with my hours and my pay, and the three weeks off every summer, and also with the good job I was doing. And I liked it there, the oily smells, the clanging noises of the shop, the easy friendships I made over coffee. I must have had a hundred good friends in that shop, all of them working on turbines. It was them that got me elected steward of the union and gave me my first taste of politics. I got it in my blood and it's never been the same for me since. Much later, when I won the special election for mayor, I pulled in the working man's vote and beat those Republicans good. I think that people saw in me a good Democrat, a hard worker, and an honest man.

THE IRISH PRINCESS

I wish my own wife would believe in my honesty as much as the voters did. Hildy hasn't spoken a word to me in months. I don't know how she can be so hard and unforgiving. It must be her German nature. I've tried to talk to her. At first, I badgered her with questions, thinking I'd wear her down, make her laugh again, make her like me a little again. But she'd give me that grim look and walk away. She thinks I took the money from her bank account.

Hildy's been saving now for years so that she could send for her mother's twin sister in Germany. All her life it has been drummed into her head that Aunt Lisl must come to this country. Hildy is a fine seamstress, I'll say that for her, and so on the side, besides keeping house and raising Peter and Gretchen, she's been making clothes for the fancy ladies from Sycaway and those other toney suburbs. She had about nine hundred dollars in her account and someone just walked into the Union National bank with Hildy's own account book and withdrew the money. I swore on a stack of Bibles that it wasn't me, but Hildy thinks it could have been no one else. I'm afraid I know who took the money and why, but I dare not tell Hildy. First of all, she wouldn't believe, and second, she'd hate me all the more for suggesting it. Third, it would break her heart. Instead, I'll bide my time. She can't be so stubborn as to never speak to me again.

Clare

I met Hildy by accident in Woolworth's the day after Danny won the election. I was shopping for cheap fabric so that Margie could do her stuffed animal for the Campfire badge she's working on. Hildy was in the notions department looking for snaps for a dress she's making for Judge Goldstein's wife.

"Hildy," I said, "please talk to me." I wasn't going to let her brush me by like she does to the rest of the Malloys. We had been good friends. We raised our babies together. I thought of the many times we'd taken Mo and Peter to Prospect Park when they were toddlers. Before the polio scare we'd let them play in the wading pool for entire afternoons while we sat and talked. And then it was Margie and Gretchen. My Margie learned to walk holding Hildy's hands. How could she just ignore that?

Hildy gave me that grim German stare of hers and tried to step by me, pushing her Woolworth's basket out in front almost like it was a barrier between us. I guess she didn't know me all that well if she thought a flimsy, little, red plastic basket could stop me.

"Hildy, I'm not moving from this spot until you talk to me."

Hildy's face seemed to crumple a little and she said, "I'm sorry about the baby, Clare."

I guess I wasn't prepared to discuss Michael then and there, for I lost my control and just started to cry, right in Woolworth's. Well, what could Hildy do? She steered me to the luncheonette counter and ordered tea for the both of us. She put her strong German arms around me and patted my back as I cried like a baby. Later, I was really embarrassed, breaking down in public like that, a professional woman like me, with a reputation to hold up. But then, I just couldn't help it. I guess it will be a long time till I really get back to my old self.

Hildy and I talked about my baby for quite a while. She confided to me that she had lost a baby last year, a miscarriage in the fourth month. That surprised me because none of the Malloys knew anything about Hildy being pregnant. But she always was the silent type, she never told us about Peter or Gretchen till she showed. Anyways, that was last year when she and Danny were still talking, or at least sleeping together.

I told her how good the campaign had been for me, what with losing the baby and then not even having a teaching job to return to till next year.

Hildy sort of glared at me and said, "Don't speak to me of Danny, Clare."

"But Hildy, what's wrong with you and Danny?" I blurted out. To me, their not speaking was incomprehensible. What could be so wrong that you could live in a house with someone and never speak to him?

"The man is a dishonest, lying schemer," Hildy said, her voice so hard and bitter-sounding, it was like someone I never knew was speaking.

"Keep your voice down," I reprimanded her, looking around. After all, my brother-in-law Danny had just been elected mayor of the city on his platform of honesty and hard work. It would hardly do to have his wife calling him a "lying schemer" out in public. Besides, I knew the Malloy family well, better than most people know them, and one thing they are is honest as the day is long. Suddenly, I was Danny's campaign worker again and someone had just made a slur at my candidate.

Hildy's face was hateful, and as I tried to calm her down, it occurred to me that maybe she had a serious mental problem. "Hildy," I said, "have you been to see Dr. Moriarty lately for a checkup?"

"I don't need no mick doctor telling me it's all in my head what Danny done."

"What did Danny do?" I whispered, trying to get her to speak lower.

"The Honorable Daniel T. Malloy stole nine hundred dollars of my hard-earned money from my own private bank account. Using my bankbook, the nerve of him."

"Oh, there must be a misunderstanding, Hildy. Danny would never do that. You must know Danny would never steal from you," I said, and what I said, I knew was true. Danny Malloy may have his faults, but cheating and stealing are not among them.

"It could be no one but Danny, Clare. He's the only one who could have known where I hid the bankbook."

"Well, other people live in the house, Hildy. And many of your friends come and go. Maybe someone else saw you hide the bankbook." I thought of Hildy's old German Bible, her precious family heirloom, and I guess I knew where she hid her bankbook, too. "Why, even the children probably knew where your bankbook was," I added.

Hildy looked at me with scorn. "Don't you dare suggest such a thing to me, Clare Malloy. You're just like the rest of that Irish mob, thick as thieves you are." Hildy stood up and threw some change on the green formica counter. "You can just cross me off your list of friends, Clare Malloy, suggesting that my Peter or my Gretchen would steal from their own mother."

She gathered up her basket and straightened her shoulders and turned and left me sitting alone at the counter.

I watched her leave, walking tall with her head high, looking straight ahead. With her blond hair pulled back tight in a braided bun and that set look on her face, she reminded me of those Valkyries, those battle maidens in the Nordic myths that I used to read to my sixth-grade class. I thought of my gentle brother-in-law, Danny, trying to cajole her out of her anger. He would never win. I thought of that boy of hers, Peter, who Bridey always said was going to be spoiled rotten by Hildy. I thought of things Mo had heard from her friends at the Academy, the school where Peter goes, about him being in trouble with the headmaster and of the times Jim had been called to use his influence with the police to get Peter out of a jam. Always, Hildy would say, "Boys will be boys," and just excuse away his petty misdoings. I wondered if Peter knew where Hildy kept her bankbook. I supposed he did.

Margie

When my Aunt Hildy stopped talking to my Uncle Danny and then to my mother and finally to the rest of us Malloys, it meant that I never got to play with my cousin Gretchen again. I felt really bad about that for a long time, because Gretchen is the only cousin who's just my age and she was my main friend at all the Malloy picnics and family get-togethers. After the special election that spring that made my uncle the mayor of Troy, I never even really got to talk to Gretchen again. Sometimes I would see her walking on the street in Troy, holding hands with my Aunt Hildy. Sometimes I'd see her from the late school bus and I'd always wave and she'd wave back. My Uncle Danny continued to come to all the family parties, but after his big victory he never brought Aunt Hildy and his kids again.

At the victory party at my Aunt Bridey's house after the election, I heard the aunts whispering in the kitchen. My mother was there, whispering, too. I'm sure they didn't want Uncle Danny to hear what they were saying and be hurt.

"Hildy wants nothin' to do with any of the Malloys," my Aunt Bridey said. "And she says we are a bad influence on her kids, so she's not allowin' them to come here anymore with Danny."

"A bad influence"? I thought of my cousin Gretchen and the fun we had pretending to be girl detectives. Did my Aunt Hildy, who used to be one of my favorite aunts, who used to hold me and Gretchen on her lap and tell us stories about the Black Forest and how it was filled with fairies and elves and bears that sometimes turned into people, did she think that I was a bad influence, too?

"She's upset about something she just can't face," my mother said, and now she wasn't whispering. My mother has strong opinions and she believes she's right all the time. "She's taking it out on Danny, because he's the easiest person to be the scapegoat, and she's extending her anger to all of us."

I went to the door of the kitchen and peeked in. My aunts were all sitting around the table with the checkered oilcloth cover, listening to my mother. They were having coffee and my Aunt Bridey had the three high chairs lined up in a row. My baby cousins, the triplets, were sitting there like eager little birds waiting for my aunt to feed them. She had one big dish of baby cereal and one spoon and she fed them like they were on an assembly line. Those babies didn't miss a bite. I didn't want the aunts to hear me listening so I just stayed there, leaning against the door, really quiet-like.

"Tell them about meeting Hildy in Woolworth's," my Aunt Bridey said.

My mother told the story and my aunts gasped when they heard the "Irish mob, thick as thieves" part.

"That was a terrible thing for her to say," my Aunt Anna said. "Why, I'm Swedish. I'm not even one bit Irish!" she added indignantly.

My mother and my other aunts laughed when Aunt Anna said that, and my mother said, "You're Irish by relation, Anna, and you should consider yourself damn lucky."

They all laughed again and then my little cousin Erin began to cry. She's my mother's favorite of the triplets.

Aunt Bridey picked her up and handed her to my mother and Erin calmed down as my mother cuddled her. Watching Mommy hold my little cousin, I started to feel real teary for my dead baby brother and I thought about him in that little white box, alone under the ground, and for a moment I just wanted to run away.

And then, strangely, as if my mother knew I was at the door listening and knew what I was thinking, she said to my aunts, "Life goes on." They all looked at her, holding that little baby, and nodded their heads, their lips fixed in little half-smiles.

"We'll just have to support Danny the best we can through this and make a good face of it."

"Make a good face of it"! I thought of the things that my Aunt Hildy had already missed, and that people had noticed her absence. Like the party at headquarters the night of the election. And she wasn't going to be at the swearing-in and neither were Peter and Gretchen, according to my Aunt Mary.

"I'll miss Hildy, because we go way back," my mother added, "and I know that Margie is really going to miss Gretchen. I doubt that any of us will miss Peter terribly."

My aunts nodded in agreement and I had to admit my mother was right again. None of us would miss that bully, Peter. But Gretchen! I wanted to cry at the thought she wouldn't be playing Nancy Drew with me.

I thought of how we called ourselves "the twin cousins" because we were the same age and we kind of looked alike. Gretchen has the same light red hair that I have. We get it from Grandmother Malloy. Mommy says it's from a recessive gene that skips a generation, whatever that means.

Anyways, if it's true about Aunt Hildy not letting Gretchen come to family parties, who am I going to play girl detective with? I thought about the last time we'd played it down in the swamp near the creek. We'd pretended that the Black Sultan, that evil man from Nancy Drew mysteries, was after us because we knew his secret hideout for smuggling stolen jewelry into the country was right there in the woods near the Wynant-skill Creek.

"His alias in this country is Mr. Peter Malloy," my cousin Gretchen announced.

"Gretchen, you can't make your own brother into the Black Sultan," I protested.

"Oh yes, Peter has to be the bad guy or I'm not playing."

Gretchen was stubborn. My mom called it "her German inheritance," because she sure didn't get it from my Uncle Danny. He could be persuaded to change his mind on everything. That's why he is such a good politician, my father said.

Gretchen insisted that Peter be made the bad guy, and he wasn't even there to defend himself. I agreed because it was just easier than to argue with Gretchen, but I asked her, "Do you hate your brother, Gretchen?"

"Yes," she hissed and she sounded so mean she just reminded me of a snake.

"Why?" I asked and again I thought of how I wished that my brother had lived and how I would never hate him, even if he got into all my things and got all of Daddy's attention.

"Because he is a dishonest, lying schemer!" my cousin said.

I heard those words again that day I was at the kitchen door at Uncle Danny's family victory party. But when I heard them, it was my own mother saying that was what Aunt Hildy had called my Uncle Danny. That was the day that I began to wonder if Aunt Hildy was confused. That was the day I began to realize that the times of playing girl detective with my twin cousin, Gretchen, were probably over for good.

8

Holy Week

April

🌿

Mo

We put away our winter cheering uniforms last week and Mrs. Tully, our cheerleading advisor, passed out the spring ones. Of course, with the *new* uniforms she just had to go over the *old* rules. No riding on the team bus, no sitting on boys' laps on the spectator bus. If there aren't enough seats, you just have to stand. No smoking or, heaven forbid, drinking. You must always remember that you represent Troy High School when you're in uniform and then act accordingly. When she said that rule, she turned her chubby, old face right to me and stared.

"As I said, Maureen, there will be no, I repeat, *no* repetition of the type of incident that happened outside the Mayflower Diner after the basketball game with Lansing High."

I really don't like Mrs. Tully most of the time, she is a prissy old teacher, but today along with the red shame on my cheeks, I could feel real black hatred inside me. I tried not to show it, though, because I wanted to stay on the squad, so I just looked down and nodded. It really wasn't such a big deal at the Mayflower, anyways. I was just trying to break up a fight between Tony Casey and one of the Lansing basketball players, and a reporter from *The Troy Record* happened to be there and snapped a picture. Then I ended up in my cheerleading uniform on the front page of the sports section with a big caption: "School Spirit Goes Awry." My friends all thought it was funny, but my parents and Mrs. Tully didn't. And of course, my father got an immediate phone call from my Aunt Bridey.

Anyways, I looked down at my saddle shoes and very politely said, "It will never happen again, Mrs. Tully." I can be a real little Goody Two-shoes when I want.

"Very well, Maureen, now if you'll help me pass out these new uniforms, we'll be able to get some practice time in."

"We'll" be able to practice! Ha, I thought. We're the ones who do the jumps and the splits and the kickline and the cartwheels. Mrs. Tully sits on her fat butt and critiques us. Sometimes I wonder if putting up with her nosy, old piggy-face is worthwhile, but I suppose it is, because the squad is really good now and the new spring uniforms are really cute. We have these short, purple-and-gold-plaid, pleated skirts and gold blouses to match. And the nicest part is the school is giving us a little necklace with a gold THS pendant.

We also got new pom-poms for baseball season. I

hope that David Markovitch is trying out for varsity baseball this year. It will give me a chance to get to know him better. He's been looking at me in Mr. Henry's physics class and I think he likes me, but he's a little shy. Maybe my short, plaid cheering skirt will help him overcome all that.

Actually, I've only got a month to work on it, but I'm expecting David to be my prom date. He's going steady with Laurie Glassman right now, but I heard through the cafeteria-gossip grapevine that they're about to break up.

She came up to my locker yesterday and said, "If you're planning on dating David, DON'T! He's already spoken for."

"Spoken for"? For crying out loud, I thought. Laurie makes it seem like we're living in the Dark Ages. I don't want to marry David Markovitch, I just want to go out and have fun.

"I think David can make up his own mind, Laurie," I said and I slammed my locker hard and walked away. Later, I saw those snotty girls from Sycaway that Laurie hangs out with, pointing at me and whispering. I guess that was supposed to bother me.

Well, at least I won't have to deal with them or Laurie for a few days. We have Thursday and Friday off because it's Holy Week and the beginning of April vacation. Everyone is planning to go to the Red Front for pizza on Thursday night, but my father has already informed me that we have to go to Holy Thursday service at our church.

"Aw, Dad, do we have to do that again this year?"
I asked.

"Maureen, this is the holiest week of the year for
Catholics, and we give up things we want to do, like
going to the movies or going out with friends for pizza,
to sacrifice to be ready for the Resurrection."

"But Daddy, all the rest of the kids are going," I
said and I thought of the opportunity Laurie Glassman
would have with David Markovitch if I didn't show up.

"All the rest of the kids are not Malloys!" my father
said and that was the end of it.

So we'll all be at church on Thursday, watching
Father Tim wash an old man's feet. I know it's symbolic
and all, but I couldn't stand having to wash some old
man's feet, even if he is the bishop of Albany. Father
Tim has to do it in our church because he's the youngest
priest.

He's pretty much given up on me for the convent.
Since that day we went horseback riding last summer,
he hasn't mentioned it at all. In fact, he's kind of avoid-
ing me, I think. Last week after mass I stopped to talk
to him to see if he'd sent that recommendation that the
College of Saint Benedict needed for my application.

He blushed a little when I smiled at him, and said
he'd sent it in several weeks ago.

"Did you also write me a letter for Syracuse?" I
asked. I'm counting on some scholarship money from
Syracuse so I can go there.

Father Tim frowned and said, "I sent in the letter
as you requested, Maureen, but I wish you would think

very clearly about your decision should you be accepted at both places. Saint Benedict's is clearly a better choice for you. I've explained that to your parents already."

Explained what to my parents? I thought. Explained it would be better for me to be taught by a bunch of nuns than to go to a big university like Syracuse? I wanted to tell him what I thought, but instead I just shook his hand and walked down the steps of the church. Of course I'd pick Syracuse over Saint Benedict's. But it all depends on the money. With Mom not working, I'll have to choose the college that offers me the most aid.

Well, while all my friends are out partying their way through Holy Week, maybe I'll use the time constructively to pray extra hard. I know I shouldn't pray for such trivial things. I know I'm supposed to pray for world peace and the conversion of Russia to Catholicism and all those kind of things, but I think I'll pray that Syracuse gives me a lot of money. I have to go there.

Clare

Mike insisted that we go to the foot-washing service and then visit several other churches on Holy Thursday. All the Malloys do that during Holy Week. I guess it is a South Troy tradition. We never did it in Granville, but then our little town only had one Catholic church.

I really would rather have stayed at home, kicked my feet up, and watched TV. Since we lost the baby, I just seem to be saying empty prayers. Prayers with no meaning, rote words from my childhood that bring me no peace and no comfort. I've spoken with Father Mullen about it and he doesn't seem to get what I'm saying.

I made an appointment to talk to him about my feelings one night last week. I felt like I couldn't go on having those black thoughts, picturing my baby's flesh just rotting in his grave. It was driving me crazy.

When I got to the rectory, he insisted that we sit in the parlor. "Let's not sit in that stuffy office," he said. "You'll feel more comfortable in the parlor." He showed me into an old-fashioned sitting room, so different from the modern look of our church that it put me off, made me feel uneasy. Our newly built church is all tile and light wood and beautiful stained glass windows. It is simple and airy, that's why I like it so much. This room with its dark mahogany furniture and worn velvet sofas and lace doilies reminded me of my aunts' houses. Did he think I would feel more comfortable in this old-style room?

"I have trouble reconciling my baby's death with the loving God that Jesus is supposed to represent, the Jesus we read about in the Gospels," I confessed to him.

"Clare, my dear," he said to me as he took my hand, "God does not give you a cross you cannot bear."

"Well, he has!" I insisted, angry with his pat answer, a platitude that held no meaning for me at all. "I can't bear this, it's eating me alive," I said.

THE IRISH PRINCESS

"My dear, you simply have to overcome this test," Father Mullen said. "Think of how Job was tested in the Old Testament. His family and home were lost to him. You still have your two lovely daughters and your husband. For their sake, you simply have to keep up your spirits."

"Simply"? I looked at Father Mullen and tried to control my feelings. I felt like slapping him and screaming obscenities to shock him into awareness of what I was suffering. I took a deep breath and closed my eyes for a second. He's just a man, only a man, I thought. I can't expect him to know how a mother feels. How could he know about losing a child? Why did I ever expect he might have answers for me? I felt a sudden, powerful feeling of loneliness and longing. Longing to hold my Michael again, loneliness in the knowledge that no one, not even Mike, could experience what I was feeling. And certainly not this old man sitting beside me, content with his quaint Irish aphorisms, his little Band-Aids for my great wound. Thinking his words would bring me comfort, as if they could help me at all. I wondered if he'd ever faced tragedy up close.

"You're angry at God for takin' your little one, Clare," he continued. "That's understandable. But just think, that precious baby is in the arms of the Lord and his Mother, Mary. He's surrounded by a Heavenly Host."

Why can't I think of it like that? I wondered. Why do I think of my Michael in a cold grave instead of in the light of Jesus?

I made my Easter duty with confession on Holy Thursday. I asked for forgiveness for my doubts, I asked for understanding. But in my heart, I didn't mean any of it. I'm going through the motions for the sake of the girls, but the truth is I just don't believe in a loving God. What kind of a loving God would let a sweet baby like Michael die?

Mike

I can't be guessing what's in that woman's head, but you could have knocked me down with a feather when I heard where she took the kids on Good Friday! I hope the good Lord is forgiving, I hope he understands that Clare is not quite herself yet, but Jesus, Mary, and Joseph, a picnic on Good Friday, the day Jesus died on the cross!

"Mike, this involves the moral education of your girls," my sister, Bridey, said when I told her about it. "You really must speak to Clare."

Bridey claims that Clare and I should never have taken the girls out of parochial school to put them in public school. She claims that now we have to work extra hard to bring them up properly in the Faith.

Clare and Bridey don't always get along that well. I think it's because Bridey is a little jealous of Clare's college education and a little scared of it.

As if she could read my mind, my sister said, "After

all, I only went to Mildred Elley Secretarial School, but I know as well as any college-educated teacher how children should be raised in the Faith. And after all, I am Maureen's godmother."

Bridey has pulled that "Maureen's godmother" bit a lot on Clare and me. Clare says it's just a convenient excuse for Bridey to stick her nose in our business, but I don't think that of my sister. I really believe she worries about the spiritual welfare of the children. Christ, before she met Paulie, she almost went into the convent herself.

I left my sister's house, wishing I'd never mentioned the Good Friday incident to her, but I did and now it was water under the bridge. I don't like to go up against Clare. I never have, because she's usually got all the answers, but I had to call her on this one, especially now that Bridey knew.

After Saturday dinner, while the kids were getting ready to dye Easter eggs, I told my wife we needed to talk.

"Clare," I said, "it was wrong to take the girls on a picnic on Good Friday. They should have been in church from one to three with the rest of the Malloys, saying the stations of the cross."

My wife glared at me. Clare does not like to be wrong, and in the past, in matters regarding the children and their education, I have always listened to her. But this time I just had to say my piece.

"Don't you start telling me *now* how to raise these children," my wife said. She stressed the word "now" as if I hadn't had any say in their upbringing before.

"For God's sake, Clare, I just want you to show a little respect for the Church. A picnic on Good Friday is wrong."

Clare's face got red and it was as if the devil himself was speaking. Surely it was not the Clare I loved.

"What's wrong, Michael, is to sit in church on a beautiful spring day, contemplating a cruel and unmerciful God."

"You can't mean that, Clare," I said. I was shocked to hear my wife blaspheme. The baby's death had left Clare not quite right, but she had never said such a terrible thing. Not thinking, I made the sign of the cross on my forehead. That seemed to infuriate Clare.

"Just call on your God to protect you, Michael. But tell me, where was he when we needed help for our baby? Where was he then?"

Clare left the kitchen and went to our room, slamming the door behind her. I could hear her crying in there and Lord knows I wanted to go to her but, as God is my witness, I was afraid. I was afraid of what else she might say.

I didn't know what to do, so I called my sister, Bridey. I thought she could help me with the woman's viewpoint.

"Not to worry, Mike," Bridey said. "I'll talk some sense into Clare at dinner tomorrow."

"No, Bridey, better just let it lie," I said and I could just picture the Easter dinner table at Ma's house, now my sister's house, strewn with purple eggs and Malloy bodies. I swear I pictured it that way!

Margie

I learned a lot about my family on Easter Sunday. I learned that Mo has a new boyfriend and he is Jewish and Daddy doesn't approve. I learned that my Aunt Bridey doesn't like Jews or Negroes. I learned that my mother doesn't really like Aunt Bridey all the time and thinks that she's superstitious. I also learned that my father is a little afraid of both my mother and my Aunt Bridey. It all started out really simple on Good Friday, but by Easter dinner, my parents were in a full-scale war and Aunt Bridey was in the middle of it.

We were all dressed to go to church on Good Friday. I had on nice pants and my new spring jacket and Mo had on her good school clothes. We were both pinning on little, white lace veils to cover our hair when Mommy came into the room.

"Forget about those veils, girls. We're going on a picnic."

I looked at my sister and I could tell she was thinking the same thing that I was. This was too good to be true. We followed my mother into the kitchen and found that she'd packed our picnic basket with sandwiches—tuna fish, of course, because it was Good Friday—and potato chips and chocolate chip cookies and soda. Mommy put on her coat and we followed her to the car.

"I don't care if it is Good Friday, girls. It is too nice to spend it inside. You'll do your praying at the Grove."

My sister looked at me and raised her eyebrows. This was definitely out of line on my mother's part, but I didn't care. The Grove was one of my favorite places. It's way out in the country near Crooked Lake. It's a picnic area full of pine trees that let spotty patches of sunlight through. The ground is covered with soft pine needles and it always smells so good. There is a little stream that you can follow back into the woods to pick wildflowers. I wondered if it would be too early for wildflowers.

When we got to the Grove, we were the only ones there. Maybe everybody else was in church praying. We spread out our blanket in a sunny spot and Mommy took off her coat and sat down.

"I have a special surprise for after lunch," she said as she handed us our tuna sandwiches.

"What is it?" I begged.

My mother held up a bag of M&M's. A big pound-sized bag! She smiled that funny grin she has and I thought, right then, that she could be just thirteen, like me. I also thought she was just the prettiest lady in the world and I was glad that she was my own mother.

After we finished our lunch, Mommy lay down on the blanket.

"Ah, the sun feels so good on my face," she said. "I think I'll rest here for a while."

"Can Mo and I go looking for wildflowers?" I asked.

"Sure, but don't go too far back into the woods. Understand, Mo?" my mother said, looking at my sister.

Mo and I walked along the creek, not talking, just appreciating our freedom. I knew my cousins and all my Catholic friends were in church and that made this picnic all the more fun for me.

I bent over to pick a violet. I had a handful that I was going to bring back to Mommy. As I parted the damp weeds to reach the violet, I felt something move against my hand. It felt cold. I jumped back because I thought I knew what it was, and I was right! A huge black-and-white snake lay coiled right near the patch of violets. I screamed because I'm really afraid of snakes, and I dropped my violets and ran back to my mother. Mo was right behind me, too. She pretends to be so grown-up, but she's more afraid of snakes and spiders than I am.

My mother was packing up when we got back to the blanket. I don't think my mother is much afraid of anything, because when we told her about the snake she said, "Show me where it is."

"Not me!" I said, and my sister agreed with me. We were not going back to see that snake.

"There's nothing to be afraid of, girls. There are no poisonous snakes in this part of New York," my mother said.

"Oh yes, there are," Mo argued. "Jimmy Rockett

found a whole nest of rattlesnakes in his backyard last summer."

"Maureen, I'm surprised at you. You know Jimmy is the biggest fibber in all of Wynantskill. Why, when I taught him in sixth grade, he had a different story every day for not having his homework done. And they were very creative stories, too," my mother added. "Besides, that big, old snake in there isn't causing anyone any trouble."

My mother was wrong about that! That snake caused a lot of trouble at Easter Sunday dinner at Aunt Bridey's.

"It's a sign from God," my Aunt Bridey said as she passed the ham and pineapples around the table. All my uncles were sort of smirking because they know how their sister can be when she gets going. They call it her "high horse." "The serpent was there to remind you that it was Good Friday and you had no business being out on a picnic, Clare," my aunt said.

My father interrupted. "Bridey, let's not bring this up now."

"I wasn't the one who brought this up, Mike. My own goddaughter brought this up when she was telling her cousins about the Good Friday picnic." My Aunt Bridey looked at Mo. "The snake was there to remind you of how Jesus conquered the serpent. Just like the statue in church of Mary crushing the serpent's head with her bare foot is there to remind us each time we see it."

"Oh, for God's sake, Bridey, don't be so foolish,"

my mother said, laughing. I could tell she was trying to make light of it so that Easter dinner wouldn't be ruined. All the cousins were suddenly quiet and looking at my mother and my aunt.

"Honestly, Clare. You should have known better, setting such an example for the children. And now Maureen tells me that she wants to go to the prom with a David Markovitch. Now what kind of a name is Markovitch, I ask you? Probably Jewish! Next thing, your girl will be going out with coloreds."

My aunt was on a roll now. Her face was getting redder and she was shaking her finger at my mother. She stood up and leaned across the table. Her green linen dress was wrinkled in spots and tight across her chubby hips. As she shook her finger at my mother, the rest of her shook, too, except for her bouffant hairdo. That puffed-out beehive didn't move at all! I knew that my mother was not going to laugh this one off. She only stands for just so much!

"Bridey, I'll thank you to mind your own business," my mother said.

"Maureen is my business. Or have you forgotten, Clare? You're the one who personally asked me to be her godmother on the day she was born."

"And a sorry choice that was." My mother stood up. "I will not sit here at Easter dinner and listen to superstitions and racial slurs come out of your ignorant mouth, Bridget."

Bridget! No one ever calls Aunt Bridey Bridget. She hates that name.

"I'm going home, Mike. You can join me if you want to. Come, girls."

My mother motioned to Mo and me, and we dutifully stood up. We were not about to cross her now.

My father stood up, too. "Bridey, I asked you not to bring this whole thing up today."

His voice sounded angry, but I couldn't tell if he was mad at Aunt Bridey or my mother, or both.

My aunt just glared at my father as he left the table and followed us to the door. The babies started to cry and all the other aunts and uncles jumped up to try to patch things up. But there was no changing my mother's mind that day. The Michael Malloy family walked out on the Easter dinner.

Later, my Aunt Bridey called my mother to say she was sorry. I think the rest of the family made her do it. My mother was very gracious and accepted her apology and eventually things got back to normal. Aunt Bridey and my mother became friends again, sort of, although my aunt still bothered my mother about us going to public school. Mo did get invited to the prom by David Markovitch and he *is* Jewish. Most important, after that Good Friday, "the day of rebellion," my father now calls it and he laughs when he talks about it, my mother began to get better and soon she was her old self again, the mother I remembered before we lost Michael.

9

The Senior Prom

May

❧

Clare

"Well now, which one of you lovely young ladies is looking for a prom dress?" Mr. Baronson asked.

Mo nearly laughed out loud at the question, but it made me feel good. I knew he was just making silly flattery, trying to turn my head into buying one of the more expensive formals for Mo, but I didn't care. For just a few minutes, I felt like a teenager again and all my troubles just lifted away. It's been more like that lately. I don't think so much about the baby anymore, and when I do it's more like a distant heartache. Not like it was at first, when I blamed myself for losing him and the actual pain of it all was like a knife stabbing in me. Looking back, I think I must have been out of my head with grief, because I don't really remember a lot of other things besides the pain.

"My mother will not be going to the senior prom," Mo answered in her sauciest voice.

"No," I agreed, "I'm afraid my social schedule

doesn't allow time for the prom this year, Mr. Baronson. But my daughter Maureen will be going and she'll need a beautiful dress."

"Beautiful dresses, we have plenty of. Let me get Mrs. Baronson to help fit you."

Mr. Baronson walked to the back of the store, calling out to his wife. I took a quick look at the price tags after he left. Good heavens, $129.98! I hadn't planned on paying that much, but somehow I'd do it. Layaway maybe. Although she hasn't come right out and said so, I know that Mo has her sights set on being the prom queen. She's joined every prom committee and I hear her on the phone lobbying for the student vote. Knowing how she can turn on the charm, I'm sure she's also working on the teacher vote in school. Most important in her plan is a beautiful gown. It's a known fact that some plain-looking girls make the queen's court if they've been hard workers and have managed to find a date, but the prom queen is always radiant. The queen is always a pretty girl in a beautiful gown. We really can't afford it, but I'm determined Mo will have a chance at senior prom queen.

Mrs. Baronson came out of the back of the store. She carried several large clear plastic bags filled with pastel satins and laces—strapless gowns, with tops shaped like women's breasts. Everything looked pretty and smelled new, as if the gowns themselves were making promises of the wonderful night to come.

"We have several new styles from Priscilla," Mrs. Baronson said, turning to me to qualify her statement.

"Priscilla of Boston . . . I'm sure you've heard of her, a very fine designer."

I nodded my head, pretending recognition. I certainly had no knowledge of any gown designers, let alone Priscilla, but I wasn't going to let on to any haughty shopkeeper. My money was as good as anyone's and no one was going to be lovelier than my daughter on prom night.

Mo picked out several gowns and walked into the dressing room. I sat down in a chair near the three-way mirror. I watched her jeans fall to the softly carpeted floor as she tried on the first gown. "I'm right here if you need help with the zipper, Mo," I said.

"It's okay, Mom," Mo said and walked out into the mirrored room wearing a short, white formal.

"Oh yes, darling, that looks too lovely on you. Your hair! Your high color! Ah, you are a vision!" Mrs. Baronson fawned as Mo turned around, looking at her reflection in the three-way mirror, the white tulle rustling.

My daughter blushed and smiled sweetly at the older woman. Mo did look lovely and she knew it. The emerald appliques on the white gown matched her eyes perfectly and the short skirt accentuated her long, shapely legs. She was prom queen material!

"That one is only $139.95, plus tax, of course," Mrs. Baronson said. "And just think, Mrs. Malloy, she can take this short gown to college with her." She turned to Mo. "Where are you going, darling?"

"I hope to go to Syracuse. If I get a big enough scholarship," Mo answered.

Mrs. Baronson looked worried. Did she think we couldn't afford this gown when Mo mentioned scholarship? I decided to set her straight.

"Maureen does very well in school, Mrs. Baronson. She's been accepted at Syracuse and Saint Benedict's. We're waiting to see which college can offer her the largest scholarship. She's worked hard and we feel she's entitled to the best."

"Of course," Mrs. Baronson answered. "And who is your date, darling?"

"I'm going with David Markovitch," Mo answered. "Do you know him?"

"A prince, that boy." Mrs. Baronson turned to me. "Have you met him yet, dear?"

I shook my head no. We've had to walk on eggshells with Mike about David Markovitch. Bridey has really had his ear about Mo dating "out of the Faith." I think it's ridiculous and I have told him so a thousand times. These are the sixties and we have to stop being so clannish. And besides, Mo isn't going to marry David Markovitch, she's just going to one dance with him. Mike has finally seen our side and has agreed to let Mo go, as long as there's no talk of going steady or wearing rings and if she's home by 2:00 A.M.

"Actually," Mrs. Baronson continued, "I'd heard that David was going with Laurie Glassman. She was in last month, looking at gowns."

"That was last month," Mo answered.

THE IRISH PRINCESS

I was surprised to hear that tone of finality in Mo's voice as she cut short Mrs. Baronson's probing.

Unabashed, Mrs. Baronson helped Mo out of the gown and asked, "Shall I wrap it?"

I nodded yes.

"How do you intend to pay?"

"Do you have layaway?" I asked hopefully.

"No, darling. You understand, these children. They think they have a date. They buy a gown. They lay it away. They break up with their boyfriend before the prom. Then they want their money back. You can see we just can't allow layaway." She smiled consolingly.

"Well, I'll have to write a check," I said, calculating how much I'd have to transfer immediately from our savings to our checking account.

"Be sure to bring us a picture, darling," Mrs. Baronson said to Mo as she wrapped the gown in pink tissue. "Ah, David is so handsome and your girl so lovely," she said to me as she closed the door behind us. "Together, they will be like a king and a queen."

I looked at Mo and she smiled. King David and Queen Maureen! I was sure that's exactly what she was thinking.

Mike

My own sister has been on my back about Mo's prom date, but Clare has insisted that we allow Mo to go with David Markovitch. "It's only one dance," she says. "What harm can there be in going to one dance with a Jewish boy?" I hope she's right. I just don't want my daughter getting too involved with him. It was bad enough last year when Mo was dating the son of the minister of the First Baptist Church. Mo finally broke that off because she thought he was too wild. I kind of got a chuckle out of that. The minister's son being too wild. It's like the psychologist's kids being messed up, or the teacher's kids being stupid. We don't have to worry about people thinking that! Mo is the living proof of what's wrong with that statement! It looks like Mo is a ringer for that scholarship to Saint Benedict's. Father Tim took me aside last night at the horse show committee meeting and said he'd received word from the dean of students, Sister Margaret Francis, that Saint Benedict's was very interested in having Mo attend. He indicated there would be a fair amount of scholarship money available. I certainly hope so. When I saw how much Clare had spent on that gown for Maureen, I nearly dropped the bank statement in shock.

"She'll be able to take that gown to college with her, Mike," my wife explained.

"Do they have formal dances at Saint Benedict's?" I asked.

"I suppose they do," Clare answered, "but I meant at Syracuse. Mo really wants to go to Syracuse."

"Bridey thinks she should go to a Catholic college," I said and the minute the words left my mouth, I knew it was the wrong thing to say.

"Michael," my wife said, "you and I and Mo will decide where she will go to college. Not Bridey!"

I decided to change the subject and leave Bridey out of it. "What time do all the festivities start on Saturday night?"

"Mr. and Mrs. Markovitch are coming here at seven-thirty to take pictures before the prom," Clare said.

"Oh, so that's what all the sprucin' up is about." I'd been watching Clare clean and polish with a vengeance for the last few days. I'd thought it was just a case of spring housekeeping, but now I realized it was an effort to put our best foot forward.

Clare looked at the faded slipcovers and the old carpet and I knew she was thinking of Mo's prom gown. With $139.95 plus tax we could have had new slipcovers. I wondered if she was thinking of the two, beautiful, antique sofas that she'd so regally given away at Aunt Lizzie's Last Will and Testament. I also wondered if Mr. and Mrs. Max Markovitch would like our daughter. Did they approve of David dating outside his faith? I suppose we'd all find out on Saturday night.

Mo

I don't care what happened afterwards. I don't care if I'm grounded for years. I'd do it all over again if I had the chance! Saturday night was the best night of my entire life.

It started out a little shaky, when Daddy and Mom had to meet Mr. and Mrs. Markovitch. They came to our house to take pictures. One look at the different cameras that the parents were using said it all. There was my mom trying to position David and me just so, so you couldn't see Binky's spot on the carpet or the thread-bare slipcovers. There was my dad taking pictures with a Brownie Kodak, while Mr. Markovitch was setting up the tripod for his expensive thirty-five millimeter camera. David's father made us all stand together—my parents, David and his mother, and me—and then at the last minute he pressed a button and ran into the picture.

My mother offered Mr. and Mrs. Markovitch a drink and passed around crackers and cheese. I was embarrassed about that. I mean, we read about hors d'oeuvres in French class and I picture snails and shrimp and fancy things and then out comes my mother with a tray of Ritz crackers and cheddar cheese and vegetables.

David's parents ate a few, to be polite I imagine, and then after they finished the Manhattans that my father had foisted on them, we got ready to leave. David's father's car is a Cadillac and the plan was that we would drive his parents home and then pick up Lucy Perkins and Jonathan Bertrand, the couple we were doubling with. Mr. Markovitch had decided that David could have the Cadillac for the night. "Beautiful girl, like Maureen here. You got to drive a nice car. Right, son?" he said. "Nothing too good for my boy! Right, Dave?" He slapped David on the back.

David nodded and looked at me. His face reddened a little and I could tell that his father had embarrassed him. I smiled at him to let him know I understood how parents can be. He looked down at his shiny black dress shoes.

He looked so good standing there. His skin was dark, from baseball practice, against his white dinner jacket, and his black, curly hair was already cropped short for the summer. I could see why his parents spoiled him.

I went to stand next to him. He smelled like Old Spice aftershave. "We have to go now, Mom," I said. "We have to pick up the couple we're doubling with."

As we walked to the front door, David whispered to me. "Thanks," he said.

"For what?" I winked at him and smiled.

"Rescue . . . from parents!" He nodded toward his parents, who were shaking hands with my mother and father and raving about the cheese and crackers.

We walked out to the Cadillac and climbed in the backseat. I felt like a queen, riding in that car.

After we dropped his parents off, before we picked up Lucy and Jonathan, David pulled the car into an out-of-the-way parking lot.

"Can I kiss you, Mo?" he asked.

It was only the very beginning of the evening but I wanted him to, so I nodded my head yes and he leaned across and kissed me, putting just the tip of his tongue in my mouth. I know you're not supposed to do that on the first real date, but I swear we couldn't help it. From that minute on, I began to have different thoughts about David; I began to realize that this was something different than my other short-lived crushes. I had never felt this way before. This might be the real thing.

The rest of the night was perfect. I was the queen of the senior prom and Lucy was on my court. David and I led the Grand March and I could feel everyone watching us. I could tell they were thinking how good we looked together.

After the prom was over, we went to Cironi's River Club and they actually served us. I'd never been served in a bar before. Actually, I've never been served, period. I've tasted liquor at parties when kids would sneak it from their parents' liquor cabinets, but this was different. They were treating us like we were adults. I ordered brandy Alexanders and David drank gin and tonics. He had to be careful not to drink too much because he had the Cadillac to worry about.

When the crowd broke up at Cironi's, we went to Frear Park. We necked for a while and then Lucy said she had to be in before 2:00. I really think she was lying about that just to get away from Jonathan. I heard a lot of "Stop that's" and "No's" coming from the backseat.

After we dropped Lucy off, we brought Jonathan home and David asked me if I wanted to go home.

"No," I answered, even though I knew it was already past 2:00 and my mother would be worried and my father would be furious. "I want to stay out till sunrise," I added, suddenly feeling like someone in a James Dean movie.

"Me too," said David and he grinned at me. "To hell with parents."

We necked for a long time, kissing till our lips were swollen and hurting, and then David undid the zipper on my gown and put his hand inside my dress. I didn't even try to stop him; I didn't want to.

We stayed out till almost dawn. It was the best night of my life. Even my father's anger when I finally came in at 4:30 couldn't ruin that night for me. Daddy says I can't ever date David again, but he can't stop me. This is the first time in my life that I've ever been in love.

Margie

I am definitely glad that I am not the first child in this family! I figure that by the time I get to high school, Mo will have broken every one of my father's rules at least once, so then nothing I do will seem as bad.

The night of the prom Mo came in two and a half

hours after her curfew and she hadn't even called to say she'd be late. My mother was so worried she made my father call my Uncle Jim at police headquarters to see if there had been any accidents. Then they called Lucy Perkins' house at three in the morning.

"Lucy's been home in bed for a half hour," I heard my mother report to my father.

"There's gonna be hell to pay, Clare, when I get my hands on Maureen!" Daddy said.

I pictured my father with his hands around Mo's neck, strangling her, and somehow it just didn't wash. Daddy had never even spanked us before. Usually, most of the disciplining was left to my mother, except in rare instances when my sister really stepped out of line. This was one of them.

The morning after the prom there was a big family conference in our kitchen. I shouldn't say "family," because I'm one-quarter of this family and I wasn't allowed in the kitchen. I think they didn't want me to hear Mo's confessions. They didn't want her to be a bad example for me. I was dying to hear what happened to make her so late, so I listened at the door.

Mo was crying and my father was ranting about the Malloy name.

"We have a name to uphold in this city, Maureen. Your Uncle Danny is the mayor, your Uncle Jim is a police captain, your own mother is a respected teacher, and I don't want to walk around my route with people lookin' at me and thinkin' that my daughter is a slut, bringin' shame to the name!"

"A slut"! My father using the word "slut" in the same sentence with "daughter"? What did he think Mo had been doing? I pushed my ear flat to the keyhole. I couldn't miss this.

"It isn't like that, Daddy. David is a nice person and we just sat in his car and talked." Mo's voice sounded shaky and even I didn't think the talking part was the truth. I couldn't imagine my parents falling for it.

"I called Lucy's house and her mother said she came in before two-thirty. Were you and David alone until four-thirty?" My mother's voice sounded suspicious. So they were alone—it wasn't like they were babies and would stick their fingers in the car lighter or fall out the door. It wasn't like David would hurt Mo. What was the big deal?

"You put yourself and that boy into an occasion of sin, Maureen," my father said.

I wasn't exactly sure what an "occasion of sin" was, but it sure did sound terrible. I decided that I'd check my Baltimore Catechism after I got done listening at the door.

My mother interrupted my father. "The thing I'm upset about, Maureen," she said, "is that your father and I trusted you and you betrayed our trust. You promised to be in before two o'clock and then you came waltzing in over two hours late. You never called. I thought you were dead on the highway. As you damn well might have been, judging from the smell of liquor on your breath."

"Liquor"! Mo had really bought it this time. I was

so excited by this new piece of information that I pressed against the keyhole too hard and the door pushed open. I fell onto the white-and-gold-speckled linoleum of the kitchen floor. Everyone stopped talking and stared at me.

"Poking your nose in where it doesn't belong, miss?" My father was not amused. His face was red and I could tell he was really angry and I didn't want to share any of that displeasure with my sister. I backed out of the room, down the hallway.

"Come right back here, Margie." It was my mother's voice.

I walked back into the kitchen.

"Since you're so nosy, you might as well hear everything, so that when you are Maureen's age you will not repeat her acts of willful disobedience and poor judgment." My mother sounded like the list for examination of conscience to prepare for confession that was in my St. Joseph's Daily Missal. My mind ran down the list: poor judgment, occasion of sin, willful disobedience, excessive amusement, drinking, impure thoughts, desires, or worse, actions? Wow! If my parents were right, Mo had really broken the bank on prom night. I looked at my older sister with new eyes. I was torn between a kind of horror and newfound respect.

"You will absolutely not see that young man again," my father said and his voice sounded mean. I'd only heard that bad voice once before, when I'd pushed my cousin Peter off the top of the slide on purpose.

"But Daddy," Mo said and started to cry.

I knew the tears would do her no good this time.

"I hate to admit it, but Bridey was right on this one. We shouldn't have let Maureen go out with David Markovitch," he said to my mother.

My mother gave him a narrow-eyed look and I couldn't tell what she was thinking, but I was pretty sure she wasn't admitting that my Aunt Bridey was right on anything.

Mo stood up and her face was red. "Aunt Bridey is a bigot and she wasn't right. David Markovitch is the nicest boy I have ever known, even if he is Jewish, and I don't care what you all think. I'd do it all again in a minute. Last night was the most wonderful night of my life."

My father had been pushed to the limit! First Mo called his sister, Bridey, a bigot, and then she said she didn't care what he or my mother thought, and then she said she'd do it all again! I was astounded; it was almost suicidal! My father, who had never laid a hand on either of us before, walked over to Mo and slapped her right across the face.

My mother jumped up as if she wanted to stop him, but then she just stared at Mo and my father.

"You will not see that boy again," my father repeated.

Mo ran from the kitchen, slamming first the kitchen door, then the hallway door, and finally the bedroom door. We all heard her yell, "Oh yes I will, and YOU can't stop me!"

And he couldn't, either. That was the day I knew that my sister had become a real person, and not just a kid anymore.

10

War

June

Clare

"Before he graduates?" I asked. I could hardly believe the story that Mike had brought home from his Thursday night poker game.

"Yup, even before he finishes up at the Academy. He's to report for his orders on Tuesday," Mike answered.

"Next Tuesday?"

Mike nodded his head.

"But why, Mike? Why was the judge so harsh? Especially now that there's a war on." I was just astounded that Peter was going into the army. He was only seventeen, just Mo's age.

"Because it's not the first time he's been caught stealing. It's not even the second time, Clare. It was Judge Cabot's decision. You remember him, don't you? He was the one that we met at the Democrats' picnic at the Grove last year. The tall, bald guy with the funny accent."

I nodded. Yes, I remembered him. He'd looked so out of place in that motley crowd of South Troy Democrats. Him, with his striped shirt and blue blazer and tie. A tie, for heaven's sake! For the Democrats' picnic! And the way he spoke, as if his teeth were clenched together, every word articulated precisely. I'd even tried to start a conversation with him, told him I was the mayor's sister-in-law and had worked on Danny's campaign. "Right" was all he could think to say and our conversation had stopped cold right there.

"Actually the judge was givin' Peter a break," Mike said, interrupting my memory of Judge Cabot. "Danny told us it was either the army or jail."

"What did Peter do, for God's sake?" I asked, trying to remember the little blond boy that I'd held so often on my knee, whose diaper I'd changed, whose cuts I'd cleaned and bandaged, who used to call me Auntie Clary.

"Well, the other incidents were just brushed off as kids' pranks. Breakin' into lockers, stealin' lunch money, throwin' stones through windows. But this one involved the headmaster's car and a lot of money."

"How much?" I asked.

"About a thousand dollars. Peter broke into the headmaster's office and took money from a school fundraiser and the keys to Brother Christopher's Pontiac. Then he went for a little joy ride."

"Had he been drinking?"

"Yeah, he was loaded." Mike sighed and then said, "My heart is breakin' for Danny and Hildy. In times like these, I'm glad we have girls."

I thought of our own son and wondered, if he'd lived, could I ever have sent him off to a war halfway across the world, a war in steamy jungles filled with death and disease, in places we'd never heard of before? Places with strange, harsh names like Saigon and Da Nang? I thought about how we rush our girls off to Dr. Moriarty at the first sign of a fever or sore throat. How we rely on our polio vaccinations and our penicillins and our vigilance to keep them safe. I was glad we only had girls, too.

"Is Hildy speaking to Danny again?" I asked.

"Yeah, it's seems that she's softened up toward him a bit. It's a good thing, too. This is hard on Danny. They're doin' their best to keep it all out of the papers."

The campaign worker in me popped up and I said, "Do you think this will hurt Danny's chances for re-election?"

"Nah, like I said, the police, because of Jim, and the politicians are keepin' the story real low. Most people probably won't even hear about it."

We sat silent for a few minutes, both of us thinking about our nephew Peter, leaving for Fort Dix on Tuesday. I was wondering what Bridey was thinking of the whole mess with her great concern with "shamin' the name." The precious Malloy name.

"You know," Mike broke the silence, "maybe it's not such a bad thing, Peter goin' off."

Trust Mike to find the silver lining in every cloud, I thought.

"What do you mean?" I asked.

"Well, maybe he'll get the discipline he needs in the army and at least this whole mess started his parents speakin' to one another again."

I shook my head and reached over to hold Mike's hand. "Life is strange," I said. "It takes Peter going off to fight in a war halfway around the world for his parents to end their own personal war right here in Troy."

Bridey

You could have knocked me over with a feather when I got that call from Hildy.

"Fine time we've heard from you, Hilda Malloy," I said. I wasn't going to pussyfoot around about her snubbing our family for the last six months. She almost cost Danny the election, for heaven's sake.

"Have you heard about Peter, Bridey?" she asked, totally ignoring my comment about her finally deciding to speak to us again.

"No," I lied. Jim had called me earlier in the week to tell me about the trouble Peter was in, but I wasn't letting on to Hildy. I wanted to hear *this* story in her own words.

"Well . . ."

Hildy hemmed and hawed and beat around the bush for a while. I cut her short. "Hildy, I'm very busy with the triplets right now; if you have something to say to me, then say it." I could hear funny little noises and I guessed that Hildy was trying not to cry.

"Oh, Bridey, it's so awful. They're sending my boy to Vietnam. And he's so young, just a baby."

Some baby, I thought. Stealing Brother Christopher's car and riding all around town drunker than a skunk. I was embarrassed he was a Malloy and I wished I wasn't his godmother. I thought about my two god-children and their upbringings. Maybe I should have tried to have more say. Maureen, Mike's girl, pretty and smart, but definitely getting her own way about *everything,* and Peter, shaming the family with his escapades. Lord, I hope none of my six kids turn out like him!

"Now, Hildy," I said, "calm down. Did Peter enlist or something?" I asked, pretending ignorance of the whole family court thing.

"Oh no, Bridey," Hildy answered and I could tell she was on the verge of tears again. "Peter got in some trouble at the Academy," she said and then she told me the whole story—her version, of course.

Peter was being railroaded for some schoolboy pranks. Those Christian Brothers at the Academy were trying to make a mountain out of a molehill and had pressed charges. Danny had pulled some strings and did what he could and Jim, too, with the police.

"I have to thank the Malloys for that," Hildy added.

"Hildy." I cut her off; I'd heard enough of her story. "Why are you calling me? I haven't heard from you in six months." I was mad. Suddenly, she needs the

Malloys around and she expects us just to jump.

"Bridey, I'm sorry," she said.

Her voice sounded funny. I know how she always thinks she's right and hates to be wrong. That's her German nature, I suppose. Admitting she might have been wrong about us must be hard for her.

"I don't know who stole the money from my bank account, but I know it wasn't Danny. And I'm thankful for all Danny and Jim have done for my Peter."

Like keeping him out of jail, I thought.

"Apology accepted," I said in my most proper voice. I didn't want to make it too easy for Hildy. I knew she'd never truly come back to the family fold after the things she'd said about the Malloys, and I didn't want her thinking that the family was just sitting around waiting for her to call and talk to us again.

"Peter's going to Fort Dix on Tuesday."

I didn't say anything.

"And then to Vietnam," Hildy added. "You're his godmother; I just wanted you to know."

I thought of that hot July day, almost eighteen years ago, when I'd stood on the altar at St. Joseph's with that tiny baby in my arms. I'd bent down so the priest could splash him with holy water from the baptismal font.

"I baptize thee, Peter Frederick, in the name of the Father, and the Son, and the Holy Ghost," the priest had said as he made the sign of the cross with cold water on the baby's forehead.

"Bad luck," my sister-in-law Mary had whispered in my ear, reminding me of that old Irish superstition about the uncertain future for babies who don't cry when they're baptized. Peter slept through his whole induction to Christianity.

"Bad luck," I said to Hildy, "him being inducted into the army at a time like this." But then I didn't have the heart to go on being mean, especially after remembering Peter as a newborn in my arms. His perfect, little mouth like a rosebud, his blond hair clinging to his ruddy scalp, his red face and his bright, bright blue eyes. So I said, "Take heart, Hildy. Maybe he won't be sent to Vietnam."

"I pray not," Hildy answered and I could picture her sitting there with her precious Lutheran German Bible on her lap, reading the verses over and over. Being a convert, she'd never been much for saying the Rosary and believing in the Blessed Virgin like the rest of us Catholics.

"I'll pray to Mary for your son," I said and I hung up.

Mo

All the boys in my senior class, even the stupid ones, are trying to get into college so they won't get drafted and what does my cousin Peter do? He gets in trouble and gets sent into the army. What a jerk! Soon my mother will be making me write letters to him and pretending like we like him. Not me. I might write a letter every once in a while, but I'm not acting like I like him. Everyone in Troy knows he's my cousin and that's embarrassing because he's such a loser. Him stealing a lot of money is no big surprise to me, either. My friends at the Academy have had his number for a long time. Kenny Masters told me Peter shakes down all the little seventh graders for their lunch money and he's been caught smoking pot in the alley in back of the school. "Good riddance" is all I can say about him going into the army. I hope he gets a real mean drill sergeant.

I don't want him to go to Vietnam, though. I'm not mean enough to wish that on anybody, even Peter. Just last week Mom made Margie and me go to the dedication of the Wynantskill Little League's new field. It was made in memory of Glenn Fogarty. He was the first boy from Wynantskill to be killed in Vietnam. His parents placed a black wreath with red, white, and blue ribbons right next to the plaque with his name on it and then they had to take his mother away, because she was crying so hard it looked like she might collapse. It was sad. I didn't know Glenn very well because he was a lot older than me, at least four years. I knew his family and his brother, Jimmy. Jimmy was the first boy I ever kissed. We got stuck as partners in a spin-the-bottle party at Carol Bradley's house at Halloween when we were in eighth grade. Actually, he was a nice kisser and it felt good, so we stayed together at that party the whole night. Afterwards, though, we were too embarrassed ever to talk to one another again. So that was that.

Jimmy was there at the memorial and he came over to us. I thought he was finally going to say hi to me, but he came to speak to Margie.

"Glenn would want you to have this, Margie," he said and he handed her an old, worn, baseball glove.

I'd forgotten that Glenn had been Margie's softball coach for three summers in a row.

All my sister could say was "Gee." So I thanked Jimmy for her.

My sister reached out for the glove and it was then I noticed her hands were trembling, so I put my arm around her shoulders.

"C'mon, Marg, let's go home now," I said.

Margie was turning that old, worn-out glove over and over in her hands and I couldn't tell what she was thinking. It was strange. I expected her to cry and I would have known how to handle that. But she just stared with a faraway look out at the poplars that are all around the Glenn T. Fogarty Memorial Field.

"Let's go home," I said again, looking around for my parents, who were over speaking to the Raffertys, Glenn's aunt and uncle. My father knows them from the horse show committee. I could tell that I shouldn't interrupt them, they were having a serious talk, so I signaled to my mother that I was heading for the car with Margie and she nodded okay to me.

We sat in that hot car for a long time waiting for my parents to finish talking. Margie didn't say anything at first. When she finally spoke, I was taken aback.

"Does God make wars?" she asked me.

I just shook my head. What could I say? All those years studying the Baltimore Catechism, all those medals for getting first place in the Religion Exams, all those awards from the Confraternity of Christian Doctrine Office. None of those things helped me with Margie's question. Not one bit.

Margie

I remember Glenn so well. I remember how he smelled sweaty. That nice, sweaty smell that people get when they're playing outside in the sun. I remember his voice telling me to arc it in over the plate.

"One more time, Marg. Soon the Giants' scouts are gonna come lookin' for ya, babe. You're gonna be the best little pitcher in the Capital District."

The Capital District was the league our team, the Red Hot Hornets, played in. We called ourselves the "Red Hot Hornets" in honor of Glenn's red hair. I think that's one of the reasons he picked me to make me into a pitcher. We both have red hair. Daddy said that was silly, I got picked because I have a good arm. But Glenn liked me before he knew I could throw. Maybe he remembered when he was little and everyone teased him about being a carrottop or having his hair on fire. Anyways, Glenn sure helped me with my slow pitch.

THE IRISH PRINCESS

When they shipped Glenn's body home from Vietnam, Mommy wouldn't let me go to the wake and the funeral with her and Daddy.

"It's too sad, honey," Mommy said. And she was right. If I saw Mrs. Fogarty crying all over the place like she did at the Little League field, I don't know what I would have done.

After they came home from the funeral, I heard my father tell my mother that they had to have a closed casket because Glenn had stepped on a land mine and was blown to bits. That's what I thought of when Jimmy Fogarty handed me that old baseball glove at the field last week. I thought of Glenn scattered in a million pieces. That scared me, thinking about Glenn in little bloody pieces all over the place.

I don't want to remember him like that. I want to think about him riding me home on the back of his bike after a practice when my father forgot to pick me up. I want to remember holding on tight to him as we flew down Pawling Avenue and seeing that patch of brown freckles on his neck close up. I want to remember the sweet smell of laundry on his white T-shirt, and his Dodgers baseball hat turned backwards. I want to remember his solid muscles, strong like he had rocks in his arms. I want to remember him in one piece, whole.

When I heard Daddy and Mommy talking about Peter going to Vietnam, all I could picture was Peter's arms and legs and eyeballs and ears and feet flying off in all directions. I imagined my Aunt Hildy, who I haven't seen in almost half a year, using her sewing stitches to try to put him back together. I haven't liked Peter very much over the last few years, but I hope he doesn't come home in pieces.

11

Pomp and Circumstance

June

☙

Mike

Graduation day was blistering hot, but I would have sat in those bleachers till hell froze over to see my girl win all those prizes and scholarships.

"Wear your gray suit, Mike," Clare had said to me in the morning when we were all fighting to get in and out of our tiny bathroom.

"I was just gonna wear a short-sleeved sport shirt, hon. It's gonna be hot as Hades today."

"I think you're going to want to walk tall today, Mike. I know I'm going to wear my best dress and I'm going to insist that Margie wear that pink sundress that Anna made for her."

"Margie's not gonna like that," I said, thinking of my youngest daughter who much preferred jeans and a T-shirt to any other outfit.

"Well, if she doesn't like it, she'll just have to lump it. We're all dressing up," Clare snapped. "It's Mo's big day."

"Mo's big day"! It just seemed like yesterday when I went to Sister Jeanne Marie, the principal of St. Joseph's Elementary School down in South Troy, to register Mo in kindergarten. She was so small they couldn't find a uniform to fit her, and a good thing, too, because when Clare got wind of their teaching methods, Mo didn't last too long at St. Joseph's.

Now, there we were at her high school graduation, sitting in bleachers, dressed fit to kill, watching all the young people in their white caps and gowns turn the purple-and-gold tassels on their caps, signifying their graduation. After all the diplomas were presented, the principal, Mr. Guy Imbersano, started in on the prizes and scholarships.

"And I am pleased to announce that one of our students is a National Merit semifinalist. Will Maureen Katherine Malloy please come to the podium?"

I watched my tall, beautiful daughter walk gracefully to the platform that held the dignitaries from the school board and the city officials. Her red curls shone beneath her cap in the morning sunlight and I remembered all the fairy tales I used to tell her of Irish Princesses with hair that leprechauns had spun from gold. I swear, I was never prouder to be a father than at that moment.

"Presenting Maureen's award will be her uncle, the Honorable Daniel T. Malloy, mayor of the city of Troy."

I saw my brother Danny stand up, beaming with approval at Mo, happy for the opportunity to stand at the podium with a beautiful girl, a blood relation, no less, who was winning all the prizes. Danny cut a fine figure, standing there in his navy suit and red tie, but for the first time I realized that he looked old. My youngest brother, and he looked old! His red hair was lighter for all the gray, and the years of beer drinking had cost him. Even his 6' 2" frame couldn't hide his paunch. He was running to fat, as we say. He took the microphone. I hoped he was thinking of Mo, but I'm sure he was also thinking of votes.

"Maureen, it is my great honor to present you with this plaque signifyin' your achievement in the National Merit scholarship competition. I would also like to take this opportunity to present you with this one thousand dollar savings bond from the Troy Lions Club, presented annually to the Outstanding Young Achiever in the Senior Class."

"Thank you, Uncle Dan," Mo said and turned to leave the podium.

Mr. Imbersano stood up and stopped Mo from returning to her seat. "Excuse me, Maureen, while you're here, I'd like to make an announcement. Syracuse University has just notified us that you are the recipient of a four-year, all-tuition-paid scholarship. Troy High School can be very proud of you."

Clare reached for my hand and squeezed it hard. Her palm was sweaty and I realized that she must have been expecting all this, that's why she was nervous, that's why we wore our Sunday best. "Now she'll be able to go to Syracuse, Mike," Clare whispered in my ear, her voice breaking a little with emotion.

I realized then that my hopes for Mo to go to Saint Benedict's College were a thing of the past. I really didn't care, but I knew I'd probably never hear the end of it from Bridey. First public elementary school, then Troy High, and now a big, secular university like Syracuse! We'd be lucky if Mo didn't turn into an atheist, according to Bridey. Well, I wasn't going to let that worry spoil my day, Mo's day.

As I snapped pictures with my Brownie Kodak, I wondered if Max Markovitch was here taking pictures with his fancy camera. I hoped he hadn't failed to notice my daughter and all the prizes she won. We might have faded slipcovers and carpet that needs replacing, but we've also got our girls and they are something to really be proud of.

Bridey

Clare and Mike had a big graduation party for Maureen in their backyard. We were all expected to come: aunts, uncles, cousins and all. I offered to bring my favorite potato salad, knowing how much it would cost to feed all the Malloys.

"No, thank you, Bridey, it's really nice of you to offer," Clare had said to me, "but Mike has arranged to have the whole thing catered by Longo's Family Restaurant and Tavern."

Catered, no less! I thought. Six months ago all Mike and Clare could do was complain about Clare losing her teaching job because of the baby and how short they'd be with Maureen's college coming up, and now they were having her party catered.

Well, it wasn't like it was pheasant under glass or filet mignon or anything special like that. Longo's just brought in big trays of ziti and lasagna and green salad and Mike cooked hamburgers and hot dogs on the grill. They had a keg for the grown-ups and a big barrel filled with Nehis for the kids. Seeing those orange Nehi bottles on ice took me back. I remembered when Papa was still alive and he would take us to the Snuggery Inn down behind First Street, right on the river. He'd go in and have a tap beer and he'd always bring out orange Nehis for me and my brothers. We weren't allowed in the tap room, being just kids, so we'd sit on the river-bank drinking the soda and sharing the bar pretzels that Papa snuck out to us. Those orange Nehis reminded me of that and I felt a special kindness for my brothers at that graduation party. I felt proud for Mike, too. He was so pleased with his girl.

"Mike," I said, "you and Clare have done good by your girl."

Mike had drunk a little too much from the keg and was standing there weaving back and forth in one spot.

"Aye, she's a princess, that girl. I call her 'my Irish Princess.' She's done the Malloy name proud today," Mike slurred.

I put my arm around my older brother and walked

him to the picnic bench. "Sit here with me a while, darlin'," I said and I held his hand. It was twilight and lightning bugs were starting to glimmer near the grass. Mike's smelly old dog, Binky, came over and lay at our feet.

"I wish Ma had been here to see Mo win all those prizes today, Bridey," Mike said.

His voice sounded really sentimental and his eyes were getting teary.

"Not to worry, Michael. Our Ma is lookin' down from heaven and she's seein' your daughter, for sure," I said.

Mike smiled and nodded, pointing toward the backyard, "Here they come, Bridey. Aren't they wonderful?"

I wasn't sure whether he was talking about the kids or the fireworks they were playing with.

The younger children ran by shrieking and twirling their sparklers that Jim had brought them.

"Got these sparklers and bottle rockets after one of our rookies took 'em off some dago kids down in the South End," Jim had told us earlier. "There was cherry bombs, too, but Mary wouldn't let me bring 'em, said they was too dangerous for the little ones."

Colleen's sparkler burnt out and she ran over to us. She's really too young to run with the older cousins, so she climbed on Mike's lap and put her head on his shoulder.

"My light's all gone, Mommy," she said to me, holding up a charred metal rod.

"That's okay, baby, it's almost time for everyone to go home, anyways," I said.

"Bridey," Mike turned to me, "when you were little, I used to hold you on my lap just like I'm holdin' Colleen. Do you remember?"

I smiled, remembering my big brother Mike, already a teenager when I was born, but I could feel the tears welling up in my eyes, too.

Mike was looking across the yard at his daughter Maureen, standing in the midst of her cousins, flushed by the excitement of the day, all the awards, all the graduation gifts from our family. "Where do the years go, darlin'? Where do they go?" he said.

For a second I thought he was talking to me, but then I realized he was staring right at Maureen and saying it to her. She couldn't hear him, of course, and would have thought he was just being an old fool, if she could, but he was asking her how she'd grown up so fast.

I put my arms around my own little girl and slipped her from Mike's lap to mine. I wanted to hold her tight, to keep her in this moment forever. I didn't want her to grow up and go away to college someplace. Away from me. I knew what my brother was feeling. He was happy and proud for such a daughter, but mostly sad that she wouldn't be just his for very much longer.

Margie

Maureen Katherine Malloy! Maureen Katherine Malloy! Maureen Katherine Malloy! I mean, I was proud of Mo and all, but I thought if I had to hear my sister's name for one more prize or scholarship I would puke. And Mommy made me wear that pink dress that I hate. It shows all the freckles on my back and the last time I wore it to church, Rollie Evans sat behind me and called me a speckled sunfish and he's been calling me that ever since. Well, I'm even more speckled now because of that darn graduation. We had to just sit there in the bleachers for three hours and besides more freckles, I got burn lines on my back. Later that day, at the party, Mommy had to rub Unguentine all over me and my cousins all held their noses and said, *"Phwew! Margie's well-done again!"*

The party was something else. I'm beginning to think that my Aunt Bridey is right about Mo being spoiled. First, Daddy had all the food brought in by his friend Frank Longo from his bar down on Atlantic Avenue. Then the grown-ups had a champagne toast to Mo. Champagne! My parents never even drink it on New Year's Eve like normal people. They say it's too expensive. Then my mother comes waltzing out with a huge ice cream cake from the ice cream store. Of course, written in frosting across the top is "Congratulations, Mo!" in big, pink letters. And the presents! My uncles and aunts chipped in and bought Mo her own stereo to take to college and my parents bought her a real typewriter.

"You'll need this, Mo," my mother said when she handed the big box to my sister. "When you go to a school like Syracuse, you're expected to hand your work in on typed sheets."

It was decided, then. Syracuse over Saint Benedict's. Aunt Bridey's nose was out of joint over that! I could tell. She was trying to be real nice at the party and not make a big deal over it. I heard her tell Mo how proud she was of "her goddaughter."

Later, when I was sitting inside, I heard her whispering to Aunt Mary.

"I hope they don't live to regret sendin' Maureen to that huge, secular school."

"I hope not," Aunt Mary agreed. She's not one ever to cross Aunt Bridey.

"When my children go to college, it will be Catholic schools, for sure."

"But Bridey, Mo got a big scholarship to Syracuse," Aunt Mary said.

"Scholarship, smolarship. I'd work on my hands and knees as an Irish washerwoman for the privilege of payin' for a Catholic education."

Aunt Mary looked a little surprised when Aunt Bridey said that. Somehow, I don't think she could picture Bridey on her knees scrubbing someone else's floor.

I walked over to my parents' record player and put

on Mo's Johnny Mathis album. It was getting dark outside and most of the grown-ups had moved onto the porch where they could hear the music really well. All the kids were playing hide-and-go-seek in the backyard, but I didn't feel like being such a kid tonight. I don't know how to explain it. I almost felt like crying. Mo was leaving us and going to college. I was going to start high school after the summer. Everything was changing. Even Aunt Bridey's babies were changing. All three had just started to walk and they toddled all over the place, always being under somebody's foot. For a minute, I thought of my own brother. He'd be almost seven months old now if he lived. Even though I never really knew him, I missed him.

I sat in the darkened living room and listened to my parents' and my aunts' and uncles' low voices, their conversation drifting in through the summer screens along with the cooling night breeze.

"Would you like to dance, macushla?" my father asked my mother.

"Don't be silly, Mike," my mother chided. "Besides, you've had so much from the keg, we'd probably fall off the porch."

My mother's voice had a laughing sound to it and I could tell that even though she disapproved of my father's drinking, she was pleased he'd called her "macushla" and asked her to dance.

"Don't be scoldin' me, Clare, darlin'. I'm just celebratin' for our wonderful girl."

"I know, Michael, I know," my mother answered.

"I'll bet Mo will dance a round with me," my father said. "Margie, I know you're sittin' in the dark listenin' to everything we say, so could you put on that Frank Sinatra record I like so much?" he called through the window.

I knew which Frank Sinatra record he wanted. The one that had "Daddy's Little Girl" on it. I walked to our record player and lifted the arm off of "Chances Are" and changed albums.

"Mo, Mo." I could hear him calling to my sister to leave the childish game in the backyard and to join the grown-ups on the porch.

Sometimes I'm sure that my parents like Mo better than they like me and this was one of those times. My sister came running, and soon she and my father were fox-trotting around the front porch, while my mother and my uncles and aunts clapped their approval. I had to admit my sister looked beautiful dancing with Daddy. She was still in her white eyelet graduation dress, but she was barefoot from the backyard game and her hair hung down in loose curls around her face. No one could resist admiring her. I wondered if my skinny arms and legs would ever be shaped like hers. I wondered if I'd look as good in white eyelet and would I win lots of scholarship prizes and would Daddy dance proudly with me someday?

As I watched from the dark living room, feeling left out from the kid's game and left out from the grown-ups on the porch, I saw my sister stand on tiptoe and whisper something into my father's ear. I leaned forward on my elbows and pushed my ear against the screen, but I still couldn't hear what they were saying. I saw my father purse his lips and tilt his head.

"Well, all right," he said in a loud voice, a voice I could hear.

Mo stood back and put her hands on his shoulders and gave him her most charming smile.

"Thank you, Daddy, I love you!"

I suppose Mo could have asked for the moon that night and my father would have reached up into the sky and pulled it down for her. In his eyes, Mo could do no wrong. I thought she must have asked for a car or a new dog or something like that. Later, I found out that was how she got permission to date David Markovitch again, and that's how all the trouble began.

12

The Fourth

July

Mo

"So, what are you doing tonight?" Susie Lavin asked me when she called on the morning of the Fourth.

"I haven't decided yet," I said, not wanting Susie to know that I didn't have plans for Saturday night, July 4th. David was away with his parents for a week down at Grossinger's. He was coming back sometime this weekend and I wanted to wait just in case he made it back in time for Saturday night.

"I'm having a pajama party," Susie said. "Why don't you come over?"

I didn't want to turn Susie down outright. She was a new friend from David's part of town. She hung out with David's friends.

"Well, I told David that I'd be around in case he got back early from the Catskills."

"All Dave's friends are coming over before the pajama party. Most of the girls that are sleeping over are dating boys from the baseball team, too. So Dave will probably show up if he gets back in time. You can meet him here. Problem solved. And anyways," Susie added, "if he doesn't make it home in time, you won't be sitting around bored to death with your parents."

I thought about staying home and my father insisting on going out to West Sand Lake to see the fireworks. I thought about being the only teenager sitting on the blanket with her parents.

"I'll ask my mom and call you back later," I said. Susie was right, I thought. Why should I just sit at home, waiting by the phone or be stuck watching fireworks with my parents? The party might be fun.

"Are you sure it's all right with Mrs. Lavin?" my mother asked when I told her about the pajama party.

"Susie said it was fine," I fibbed. Susie had never mentioned her parents at all. I just assumed it was all right. "If David calls, tell him to call me over there, okay?" I added.

"Sure, honey. Have a good time. Oh, and don't stay up *all* night," my mother said as she kissed me good-bye.

Later, when Daddy dropped me off at Susie's, he bent across the front seat of the car and kissed me on the forehead. "Be a good girl, darlin'," he said. He always says that instead of good-bye. As long as I can remember, he's been saying that.

I watched him drive away in our old blue Dodge and I waved after him. I felt a little sad watching that old car chug up Susie's hill. I wished Daddy could, for once, have a new car instead of having to always buy secondhand. I wished he could have a chance at a better job than a mailman. I wondered why he couldn't have a Cadillac and own a dress factory like Mr. Markovitch. He was as smart and as handsome and just as nice. I thought about going to Syracuse and the chance I was getting and then I walked to Susie's front door and rang the bell.

Susie opened the door. She was holding a can of beer and a cigarette. "Party time!" she said.

"Susie! My father just drove away," I said, looking up the street after the old blue Dodge. "What are you doing?"

"Daddy and Mother had to go away on a business trip and I convinced them that since I'm going to be living on my own at Oneonta State next year, they should trust me here alone for the weekend."

Susie was already slurring her words and I wondered about all that trust that Mr. and Mrs. Lavin were dumping on her. I put down my sleeping bag and my overnight case and steered her back into the house. The lights were off and a bunch of kids were in the living room. It was dark and all I could see were little, orange cigarette dots winking around the room. Ray Charles' "Georgia" was playing on the stereo.

"Looks like the party started without me," I said, trying to sound cool and not uneasy, which is what I was really feeling, thinking about my father just driving away and my mother possibly calling to check on me later.

"Mo, baby, you're here." David came out of the

shadowy hallway. He had a bottle of beer in his hand and he grabbed my arm and pulled me toward him. "It's hot," he said and then he ran the cold beer bottle along my cheek and then down my neck and along the top of my shirt. It made me want to kiss him. "I called your house and your mom said I just missed you."

He led me to a makeshift bar on the dining room table. "Susie's old man keeps quite a collection," he said, pointing at the variety of liquor bottles on the table. "How about a rum and Coke?" He poured a big shot of the dark brown liquid into a water glass before I even had a chance to answer. "Now, we'll just have to find some Coke and ice," he said.

"I don't know, David, do you think we should be doing this?" I looked around the room. Now that my eyes had adjusted to the dim light, I could see kids making out on all the chairs and the couch. "Won't Mr. Lavin notice that his bottles have less in them?"

"Nah," David smiled. "He's almost an alcoholic, anyways; drinks like a fish. He probably won't notice anything."

I looked around again, hoping Susie wasn't close enough to hear David say that about her father. I thought it was a little mean of him.

"Besides," David continued, "this is what we do." He held up a bottle of gin and pointed to a piece of tape halfway down the bottle. "We mark where the liquor was before the party and then, when the party's over, we fill the bottle with water to the tape mark. Works every time. They never suspect a thing."

It sounded like this was old hat to David. His crowd is a little cooler than most of my friends. I supposed that they'd done this before.

"I imagine Laurie Glassman let you make her some pretty powerful drinks," I said and I could feel myself getting jealous and flushing at the thought of Laurie and David together. I was glad it was dim and David couldn't see my hot color.

"Laurie was history the day I first saw you, Mo. I mean that, I really do."

David pulled me to him and kissed me, putting the tip of his tongue in my mouth. It felt good, but I pushed him away and said, "Let's find a seat." I felt funny standing in front of all his friends and kissing like that.

I don't remember most of the night very well after that. My second rum and Coke made everything into a pleasant blur. I do remember Steve Ryan trying to do the limbo under Mrs. Lavin's broomstick and stripping his jeans off because they kept him from bending down low enough. I do remember that everything anyone said struck me as funny. I do remember that every place that David put his hands on my body felt wonderful.

Around midnight the couples started drifting off to the bedrooms.

"We shouldn't," I said as David walked me toward Susie's parents' bedroom.

"It's all right, Mo, I'll get some protection," he said and steered me into the room. "Be right back, gotta find Keith or Steve," he added and then staggered down the hallway.

I wondered for a moment what he meant when he said "protection" and then I knew and then I didn't know. I laughed to myself as I pictured David in a coat of protective armor, riding a white horse, and then I laughed again when I pictured him putting the other kind of protection on. I was drunk and, I don't know, it just struck me as funny.

I lay down on the Lavins' double bed and I closed my eyes. I guess you'd call it passing out, but I really wasn't unconscious. I just felt like I was sinking down into the mattress, almost like the puffy, black bedspread was a big, dark marshmallow and it was swallowing me up. The darkness, and the sinking down, and the letting go just felt so good. For a minute, I thought of Mr. and Mrs. Lavin sleeping in that bed and then I thought, oh, who cares. I certainly wasn't caring too much about anything at all right then.

Then David was there and his hand was inside my blouse and then on my stomach. I remember everything after that very well. I'll never forget it. I can't blame the rum, I knew what I was doing. I could have stopped everything, but I didn't. I wanted to be with him.

"I couldn't find Steve," David whispered in my ear.

"I don't care," I said. And I didn't, then.

The next morning I had a terrible headache. It felt like Ping Pong balls were bouncing off my temples and my mouth was dry and fuzzy. I was also embarrassed, waking up in a bed like that, with a boy.

"Let's get you some Coke," David suggested. "Or

orange juice. Orange juice and aspirin is just what you need."

We walked into the living room on our way to the Lavins' kitchen. Kids were sprawled all over the furniture and the floor. It looked like half the senior class from Troy High had spent the night there. I looked around at the Lavins' living room. There was beer spilled on the carpet and empties thrown all around. Ashtrays were filled to the brim with cigarette butts and I even noticed a burn hole on the furniture. I tried to remember if I'd ever seen it there before.

"Let's find Susie and help her get this place cleaned up before her parents come home," I said.

"Relax," David replied. "We can party all day. They're not coming home till tomorrow. Susie managed to tell me that right before she passed out last night. You're such a worrywart sometimes, Mo," he added and pulled me close to him and kissed my forehead. "I love you, anyways," he said.

"I think I'd better go home," I answered. I loved him, too, and I wanted to say so, but I felt weird about last night and I felt scuzzy. I thought about taking a hot shower, how good it would feel. I wanted to get the smoke and beer smells off me. "I'll come back later," I said, "to help clean up. Let's find Susie so I can tell her I'll be back."

We walked through the house, climbing over sleeping people, knocking on closed doors. In the bedroom hallway we found Steve banging on the bathroom door. He was hopping from one foot to the other.

"C'mon, Sue. Hurry up!" He pointed to the door. "She's been hogging the john all morning and she won't even answer me."

"Let me go in," I volunteered. "I'll get her out."

The minute I saw Susie's face I knew we were all in trouble. It was greenish, almost the exact color of the floor tiles, and the bathroom stunk to high heaven from the smell of someone being sick. Her eyes were rolled back in her head.

"Help me get her out of here, will you?" I shouted to Steve and David, who were just standing there, staring at her.

They helped me lift her up and we carried her between us to her bedroom.

"She looks really bad," David said. "Should we call someone, the police maybe?"

"The police"! I thought of Uncle Jim showing up and all the kids sprawled in the living room, half of them underage and most of them still drunk.

"No," I said. "We'll bring her to my mother. She'll know what to do."

"I'll get Keith's keys," David said. His voice sounded nervous. We'd all heard in health class about the effects of alcohol poisoning and how some kids die from it.

We drove as fast as we could through the early Sunday morning streets of Troy. Out Pinewoods Avenue and into Albia. There was no traffic and, except for an old man walking his white poodle, we saw no people. We got to Wynantskill in eleven minutes, record time.

"Do you want me to come in with you?" David asked. I could tell by the way he asked, he was hoping I'd say no.

"No, just help me get her onto the back porch," I said. On the ride out to Wynantskill, my mind had been reeling with the stories I'd have to tell to explain all this and if my mother or father saw David Markovitch, there'd be no believing anything I said. "Just help me get her to the porch," I repeated. Just then, I was more concerned with Susie than I was with the stories I'd have to make up. I wasn't even thinking about what had happened the night before. I didn't have time to worry about that then. I was too worried about Susie. She looked really bad.

Mike

I have to leave for the post office every morning at 5:30 A.M. and you'd think that on my one weekend day off I'd like to sleep late, but I don't. I always get up early on Sundays, too. I really like the house in the early morning before all the commotion starts. I make a big pot of coffee in the percolator and then I go out to the mailbox for the papers. I do that every Sunday morning; it's something I really enjoy, reading the papers and doing the crosswords and sipping coffee. When the kids were little, they'd get up early with me, too. I'd make them a big breakfast of bacon and eggs, and home fries or pancakes, so that Clare could sleep in. Now they all sleep in and, I have to confess, I enjoy the solitude.

After I have my coffee and finish the crosswords, I head over to St. Jude's. I'm in charge of the ushers for the early mass. I have to get there before eight o'clock to round up all the ushers and assign them their places and to make sure all the altar boys show up. When the mass is over, I usually stay through the nine o'clock service to count the money from the collection baskets. I don't mind staying at all; it's helping out, and besides, by the time I get home my family's just waking up.

Last Sunday, when I got home at 10:15, no one was around. I checked Margie's bed and then Clare's. They were empty and unmade. I saw the half-eaten bowls of cereal on the table. That gave me the idea that there must have been an emergency. I swear I broke out in a cold sweat wondering what had happened to my family and assuming the worst. I was just about to call Jim or Bridey to see if they knew what was going on when I saw Clare's note taped to the refrigerator: "Mike back soon Explain later—don't worry Clare." No teacher punctuation, no periods or commas. I knew she left in a hurry.

I wondered where they were and St. Mary's Hospital kept popping into my head. I decided I couldn't just stand around and wait, so I called the emergency desk there to ask if a Mrs. Malloy had been in. I could hardly believe my ears when Bernadette O'Rourke answered the phone. We'd gone to grade school and Catholic High together and I knew she worked as a nurse's aide, but I never expected her to answer the phone at St. Mary's on a Sunday morning.

"Not to worry, Mike," she said. "Your family was just here and everything's fine. They brought in a little girl, friend of Maureen's. We had to admit her, but she's okay. They just left, matter of fact, so they should be home any minute."

I wanted to ask who, what, why, all those kinds of things, but Bernie said, "Ooops, gotta go, another call coming in. God, we're busy this morning," and hung up.

I wondered who they'd brought to the hospital and what the hell Mo was doing home, anyways. I wasn't supposed to pick her up at the Lavins' till 10:30 so she could make eleven o'clock mass.

I walked out to the back porch and watched the road, hoping to see Clare's old station wagon driving up the street. It seemed a long time till they drove up, but when I looked at my watch I realized it was only fifteen minutes. They all looked bedraggled when they climbed out of the car, especially Mo. I was surprised to see Helen Dietz with them and she looked really peculiar, carrying her nurse's bag and wearing big, pink slippers on her feet.

"Thanks, Helen," I heard my wife say. "I don't know what we would have done without you." I watched Helen walk away toward her place wearing those big slippers. I'd never even seen her out of uniform before.

"Where the hell have you been? I've been worried

about you!" I said and then Clare and Margie both started talking. Mo was silent and she looked worn out. She walked down the hall to her room.

Then Clare told me about Susie Lavin and the alcohol poisoning and how they still hadn't gotten in touch with her parents, who were over in Williamstown for the weekend.

"Christ, Clare, you didn't leave the girl alone at the hospital, did you?" I asked.

Clare gave me an exasperated look. "You know me better, Mike. Of course I didn't. Susie was just conscious enough to give us her aunt's name. The poor woman lives up in Sycaway, so she got there in about five minutes. I must say she was shocked when she saw her niece. You'd have been shocked, too, Mike. She was practically in a coma from the alcohol. You'd have been really shocked if you saw the girl," Clare repeated.

I sat my wife down in a kitchen chair and poured her a hot cup of coffee, spooning in two lumps of sugar and lots of cream. I handed the mug to her. She took it in her two hands and held it close to her face, not drinking it at first, but letting the steam curl around her. She looked more worn out than Mo did.

"Alcohol poisoning and no parents?" I asked.

"Teenagers make mistakes, Mike," Clare said quietly. She sounded resigned. "That's part of being young." She took a sip of coffee and closed her eyes. Then with her eyes still closed she motioned to the bedroom hallway. "Could you call Mo back in here, Mike? She's got a lot of explaining to do."

Margie

Susie Lavin came home with Mo on Sunday morning and she didn't look too good. Her face was greenish-yellow and her eyes, when she opened them, were really bloodshot. She looked like she hadn't combed her hair in two weeks and she had stains down the front of her shirt. I've never seen a teenager look so bad.

"I was afraid to leave her, Mom. She's really sick," my sister explained to my mother.

Mommy put her face close to Susie's. "I think you mean she's really drunk," my mother said and her voice sounded nasty to me. I know that tone in my mother's voice and it's one you just don't fool around with. "Susie, look at me!" Mommy said and she shook her real hard, but Susie just slumped to one side and her mouth hung open. Drool was coming off her lower lip.

"Margie, go get Mrs. Dietz," my mother ordered. "Right away!"

I ran out the door and down the street to number 15, Mrs. Dietz's little, red house. Even though it was early, it was already hot and the white geraniums in Mrs. Dietz's window box were wilting, like she'd forgotten to water them. I pounded on the door. Mrs. Dietz opened the door wearing big, pink rollers in her hair, and shorts that showed the ripples on her thighs. On her feet she had huge, pink, fluffy slippers. I almost laughed out loud when I saw her because I've never, in all the years we've lived on this street, seen her out of her white nurse's uniform. White dress, white stockings, white shoes, and even a white cap. My father calls her "the white tornado."

"Come quick," I said, "one of Mo's friends is really sick."

Mrs. Dietz started pulling those pink rollers out of her hair like there was no tomorrow. I wanted to tell her there wasn't time for that, but I didn't. I just stood there and watched. The curls that the rollers were in just stayed perfect when she took the pink plastic out, just like Shirley Temple's curls in the old movies I used to watch. She looked around and I thought she must be looking for a brush, but she said, "Ah, there it is," and grabbed her nurse's satchel, a little, leather bag filled with all the things a visiting nurse needs. She always has it with her when I see her leaving for work. She pushed me out the door and slammed it hard behind us. I hoped Mr. Dietz wasn't sleeping because if he was before she slammed the door, I'm sure he was awake now. We ran back to my house. Mrs. Dietz couldn't run as fast as me because she still had on those pink slippers.

When we got there, my mother was holding a wet washcloth to Susie's forehead with one hand and shaking her shoulder with the other.

"Come on, Sue, wake up. Talk to me," Mommy said. "Right now, Susan!" Mommy commanded. She was using what we call her "teacherly" voice, the one that means "no nonsense," the same voice she uses when she sends kids to the principal's office. But there was something else. I guessed she was trying to sound firm so that Susie would wake up, but I could also hear that my mother was scared and that made me scared.

"Let me take her blood pressure, Clare," Mrs. Dietz said, pulling open her nurse's satchel.

They clustered around Susie, whose head was flopping from side to side.

"How much did this girl have to drink, Maureen?" Mrs. Dietz asked my sister.

"I don't know," my sister answered. "I wasn't with her all the time," she added.

I could tell from Mo's voice she was trying not to cry. My mother shot my sister a questioning look. I guess she was wondering where Mo was if she hadn't been with Susie.

"Where are her parents?" my mother asked.

"They . . . they had to go out of town . . . suddenly. I didn't know, Mom, I swear I didn't."

My sister does a lot of "I swear, cross my heart, hope-to-die" stuff, but this time I really believed her. I wondered if Mommy did.

"We'll discuss it later," Mommy said and turned her attention back to Susie. I don't think she wanted to get into it all with Mrs. Dietz standing there listening.

"I hate to say this, Clare, but I think this girl needs to go to St. Mary's. I think she has alcohol poisoning," Mrs. Dietz said.

Mo started to cry, but my mother remained calm.

"All right, should we call the Volunteer Rescue

Squad ambulance or take her there in my car?" my mother asked.

"If you can drive, we're better off not waiting for the ambulance," Mrs. Dietz said and looked at her watch. "It's too early for the streets to be crowded and I'll sit in the back with her. We'll probably get there faster on our own."

We all know about the Volunteer Rescue Squad. They mostly join up because they like fires and like to drive fast. If you have an accident, you can only hope it happens within the Troy city borders so that the Troy police ambulance gets you. I agreed with Mrs. Dietz, we'd be better off going on our own and besides, then I wouldn't miss all the excitement.

As we eased Susie into the car, Mrs. Dietz said, "I'll feel a lot better when a doctor looks her over. I'm sure they'll want to IV her. She's lost a lot of liquids."

My mother wrote a hasty note to my father, who was already over at the eight o'clock mass counting the money. I saw what she wrote: "Mike back soon Explain later—don't worry Clare." I wanted to be around for the "explain later" part. Especially if my sister was doing the explaining.

When we got to St. Mary's, Mrs. Dietz ran in and got two orderlies to come out. They were both Negroes, but they didn't talk like Troy Negroes. It was like they spoke a foreign language. Some words I could understand and some I couldn't. Their speech was pretty, almost like they were singing. Mommy told me later they were from Jamaica. They picked Susie up and told her she was "gwan be fine"—that part I understood. But she didn't look fine to me, she was just lumping all over the place, almost like she was a big sack of potatoes. I watched them disappear through the sliding doors of the emergency room.

That was the last time I ever saw Susie Lavin. It's not like she died or anything. It's just that after that night of getting so drunk that she poisoned herself, my parents didn't want my sister to hang around with her anymore.

On the way home in the car, everyone was quiet. My mother was not going to open up this discussion in front of Mrs. Dietz. Like my Aunt Bridey says, that would be "airin' the family's dirty laundry in public."

My father was waiting at home when we got there. He was worried, even though Mommy had written him not to be. We could see him pacing on the back porch as we drove up the street. We all walked into the kitchen and I noticed it was already eleven o'clock. I pointed that out to my mother. "We've missed the last mass," I said and I tried not to sound too happy.

"I'm sure the Good Lord understands, Margie," my mother said and then, turning to my father, she added, "I just hope I can be understanding."

I looked around and noticed that my sister had slipped out of the room. She must be hiding out in our room, I thought. Probably gathering courage for the showdown in the kitchen. I pictured my sister dressed as a gunslinger, like somebody from *Gunsmoke,* and my parents like Matt Dillon and Chester. There'd be smoking guns today, I was sure of that.

"Call Mo back in here," my mother said to my father, interrupting my silly daydream of showdown at the Malloys.

My father called my sister back in and she came right away. She was acting very meek. They sat her down between them and started firing questions. Who was there? When did Susie's parents leave? Who slept over? Mo told her story. From the part when she got there and was surprised to find that Susie's parents weren't home to the part where the boys started drinking Susie's dad's liquor. My parents frowned through the whole thing and my sister did her "cross my heart, hope-to-die" swears. There were a lot of tears and Mom was harping about trust and all that stuff. They weren't paying any attention to me and I felt like I should be taking notes so that I'd know what to do if this ever happened to me when I got to high school. I couldn't picture any of my friends ever getting sick on alcohol, though. Dani Jacobs told me she snuck a taste of her father's martini once and it was *"phooey,"* really bad-tasting stuff. We made a pact then that we'd never drink, or smoke, either. That was back in seventh grade.

"That's all, Mom. I swear," my sister said. So the story was over. I was kind of disappointed. I was hoping for more. Something tragic, or maybe a fight over a girl and they had to call the police to break it up. But Mo swore that was all.

"How did you get home this morning?" my father asked.

I saw Mo take in a deep breath and I thought to myself, now she's going to tell a lie. I don't know why I thought that, I just did. I hope she wouldn't do any of that "cross my heart, hope-to-die" stuff because I always worry about lightning bolts killing people who say that and then tell lies.

"Traci McNeil just got her license," Mo said. "She drove us here in Susie's mother's car. We were just so afraid, Daddy, we didn't know what to do." Mo started to cry again. "I knew if we got Susie here to Mommy, she'd know what to do," she whimpered.

"You did the right thing, Mo," my mother said.

The tears must be working, I thought, because suddenly my parents were all over Mo, rubbing her back and patting her cheek and telling her everything would be all right, believing everything she said.

I wanted to ask more questions and I said, "But Mo, what about David, when did he . . ."

"Margie, stop pestering your sister," my mother interrupted. "She's had a traumatic experience."

My father nodded in agreement and said, "Why don't you just go out and shoot some baskets, young lady."

They wanted to get rid of me, for sure. I got up and went to the back porch to look for my basketball. I called the dog to come with me. Since I was free from church, and that was really unusual for my family, I might as well go have some fun. I watched them fussing over my sister. Boy oh boy, I thought, as I dribbled the ball out of the house, sometimes parents can really be dumb!

13

Picnic

August

&

Mo

The morning of the Malloy family picnic was the first day I began to worry. It was hot and I woke up really early, even before Daddy. It was just getting light out so I think it must have been before 5:00 A.M. I had to go to the bathroom and when I climbed out of bed, I thought I was going to throw up on the spot. Being as quiet as possible so I wouldn't wake Margie, I ran the length of the house, past my parents' room, down the hallway into the kitchen, and finally to the bathroom. I threw up what was left of last night's dinner and then tiptoed back to my room.

Margie was sleeping so soundly that she was snoring. I watched her as she slept, thinking how long she looked and remembering when we first started sharing this room and her little three-year-old body only took up a third of the twin bed. She had kicked off her covers, and even though it was warm, her skinny legs looked bluish and chilled, so I pulled the cotton blanket up to her chin. She started to mumble something and I patted her on the back and said "there, there" like Mom does and she rolled over and went right back to sleep.

I went to the desk that we both share and rummaged through the top drawer, my drawer. I pulled out my calendar and tried to figure backwards to the last time I had my period. I'd never marked up my calendar with menstrual dates like some of my friends do or like they tell you to in *Seventeen*. I never really had a reason. I tried to remember from events. Did I have my period when we went to Buttermilk Falls swimming? No. But when we went to Glass Lake Beach on our class picnic? Yes. That was easy to remember. That was the first time I'd ever tried to insert a tampon, so I could wear that little bikini that I'd had to sneak out of the house. I bought the bikini with my own money from my baby-sitting jobs and Daddy would flip if he ever saw how small it is. That picnic was six weeks ago. I put the calendar down on the top of the desk and counted out the days with my fingers . . . forty-two. My cycle isn't all that regular, so I might have been only a week over-due, but it was the throwing up in the morning that had me worried.

I climbed back into my own bed and pulled the covers up around my face. They smelled so good. Clean, like the sheets had been hung out to dry in the hot sun. I held them close to me and sniffed them, hoping the sweet scent of the fabric would take away the bitter smell in my nose and the taste in my mouth.

I'll have to talk to David today, I thought. What

would I say? How would I tell him what I feared? "David, I know it seems impossible from only one time, but I might be pregnant," or "I think I'm going to have a baby," or "Help me, I don't know what to do." I imagined his face, the look that would cross it when he heard what I had to say. Surprise? Anger? But it's his fault, too, just as much as it's mine, I thought. And besides, I do love him and I know he loves me. We'd even talked about getting pinned next year. We'd talked about the future.

And what about telling Mommy and Daddy? I thought. That idea made me cringe. I pulled the covers closer around me to cushion the chill I was feeling at the thought of the look that would be on my father's face. How could I tell them that I might be pregnant?

And what about Syracuse? If I really was pregnant, would they let me in? Would I lose my scholarship? What would it be like to go there and have people pointing at me behind my back and whispering on the dorm floor about me? "There she goes, she's the one who's losing her scholarship because she's three months pregnant."

Well it can't be, I thought. It would ruin everything for me and probably David, too. Maybe I just have a stomach virus. Lots of girls miss one period. Maybe I shouldn't tell David. Maybe I'll wait and see.

I can't tell him at the picnic, anyways. How could I tell him and then make him meet the whole Malloy family for the first time? All the uncles, all the aunts, all looking him over. No, I'll wait till it's over and tell him later. I'll go to the picnic and pretend to have fun, pretend to have no cares, pretend to be hungry and try not to gag on the hamburgers, and then later I'll tell him what I suspect. Maybe he'll know what we should do.

I lay in my bed the morning of the picnic with the covers pulled up over my head and I thought all those things. I prayed, too. I looked at the picture of the Sacred Heart on our bedroom wall. I looked at that heart, pierced with thorns and dripping blood. I looked at the gentle face and I prayed. "Please, God, don't let it be true. Please, please, not now. Not now, when everything's before me."

Mike

We had the Malloy family picnic at Prospect Park because of the pool there. It was supposed to be in Jim's backyard, down in South Troy, but this summer has been hotter than hell, so we all agreed to move it up to the park overlooking the city. We brought our coolers and our blankets and Danny even brought a long aluminum table with fold-out seats just in case we couldn't find enough picnic tables to fit us all. We couldn't bring a keg because of the city ordinance and how it would look to have the mayor and a police captain ignoring the law right under everybody's nose. We did bring plenty of six packs, though, and so that day we drank our beer out of white paper cups. I don't really suppose the people strolling by our tables were much fooled into thinking the Malloys were having coffee and tea at their picnic, but His Honor, my brother, the mayor, felt better about it.

Jim set up a poker game at one of the picnic tables that was in the shade of an old sycamore tree. I remember that tree from when I was a kid. We used to climb it and from the highest branch you could see all the way down the river to Albany. My brother Danny used to claim he could see New York City and we all went along with him, asking him the score of the Yankee game or could he see the Babe swinging away. Exaggeration was a way of life to Danny. He was born to politics, I guess.

"Pat would have loved this day," Jim said and we all nodded and smiled at the memory of Pat's card-playing abilities. It's more like that now. We can talk about Pat and Johnny and remember all the good times without getting too choked up. On a day like this in Troy, so hot and steamy, it's hard to believe that our brother froze to death in this city.

Pat and Johnny's kids were with us, too. Looking to uncles instead of fathers at the Malloy picnic, caught in the big safety net of the family, that's how I like to think of it. Pat's little girl, Gracie, came over to me just as I was picking up my first hand. She was wearing a pink bathing suit with big, yellow polka dots. Her fat little stomach stuck out just enough to catch the drips from the red popsicle she was eating. Clare had taken all the little ones over to the Good Humor Ice Cream truck that winds through the park on these dog days. The kids hear those bells and there's just no denying them.

"Uncle Mike." Gracie's voice was whiney and I suspected the older children had been teasing her. "Uncle Mike," she said again and leaned her plump, freckled arm on my leg, dripping popsicle on me, too. "Aunt Bridey says we can't go swimmin' 'cause of the germs in the pool."

"Don't be silly, darlin', they chlorinate that pool every day. You go tell your Aunt Bridey that I said you can go swimming if one of the older kids or one of the aunts goes with you." I was anxious to get back to my hand and I didn't really want to walk Gracie over to the pool on the other side of the park. It was so pleasant sitting under those old sycamores, looking out over the city and watching the Hudson's muddy waters snake under the bridges down below, that I didn't want to budge an inch.

Gracie pulled on my arm again. "She says the germs are from all those kids that don't get their shots. She says all those kids pee in the pool and Aunt Clare just told her not to be silly."

Just as I was enjoying my own peace, Clare and Bridey start in again, I thought. I laid down my cards and stood up, taking my niece's sticky hand. "C'mon, Gracie," I said. "Let's go over and talk to your aunts. I'm sure the pool is fine for swimming."

I walked over to the table where the potato and macaroni salads and all the chips and pretzels were set out. The women were getting ready to start the charcoal grills and Anna had just put out her seven-layer bars. They were making themselves busy and I could tell there had been an argument.

"Here comes Mike. Just go ahead and ask your husband what he thinks," I heard my sister say to my wife.

Clare gave me an exasperated look and turned to Bridey. "You know, Bridey, I wouldn't let my own children swim in the pool if I thought it was unsafe," she said.

"Now, ladies," I said, trying to make my voice sound comical, "Gracie tells me someone's been peeing in the pool." I looked to Clare and she had a perturbed look on her face and pointed her thumb at Bridey.

"Mike," Bridey said, "I just don't think the kids should be swimming with all those coloreds from up around Ninth Street. You know how those kids are treated. They probably haven't even been vaccinated for polio."

Polio, the old scare word that used to make us keep the kids out of the water when they were little, before Jonas Salk.

"For heaven's sake, Bridey. Our kids have all been vaccinated. We don't have to worry about polio. Why can't the kids go swimming?"

"You don't know what other germs those people might have," my sister said.

Clare spread out a checkered cloth on the next table and laid out some plastic forks and paper plates. She brushed her hands together and picked up her towel.

"When Mo comes with David Markovitch, tell her I'm over at the pool swimming with Margie," she announced. "C'mon, Gracie, you can come with me," she said and held out her hand to our niece.

Bridey watched Clare, with Gracie in tow, walk away toward the big white pool house and the noises of kids swimming that traveled across the grassy open space between our grove of trees and the pool.

"Well," she huffed. "I just hope they don't come down with some strange sickness next week. If they do, we'll know just who to blame."

I shrugged my shoulders and went to look for Mo and David Markovitch. I didn't want some outsider seeing our petty family squabbles. If they came soon, I'd send them off to the tennis courts till things simmered down.

Clare

When I saw Mo and David walking hand in hand across the open field between the tennis courts and our picnic spot, I was struck by what a grown woman my daughter had become. And I'm not prejudiced when I say that she had become truly beautiful, irresistibly beautiful. Irresistible to David Markovitch, I was sure. And he irresistible to her, also. I could tell just by watching them, the way they held hands, the way they looked at each other, the way they tried to get close. Even from a distance I could see that. It reminded me of the first summer I knew Mike. How we needed to be with each other. Watching my daughter, her red hair shining in the hot sun, her face flushed from the tennis match, her white shorts revealing long, slender legs, made me wonder what Father Tim would think now of his farfetched plans for making Mo into a nun. I wondered, too, if Mike saw his daughter through a man's eyes. Did he realize how lush she was, or did he still think of her as the little girl he had brought to this same park on days just like this, when it was too hot in our house? Those days, when Mo was like Gracie is now, when we pushed her on the swings and spun her on the old metal merry-go-round, are gone for good. For just a minute, a wave of sadness hit me when I thought that if Michael had lived, Mike would probably be pushing him in the toddler swing right now. Or maybe holding his hand as he tried his first steps with bare, baby feet on the soft grass of our picnic spot.

I made myself stop thinking thoughts like that; I didn't want to ruin the day.

"Hi, Mom," Mo said, smiling at the aunts and giving little waves over to the table where Mike and the uncles were playing cards. "We're starving. Are we eating soon?" She held David Markovitch's arm protectively, as if she could guarantee him safe conduct through the gauntlet of Malloy aunts, uncles, and cousins that he was soon to run. They looked so good standing there together.

"We're waiting for the coals to die down. Why

don't you introduce David to your aunts," I suggested.

David looked a little uncomfortable, but nodded in agreement and followed Mo's lead over to the table where Bridey, Anna, Mary, Meg, and even Hildy were shaping the raw meat into hamburger patties. I followed along, a little anxious that the introductions would go smoothly and ready to be there just in case Bridey made another ignorant comment. I'd tried hard earlier to bite my tongue when she didn't want the kids to go swimming because of the Negro children in the pool.

"This is my aunt, Mrs. O'Sullivan," Mo pointed to Bridey, "and my aunts Mrs. Malloy, Mrs. Malloy, Mrs. Malloy, and Mrs. Malloy. That makes it real easy for you, David." Mo smiled and pushed David forward toward the aunts. "Aunt Bridey, Aunt Anna, Aunt Meg, Aunt Mary, Aunt Hildy . . . this is David Markovitch."

"Is this the young man you went to the senior prom with, Maureen?" Mary asked.

Mo smiled and nodded, grabbing David's arm possessively. I could tell she was thinking about the Grand March when she was queen of the prom and he was king. What I was remembering was the brouhaha that David Markovitch's name had caused at the Malloy Easter dinner. I wondered if my sisters–in–law were remembering that, too.

"Take David over and introduce him to your uncles, Mo," I commanded, suddenly uneasy, remembering Bridey's objections to David being a Jew.

Mo pulled David away toward the men's card table, laughing and saying something in his ear that we couldn't hear. I watched her turn her back to us and walk away, holding David's hand, and I realized how empty our house would seem when she was gone in September. Her loud music, the silly fights with Margie, the chants, "Let's go, THS," while she endlessly practiced her cheerleading hand motions in the living room, even her back talk to Mike and me. I'd miss it all.

"He seems like a fine young man," Anna said, interrupting my thoughts of Mo leaving and pulling me back to this day.

"Yes, Mike and I like him very much," I said.

"Where will he be going come September?" Bridey asked. Her question seemed innocent.

"David's going to Cornell."

The other aunts nodded approvingly.

"He must be a very bright boy," Bridey said.

We all knew that really good students from our high school go to Cornell. We also knew that Cornell's Ivy League tuition put it out of our league.

"His parents must be wealthy to send him to a fancy school like that," Bridey said.

I thought of Max and Ruth Markovitch and how they were dressed on prom night and their expensive thirty-five millimeter camera and their Cadillac.

"I suppose they are," I said.

"That's how it's always going to be in this city—the Jews have all the money," Bridey said.

My other sisters–in–law looked at me to answer, but I wasn't taking the bait on this one. I just decided I'd let Bridey go on believing what she needed to believe.

At this point, I wasn't going to be able to change her mind about Negroes or Jews, or the Italian kids that are always picking on her oldest boy, or the Polish butcher who she claims always shortchanges her. And I certainly didn't want to get into it now, with David Markovitch joining us for a picnic lunch.

"Do you suppose he eats hot dogs?" Bridey said, pointing over at David. "Some Jews don't eat pork," she added.

"I don't know, Bridey. Why don't you ask him yourself?" I said and I walked away.

Margie

I think Mommy gave in and let me go to the Schaghticoke Fair with David and Mo the night after the Malloy family picnic because of the bad thing that happened that day at the park. I think Mommy wanted me to get it out of my mind. Even Daddy gave me fifteen dollars and told David, "Take her on every fast and scary ride, make sure she has a good time." Fifteen dollars is a lot of money for carnival rides and at two rides for a dollar, that's a lot of rides. He must have wanted me to have a *really* good time.

"There's no sense dwelling on it, Margie," my mother had told me when we got home from the park. "It was a terrible accident. It was no one's fault and there's nothing we can do about it."

Easy for her to say, because she wasn't there when they pulled the little boy out of the pool. In fact, Mo and David and I were the only people from the Malloy family picnic to see the whole thing.

We had gone over for a final swim around four o'clock. I know the time exactly because we had to sit and watch the minute hand move on Mommy's watch until 3:55. We always have to wait one whole hour, never any less, after we've eaten to go swimming. That's one of Mommy's rules that never changes, no matter how much you beg or tease. So at 3:55, we headed over to the pool.

We walked into the pool house and sat down on the green benches near the changing rooms to take off our shoes. We didn't really need to change because we all had our bathing suits on under our shorts. I slipped off my shoes and put my feet down into the little puddles of greenish water that were all around the pool. I guess I splashed down a little too hard because Mo said, "Damn it, Margie, you got my socks wet." Mo hardly ever swears around me, and Daddy would really get mad if he heard her use curses, but I knew she was trying to show David Markovitch that she's grown up and cool.

"That water is disgusting," she said and she held her sock up to me, pointing to the greenish smudge on the white cotton. The water did feel kind of slimy and I wondered if maybe Aunt Bridey was right about germs and all. I bent over to study the water really close. I thought maybe I'd see an amoeba or at least a little worm. I was bent so close to the puddle that the chlorine smell almost made me sick.

"C'mon, Margie, let's go off the high dive," David said.

I jumped up, forgetting about the puddle, ready to do anything that David Markovitch could suggest. We were heading toward the pool's biggest board when we heard yelling and a lot of commotion coming from the deep end of the pool. We ran to see what all the noise was about.

Just as we got to the edge of the pool near the high dive, they were pulling him out. His skin was so brown and shiny it looked like Easter chocolate. His eyes were closed, but his pink mouth was open and there was blood coming out of his ear. I could see his teeth, they looked so white against his brown skin. He was a little bit bigger than my cousin Gracie.

"Jesus," the head lifeguard said, "he must have hit his head on the bottom. How the fuck could that happen? It's fifteen feet right here."

"Never mind that, Jerry," one of the girl lifeguards yelled. "Start the mouth-to-mouth. Ginny," she screamed to a pool assistant, "call for an ambulance!"

That ambulance siren set the Malloy family picnic on its ear. My parents and aunts and uncles came running to the pool. My mother was sure that either Mo or I had drowned. My Uncle Jim showed his badge and told people where to stand and he helped the lifeguards with the boy's body. My Uncle Danny was talking to all the reporters, who showed up right behind the ambulance, telling them how tragic it all was.

While the men in the Malloy family stayed at the pool to help, my mother and my Aunt Bridey led us children away, back to our grove of trees.

"It was part of God's plan," my aunt said. "We don't know the mind of the Almighty," she added and then she made us all kneel down to say the Rosary for the dead boy's soul, right there in the park. All of us except David Markovitch, of course.

"I'm going home, Mo," he said. "I'll call you tonight."

I was standing near my sister when he said that and I heard her whisper back, "Call me around nine. We need to talk." Her voice sounded sad and serious and I supposed they'd be talking about the dead boy.

David picked up his tennis racket and his towel and walked over to tell my mother he was leaving. I think he might have felt left out with all of us praying like that.

My mother walked with him to his car, her hand on his shoulder. I heard her ask him if he was okay to drive and then she said, "You should be with your family now." When she came back, she dropped to her knees and joined in on the second decade. I watched her face as we recited the prayers for the dead boy, "God's little lamb," my Aunt Bridey called him. My mother looked so sad. As we prayed together, I wondered if my aunt felt just a little bad about making the big fuss about germs before.

Later, when all the commotion was over and we

were driving home, my mother said to my father, "How can God allow such sadness? I thought my heart would break open when that boy's mother got there. I knew every pain she was feeling. He was such a beautiful boy, too."

When she said that about being beautiful, I wondered if she was talking about the boy who drowned or my brother, Michael.

The next night on the carnival rides, the dead boy and my brother were all mixed up in my mind. If the ride was too high, or if I was upside down or spinning too fast, I'd close my eyes, and whenever I did I'd see that brown skin glistening and that boy's body and then I'd see Michael's tiny white face, just like the last time I saw it, just as beautiful, but dead, too.

I couldn't put it out of my mind. I kept thinking that we were on our way to the high dive. I could have hit my head, just like the dead boy. It could have been me and then it would have been my mother shrieking and moaning on the green grass outside the pool house.

Mo must have been thinking the same thing, too, because at the fair that night, she looked really unhappy and she said the rides and the cotton candy made her feel sick. On the last Ferris wheel ride before we went home, we all squeezed into one seat. Mo and David were holding hands and whispering. I heard my sister say something like, "I don't want to think about it," and I wanted to ask her if she was still thinking about the dead boy, too, but just as I started to ask, the ride ended.

THE IRISH PRINCESS

I didn't want breakfast the next morning, either, but Mommy made me try to eat. She made chicks in the hole, which is just a fancy way of cooking poached eggs and toast. She always makes it for us when we're sick or need cheering up. She made it for Mo, too, and she watched to make sure Mo ate every bite. Later I heard Mo throwing up. I guess she's still sick about the whole thing. Just like me.

14

Confirmation

August

❦

Clare

"Take all your clothes off and put on this gown," the nurse said as she held out a blue paper hospital gown to Mo. "Make sure the opening is in the back. When you're changed, just sit right up there." She pointed to the examining table. "The doctor will be with you soon," she added.

Mo looked at me and I nodded, yes, go ahead, do as she says; be obedient to this crisp, perky woman in a white, starched uniform. I looked at the stirrups of the examining table and the tray of metal instruments that the doctor would use to check my daughter and, inadvertently, I thought of the sweet days of her girlhood and adolescence. Gone for good now.

We had driven down to Hudson for this confirming appointment. We couldn't very well go to Dr. Moriarty. Not yet. I'd heard about this doctor at school, from a teacher who lived down the river in Delmar, near Albany. I hadn't asked around, of course. We're trying to keep this as quiet as possible, at least until we know for sure. I'd remembered Kate Stagnito talking about her gynecologist in the teachers' room last year. She'd said he encouraged natural childbirth and breast-feeding and that he'd graduated from Harvard Medical School and had just opened a practice in Hudson, of all places. I was still pregnant then, so the conversation interested me.

It's strange to think that I was pregnant at this time last year. That was before we lost Michael. It's weird how I think of time now. Everything seems to revolve around Michael's birth and Michael's death. It's like a big separating line in my life, a dividing part. Before Michael, after Michael. It would appear that way on a time line. Johnny and Pat never knew my son, they died before Michael. Bridey's triplets were born before Michael. Danny was elected mayor after Michael. Mo's childhood was before Michael. Mo met David Markovitch after Michael.

I watched Mo undress, carefully folding her blouse and her skirt and rolling her white socks into a neat, little ball with the rest of her underwear. I remembered how fastidious she was with her things as a younger child. Always putting them away without even being asked. Taking special care to hang her clothes up and organize her barrettes and hair ribbons. A lot like me in that way, needing to be orderly. So different from Margie, who can never find her left basketball sneaker or the book she needs for homework, who flings her clothes off and the devil may care where they land.

When Mo finished folding her things, she climbed up on the examining table. She looked so forlorn sitting there that I reached over for her hand. Her fingers were icy cold and I could feel her trembling. The blue of the medical gown made her white skin look even paler. I put my arm around her and assured her. "We'll work things out, Mo," I said. She put her head on my shoulder and took a deep breath. I was afraid she was going to cry, so I said, "It will be all right," not knowing, of course, if it would. It was a white lie I told, a fib, to get us both through the next half hour. The half hour that would determine Mo's plans, perhaps change her life.

There was a knock on the door. It was only a little tap, but I had to steel myself against what was to happen. The doctor opened the door and walked in. I was taken aback by how young he looked. His hair was sandy brown and he had blue eyes and freckles. Though he stood there with his white coat unbuttoned to show a three-piece suit and a blue button-down shirt and tie, his face somehow reminded me of Huck Finn. I knew from what I'd heard of his practice and his education that he must be in his early thirties, but he looked like a boy to me.

He walked into the room and picked up Mo's chart that the nurse had left for him. He was very matter-of-fact. "I've read your history, Maureen, and the vaginal exam will surely give us an idea of what's going on. We'll do some tests to confirm, of course. You're not married, I see, so if there is an intact pregnancy, it will be a problem for you, I assume."

"An intact pregnancy. . . ." I wondered at his choice of words, his use of medical jargon. Did his words give him the distance from us that he needed? An intact pregnancy, a baby, a living thing, a being becoming, possibly growing as we spoke, as we sat there waiting for the diagnosis. We had no control over the cells dividing and multiplying, nor did he. He would tell us yes or no. He would say "intact pregnancy" or "false alarm." He would say "intact pregnancy," not "baby," not "child."

"Lie down and put your feet in these stirrups, please. Try to slide way down on the examining table," he commanded.

Mo did as she was told, but reached for my hand again.

"Try to relax, Maureen, take some deep breaths." His voice seemed gentler now, as if the medical procedure he was about to perform made him feel more comfortable, abler to be sympathetic. "This won't hurt you, but it will probably feel strange."

My daughter closed her eyes tightly as the young doctor began the vaginal exam. I remembered all those well child visits to Dr. Moriarty and how she'd squeeze her eyes shut tight when it was time for the vaccinations, as if by shutting out the sight of the doctor with the long needle, she could shut out the reality of it. I wondered, was she trying to push down the possibility of the unborn child with her tightly shut eyes and her vise-like grip on my hand?

"Yes, definite fullness in the uterus," the doctor

said, probing Mo's abdomen with his other hand. "Very early, about six weeks along, I'd say. Conception occurred sometime in early July."

Mo opened her eyes and looked right at me. Apology, sadness, fear . . . all those things I saw in those green eyes. July Fourth, I thought. Susie Lavin's sleepover party. "Conception occurred"—just another medical term for what really happened. Conception occurred at Susie Lavin's house. I was sure of that.

"We'll have to do some blood work and urine tests to confirm, of course, but I'd say early April. Yes, due date, early April."

I felt the deep, sad sigh escape from my body before I could control it. The young doctor and Mo looked at me. I stiffened my shoulders and said, "What options does my daughter have, Doctor Martin? She's only eighteen; she's supposed to start college in September."

"What are you suggesting, Mrs. Malloy?" The doctor's voice was cool.

What was I suggesting? Was I suggesting anything? Was I thinking out loud of the next step? God knows. I guess I was asking for help or guidance. But how could he help us? Could he help me break the news to Mike? This is the kind of thing that Mike can't handle, all the feelings that come with being an Irish Catholic, feelings about his daughters, the Church, the shame to the name. God, how was I going to tell Mike? And it would be me that did the telling, for sure. Mo would never be able to tell him. And what about the Markovitches?

They'd have to be told, too. What about David's responsibilities?

Suddenly, I felt really angry. Angry at Mo for being so foolhardy and throwing away her chances. Angry at David for jeopardizing my daughter. Angry at the Markovitches for being David's parents. Angry at the doctor standing before me with his positive diagnosis. For the first time I fully realized the meaning of the ancient posture, "Kill the messenger." I just wanted to kill that young doctor in his three-piece suit for telling us that Mo was indeed pregnant.

"Her options, in the state of New York, are quite clear. Go through with the pregnancy. Marry or put the child up for adoption."

The "child"? I thought. The child. I half-expected him to say the "intact pregnancy," the "product of conception." This is a child, I thought, and the idea of it overwhelmed me.

The doctor continued, "There is no legal termination of pregnancy in the state of New York. I can't advise you what to do. However, there are flights out of New York City every day to Puerto Rico."

"Legal termination of the pregnancy"? Was that what he thought I meant by "options"? No, I don't know what I was suggesting. Options? There were none, as far as I was concerned. For Mo, Puerto Rico might as well be the moon, as distant and unreachable.

"After the nurse takes the blood sample, get dressed and come into my office. I can give you some medication for the morning sickness. And you'll need vitamins, of course."

I looked at my daughter and could see the tears welling up in her eyes. She needed a lot more than vitamins right now. Suddenly, I remembered my last pregnancy and the pills I took to ward off the nausea and the vitamins I took to make Michael healthy and strong. Again I felt the sadness for my sickly baby rising up in me and I thought I, too, would cry, but I quelled it. I had to be strong now for Mo, my first baby. I had to get her through this. Somehow.

Mo

"Tests to confirm." I heard the doctor's words as I lay there on that cold examining table, and instead of the confirmation of the life growing inside me, I thought of the day I was confirmed by the bishop. It seemed so long ago. I pictured myself, waiting there in the vestibule of St. Jude's Church with the other thirteen-year-old girls. Standing there in my white gown and red beanie, my hands folded in prayer, waiting for the bishop's slap, making me into a soldier for Christ, confirming me with the name Jean, the saint's name I had chosen after my godfather, Uncle Johnny. Uncle Johnny was there, too, in my memory, standing with his hand on my shoulder, sponsoring me for the sacrament. And then I thought about Uncle Johnny being dead, and Uncle Pat, and my brother, Michael, and that boy at the pool and I wished with all my heart that I were dead, too. It would be better to be dead than to face my father with the news of this confirmation.

"The blood tests will confirm," the doctor repeated, and I could feel goose bumps all over my body and the hairs on my arms standing up. I thought for a minute that I would throw up again or faint.

My mother was talking about options and I pictured Mrs. Fitzgerald, our twelfth grade economics teacher, standing before the blackboard with her pointer and talking about bears, and bulls, and options. Nothing seemed to make any sense to me. It was like my own mind was shutting down and not letting me know what I already knew. That I was going to have a baby, David's baby.

I remembered the night that I told David what I suspected. He was mad at first. "You know we didn't use anything for protection," I had said.

"I know, I know. But damn!" he'd answered. "Are you sure?"

"No, not positive. We're going to a doctor down in Hudson. Mom has arranged it."

"Does your father know yet?" he had asked.

"God, no. We're not telling him till we're sure. We won't tell him till we have to."

"He'll probably kill me," David said.

I didn't disagree. I could just picture the look on my father's face if we had to tell him. First shock, then anger, then disappointment. He would be disappointed forever. I could picture him with his hands around David's neck, strangling the life out of David for what he'd done to me. But of course, we all knew it wasn't just David's fault. I was equally to blame. Me, the Irish Princess, the straight-A student, Daddy's little girl. I was guilty, too.

"Vitamins," I heard the doctor say and I remembered all the pills that my mother took after she found out she was having Michael. Iron pills that looked like M&M's and something called Natalin. And I remembered her being sick in the morning, just like I was, and then while they talked over my body about vitamins, I remembered the night at Lake George when she told me that she was going to have a baby. It seemed like years ago, but it was only last summer.

She'd come into my little cubbyhole room at the cabin and sat down on my bed.

It was late, around eleven, and I'd been reading *Gone With the Wind*. I was on the part where Scarlett returns to Tara. I wanted to keep reading. I hadn't really wanted to talk to Mommy, but she insisted.

"I just wanted to try to explain why I lost my temper earlier," she'd said.

I remembered her screaming at my father about having a "goddamn baby of your own" and then stomping out of the cabin.

She explained about her unplanned pregnancy and how worried she was about having to give up her teaching job and how she didn't know where we'd get the money for my college. She didn't say it in so many words, but I knew that she didn't really want to have that baby. That's how she felt then. Later, when Michael was born and had almost no chance to live, I know she would have moved heaven and earth, if she could have, to keep him alive.

Did she at first pray to God that it couldn't be true, like I did? When she first suspected, did she pray that she'd wake up in the morning with cramps and bleeding? Did she pray for a miscarriage? Can you pray for something like that? I wondered. If this thing inside you isn't really a baby yet, can you pray for it to go away? To die?

"Get dressed now, Mo," my mother said in a soft voice and I had to pull myself back to that fruitwood-panelled examining room, that room with all the boastful degrees from Harvard and Yale hanging on the walls. The nurse helped me down from the table and my mother handed me my clothes.

The doctor had already left the room to see the next patient. I pictured a largely pregnant, immaculately groomed, straight-haired blonde with a flowery maternity dress and a big, thick wedding band on her left hand, waiting in the next examining room for the young doctor. I pictured her patting her stomach tenderly, and I hated her.

I turned to my mother and asked, "What's going to happen now?"

"I guess we'll have to talk with your father tonight," she said, "and then with David and his parents."

I felt the blood drain from my face at the thought

of that confrontation. First my father, and then the Markovitches. What would they all think of me? I sat down quickly. I thought I might faint. My hands were shaking.

"Are you all right, Mo?" my mother asked.

"Could you get me some water, Mom?" I said.

My mother left the examining room to find some water. The nurse had gone to assist the doctor with his next patient. I looked at the sharp metal instruments on the counter. I wished I had the courage to take one of them and slit my wrists and just watch the blood seep out of my body. It would be easier than facing my father.

The nurse came back with my mother. She held out a cup of water and a little white pill.

"Here," she said in a falsely cheery voice, "the doctor says this will help your nerves."

I took the water and obediently swallowed the pill. I handed the empty cup back to her.

"All righty, you'll feel just fine in a few minutes," she said and left the room smiling. My mother helped me finish dressing.

By the time we left Hudson and were on the thruway driving north toward Albany, the nurse's prophecy had come true. I did feel just fine. In fact, I felt terrific. I thought if I could have one of those little white pills every day of my life, things would be just dandy. I felt like things were going to turn out all right. I forgot all about the baby. I pictured myself packing for Syracuse, putting wool sweaters into black-watch plaid suitcases.

Putting fresh notebooks with clean, white paper and newly sharpened, Number Two pencils into boxes and closing them with shipping tape. I pictured myself sitting in a big lecture hall, listening to a handsome professor and then raising my hand and asking the first of many brilliant questions. I pictured meeting David for Homecoming Weekend and Cornell fraternity parties and Syracuse football games. All the way home to Wynantskill, I had those rosy thoughts from that little white pill.

Then we found Margie crying on the back steps and that's when my stupid daydream about really being able to go to college fell apart.

Margie

It happened while Mom and Mo were out shopping for the afternoon, so there was no one here but me. I couldn't call Daddy because he was out on his route, so I had to take care of it myself.

It was really hot and I decided to quit the softball game at the school diamond and go home to watch TV. It was around two o'clock and I figured that cartoons or soap operas would be on, and though I don't like either very much, it would be cooler than the pitcher's mound. I fixed myself a bowl of vanilla ice cream and some lemonade and then turned on the living room fan and plopped down on the couch.

Right in the middle of *Search for Tomorrow*, the doorbell rang. I almost didn't hear it because of the fan. I got up to see who it was. Almost no one comes to our front door—we all use the back—so I figured it must be someone who didn't know us well. I was right. A man was standing there with his baseball cap in his hand. I had never seen him before. His shirt said "Eddie" on one pocket and "Steve's Auto Repair" on the other. I figured he must be Eddie. I didn't open the door to him, because I'm never supposed to do that if I'm home alone. I just stood there looking at him through the white curtains.

"Is your mother or father home?" he asked.

I'm never supposed to answer that question to a stranger, either. We know all about not doing that because there was a child kidnapped from Wynantskill two years ago. His name was Billy Rosen. My family didn't know him because he lived over in the Whiteview section and he went to private school. Someone saw him get into a fancy sports car. They found him dead out in Berlin. They never found the murderer, either, so all the kids in Wynantskill know better than to talk to strangers. The killer could still be around.

"Why do you want my parents?" I asked the man I thought was Eddie. I had to shout because both the front door and the storm door were closed and I wasn't about to open them.

"Your dog's been hurt," he said. He looked down at the Yankee cap in his hand and fingered the brim. "He just ran right out in front of me. I'm awful sorry."

He looked up from the cap at me. "Maybe you want to call your mother," he suggested. He pointed down the hill, "He's down near Main Avenue and he's hurt pretty bad."

I thought about Binky following me home from the softball game. When I'd picked up my mitt and my bat, he'd been right there behind me. Had he wandered back down toward Main Avenue after I'd come inside? Was it my fault? I could feel my eyes filling up with tears.

"My parents aren't home," I admitted.

The man looked bewildered, like he wasn't sure what to do, and I sure as heck didn't know what to do. I couldn't even get Binky to our vet. I didn't drive yet!

"Do you have a neighbor you can call to help you?" he asked.

Mrs. Evans, Rollie's mother, might be able to help, I thought.

"Yes, I'll call someone," I said, trying to stop crying, but not being able to.

"I better get back to the truck," the man said. "I'll wait there, near the dog, for you."

I dialed Rollie's number and he answered. He didn't recognize my voice, because I was crying so hard. I had to tell him it was me. He said his mom wasn't home, either, but he'd run right down to help me. Some help, I thought, remembering how he'd killed our fish last summer. I hung up and ran out of the house.

I ran down our hill. I don't think I've ever run that fast before. It was almost like I was flying, my feet barely touched the ground. When I got to Binky, almost all the kids from the neighborhood were already there. They'd heard the screech of the brakes over at the baseball field. They'd told the truck driver which house to go to.

I dropped down on the concrete next to Binky. There was a little dog blood, but not much. Binky was shivering and his eyes were open. He was laying on his side and he wasn't moving at all. His one eye, on the side that was up, stared at me and he whimpered.

"It's all right, Binky boy," I said, petting his fur. I was afraid to touch him. I was afraid I would hurt him. He made a sad, crying kind of noise and he tried to get up, but he couldn't.

The Wynantskill police pulled up. Well, I should say the Wynantskill policeman, our sheriff, because we only have one person in the whole department. His name is Randy Jones. We really don't even need him all that much. Except for that kidnapping two years ago, which the FBI worked on, anyways, the most serious crime we ever have is kids throwing snowballs at cars in the winter.

"You all stand back now," Mr. Jones said as he bent down near me and touched Binky's head. All the kids backed up a step or two. "Looks pretty bad for your dog, Margie."

I just nodded my head because I had so many tears in my throat that I couldn't talk, it was like choking.

"What do you say we get him in my police car and take him over to Doc Frita?"

I nodded again.

Mr. Jones looked around at the crowd. He knew all the kids. He makes that his business. He comes to every first grade class in Wynantskill School and gives the same speech. "I'm Randy Jones," he always says, "I'm the only officer of the law this little town has and I want to be your friend." He's also the after-school crossing guard, so we all know him. Some kids even call him Randy, but my mother told me never to do that. She's says it's disrespectful.

"Bobby," Mr. Jones said to one of the kids standing around. He pointed to Bobby's house on the corner of Main Avenue and Atlantic. "Run inside and ask your mother for an old towel."

Bobby did as Mr. Jones asked and was back really quick. I guess he didn't want to miss any of the excitement.

We wrapped Binky in that ragged, green Turkish towel. While we were lifting him, he cried a lot and he just kept staring at me. I cried a lot, too.

Mr. Jones told me to climb in the back with Binky and he jumped in the front and turned the siren on. I'd never ridden in a real police car with the siren going. Once, Uncle Jim took me around the block on his police motorcycle, but we went real slow and he didn't put the siren on.

We didn't go slow in Randy Jones' cruiser. We went so fast that the houses were whizzing by. I could see people on the street turning to watch us pass. Binky was down on the floor and I wondered if the people could see me. I wondered if they thought I was being arrested by Randy Jones.

We got to Dr. Frita's office in about two minutes. Mr. Jones ran in to get the vet and I just sat there stroking Binky. I had stopped crying then, even though I knew Binky was going to die.

The vet ran out. He's a short, chubby man with a bald head. His hair shoots out on the side like he never combs it. He had on his white doctor coat and I thought it wouldn't look so clean in a few minutes, after he picked up Binky.

They lifted my dog out of the car and carried him into the Friendly Animal Clinic. I've always wondered about that name. When I was little, I thought it meant all the animals in there were friendly. Now that I'm older, I'm sure it means that they're friendly in there to animals. Dr. Frita certainly was. He was speaking in a gentle voice to Binky.

"There, there, it's okay, old fella," he said. Of course, we all knew it wasn't okay.

He turned to me and asked, "Where are your parents, Margie?"

I explained that Mom and Mo were out shopping for college things and Daddy was at work, that I'm hardly ever completely on my own, but wouldn't you know, today would be one of those times.

Dr. Frita took my hand. He looked out at me from behind big, thick, horn-rimmed glasses. His eyes were squinty, but they looked kind, too. "Binky's back is broken, Margie. He's in a lot of pain. We have to put him out of his misery."

I nodded, because I understood. I had looked at that one, sad Binky eye in the police cruiser, all the way over to the Friendly Animal Clinic. I knew it was bad.

"We have to do it right away," he explained. He turned to Mr. Jones. "Randy, since Margie's parents can't be reached, will you take the responsibility?" he asked.

Mr. Jones nodded and the vet turned back to me. "We must have an adult signature, Margie, but you may sign, too," he said.

I thought it was kind, what he said. It was for my sake, I know. It was like he understood that all the adults in the world could come in and sign, but it was really my decision. It was really up to me because Binky was my dog.

We both signed our names on the dotted line and then Dr. Frita said, "I'll leave you alone so you can say good-bye to Binky." He left the room and so did Mr. Jones.

I sat down near my dog, who was breathing really fast now. I said some stupid things and I started to cry again. Binky tried to wag his tail. "I'll miss you, Bingo Bink," I said. "You are the best dog in the whole world." I choked out those words and then I couldn't talk anymore.

The vet came in with a long needle and Mr. Jones took me out. About five minutes later Dr. Frita came out and sat down next to me. I was still crying.

"You did what had to be done, Margie. You're a fine, brave girl and a credit to your family," he said.

I couldn't say anything, so he just kept talking. "We can keep Binky here till your parents come home, or I can wrap him up and Mr. Jones can help you get him back to your yard. I'm sure you'll want to bury him there."

I thought of the little, makeshift cross of popsicle sticks in Mommy's flower garden. That was where we buried the sick baby bird that we had found last month. We had kept it in a shoebox with cotton balls and grass and we'd tried to feed it bugs and worms. Daddy even tried to give it milk in a washed-out eye dropper. But it was too young to live without its mother. "That baby needs its mother," Daddy had said.

As I thought about burying Binky out there in the lily of the valley patch, near the baby bird, I realized that I needed my mother, too, and then I started to cry really hard. I was feeling so sorry for Binky; I'm sure he didn't want to be dead. But I was feeling sorry for myself, too. Things would be different now. I had no memory of life without Binky. We got him when I was two, so he was always there. It wasn't even like right after our baby died. We could at least remember a time before him. I couldn't remember any time before Binky.

As we drove home in the police cruiser, I thought about all the times I'd been mean to my dog. Like when I slapped him on the nose for chewing up my softball. Or the time I let my friend Mary convince me it would be a good experiment to tie Binky's legs together with string and then time how long it took him to chew his way out.

"I'll stay here with you till your Mom or Dad gets home," Mr. Jones said as we pulled up to our driveway.

He helped me lift my dog's body out of the trunk and then we laid him on the ground in the shade of the backyard maple tree. Dr. Frita had wrapped Binky in some plastic stuff that looked like heavy-duty trash bags and then taped it all together. I wanted to undo it all to see his face, but Mr. Jones wouldn't let me.

"Best to keep the flies off him right now, Margie," he said.

We sat together on the back porch steps, waiting for my mother or father. It seemed like days, but it was really only about an hour. We talked a little. Well, Mr. Jones talked. I listened. He told me that he had a dog when he was a kid and someone had poisoned that dog and that was when he decided to be a policeman when he grew up. To catch people who would do mean things like that. While he talked, I thought about the mean killer who had murdered Billy Rosen. That must really bother Mr. Jones, not to catch that criminal. Killing kids is about as mean as you can get.

We sat there together, him talking, me thinking about the child murderer, and Binky, of course, and then we saw my mother's car driving up the hill. When my mother saw the police cruiser parked in front of our house, she really stepped on the gas. So much so that she had to come to a screeching halt. Mr. Jones walked out to talk to her and calm her down.

While Mr. Jones and my mother talked, Mo popped out of Mom's car with a really silly grin on her face, like she suspected nothing strange was going on. I mean, it isn't every day that a police car is parked in our driveway. She skipped up to me. She didn't have any packages and neither did my mother. I thought she looked awfully happy for such an unsuccessful shopping trip. She was asking me a lot of dumb questions, like "Did David call?" and had I seen her green jersey and was there any vanilla ice cream left. I couldn't imagine what was wrong with her that she didn't notice my red eyes and sad face. Finally, I got a word in edgewise.

"Binky's dead," I said.

When I told Mo what had happened, it was like she was one of those porcelain dolls and someone had just cracked her face open. It was just like that, I swear. One minute she's standing there with that stupid, doll-like smile, and then, *wham,* her face is in smithereens. It was just like I'd hit her with a hammer.

Her legs seemed to crumple and she sank down on the step right next to me. "It's so, so sad," she said.

I took her hand and we sat there. We held hands for a long time.

When Mr. Jones left, Mommy came over and sat with us, too. "When Daddy gets home, we'll bury Binky in the garden," she said.

We sat on the back steps, the three of us, and waited for my father. Every so often I'd look over at that package under the maple tree. Three hours ago it used to be my dog, I thought. Every time I thought that, I'd start crying again and that would start Mommy and Mo. We cried a river of tears that day.

Later, after we had the burial at sundown with candles and all, Daddy tried to cheer us all up.

"I declare, I've raised you girls in the best Irish tradition," he said. "That was as fine a funeral as any dog ever had."

My mother smiled when he said that and said, "Oh, Mike."

I wasn't sure what he meant about the "Irish tradition" stuff, but I had to admit, it was a grand funeral.

All the kids in the neighborhood had loved Binky, so they all came over for the burial. Rollie Evans had even organized a five BB-gun salute. Carolyn and Judy Wallace had picked bouquets of zinnias and marigolds from their mother's garden and Mrs. Wallace had baked chocolate chip cookies to cheer us up. I composed a poem. I read it when Daddy put Binky in that deep hole in the flower garden.

> *There never again will be, I think,*
> *A dog as good as our dog, Bink.*
> *Sometimes he ate a ball or two,*
> *And once he ate my father's shoe,*
> *But he was a friend, true blue.*
> *He always guarded us at night,*
> *He kept us from a midnight fright,*

We didn't even sleep with a light,
Knowing Binky was there.

"A masterpiece," my mother said when I finished, and the other kids said "Amen." Then Daddy covered Binky up with dirt and we all went inside because the mosquitos were getting really bad.

I fell asleep really early that night. Almost right after the funeral. I was so tired from all the crying. I woke up once, thinking it was morning, but it was still dark. I heard voices in the kitchen—Mom's and Dad's and Mo's. I looked at my watch on the bed table. It was midnight and they were still up talking. I rolled over and went back to sleep. I wanted that day, the day Binky died, to be over.

I woke up again, much later. It must have been around three. I heard someone crying. No, not crying, sobbing. It was my sister. She was in her bed, lying on her stomach and her whole body was shaking. My mother sat beside her, rubbing her back. Somehow, she made me feel disloyal to Binky. After all, I had fallen right to sleep and there was Mo, still crying at three in the morning.

"All right, hush now, sweetheart," my mother was saying. She kissed Mo's forehead. "Things work out, Mo. They always do, somehow," she added in the sweetest voice, the voice I just love. Mo had known Binky a lot longer than me, so I guess that's why she couldn't stop crying. I don't know how Mom thought things would somehow work; even so, lying there in the darkness, I believed what she said. My sister must have believed her, too, because the sobbing stopped and she blew her nose. Still, Binky was dead and buried. There was no changing that.

"What will I do, Mommy? What will I do?" my sister wailed.

"For now, you'll go to sleep, Mo. You need your rest," my mother said. "And we'll face it in the morning. Things will seem better in the morning. They always do."

I wondered about that. How would Binky being dead seem better in the morning? Would we be talking about a new puppy or something? I don't know about Mo, but that thought gave me comfort. I closed my eyes and saw Mo and me holding a little bundle of brown fur and soon I fell back to sleep.

15

Leavetaking

September

✣

Mo

David came to say good-bye today. We're not supposed to be seeing each other. Both sets of parents have laid down that rule. The Markovitches started it when I couldn't go through with the plan to get rid of the baby. They said they wouldn't stand by and watch us ruin our lives. They said I had made my choice and they were making David's. He was going to Cornell and that's that.

My mother let David in, even though she agrees with my father that I can't see him anymore, especially now that I'm to marry Richard O'Connor.

I was in the kitchen, fixing myself some saltines and butter. I don't have as much trouble keeping them down now and sometimes I'm even hungry.

"Mo," my mother called from the front porch. "You have a visitor."

It was hot and I was wearing just a loose shift, with only bikini panties underneath. My hair was unbrushed and just hanging down all over the place. I was barefoot. I wasn't expecting company.

"Go right in," I heard my mother say. "She's in the kitchen."

I walked into the hallway to see who it was and saw David standing there. It was dark in the hallway because we have all the lights off to make the house cooler, but I could still tell that he was crying. I went right to him and put my hand on his face. I guess I've seen that gesture a million times in movies and soap operas, but it seemed like a natural thing to do.

He put his head on my shoulder and wrapped his arms around me. He could probably tell that I had hardly anything on under the cotton shift, for he rubbed his hand up and down my back. I held him tight to me, feeling him pressed against me and I didn't much care that I was in my own kitchen hallway, with my own mother sitting on the front porch not even two rooms away.

"I hate them, Mo, and I'll never forgive them. Never!" he said. "They say I'll forget you when I get to school, but they're wrong. I'll never forget you."

I wanted to shrink up when he said the word "school," for I could suddenly picture David Markovitch wearing a red-and-white Cornell sweatshirt, holding a can of beer, laughing his way into the football stadium with some pretty Jewish girls from Long Island on his arms. His parents were probably right; he would forget about me.

I thought of Carol Forbes, the girl from Massachusetts who was to be my roommate at Syracuse. She'd sent me a letter and a picture of herself after we received our room assignments. Her picture showed a pretty girl with a long, blond ponytail. She wore a red-and-black cheering uniform with a big M on the chest. She had thin legs and a big bust. She wrote that she liked the Beatles, she played field hockey, she was going to major in Fine Arts. She seemed nice. I would never get to know her.

I thought of how I'd planned to decorate my side of our room at Syracuse, of the posters I'd been saving, the old stuffed animals and pennants from my high school that I had wanted to bring. I pushed David away.

"You'd better go now," I said and I could feel my lips starting to tremble. I wanted him to hold me and touch me again, but I was also angry and so, so sorry for what we had done.

"She made her bed, now let her lie down in it!" My Aunt Bridey's words echoed in my ears. David was going away to a different life and I was lying down in my bed, thanks to Aunt Bridey.

I pushed him out the back door. "Go away," I said. "I don't want to see you ever again."

"But Mo," he protested, "I love you. You're the only person I'll ever love."

I wondered, if he really loved me so much, why he didn't tell his parents off and insist on staying with me? We could have done it. We could have both gone to Albany State. My parents would have helped us. I think. Instead, I was to be married in three weeks to an older man and David Markovitch would be gone.

I slammed the door in his face. I looked through the glass at him. He looked hurt and angry, too.

He raised his hand slowly, in a farewell gesture. "Have a nice life, Maureen."

I closed the back door blinds. I knew he stood there for a long time, because I could see his shadow through the slats. Finally, I heard him walk away.

I went into the bathroom and threw up. Pieces of saltines swarmed into the toilet bowl and then green bile and then I retched and nothing came. Dry heaves, my mother calls it. When my stomach finished revolting, I opened the mirror door of the medicine chest and took out the bottle of aspirins. I poured thirty or forty of them into my hand and just looked at them. I wanted to swallow them. I thought of everything that people would say when they found me. David's mother: "See, I told you. She was the wrong kind of girl." My Aunt Bridey: "She shamed the Malloy name. She should have been sent to Catholic school and none of this would ever have happened." Father Tim: "She can't be buried in consecrated ground." I thought of my own family. Of my mother losing another child. Of my father, who had been so proud of me at graduation. And I thought of Margie, watching me with that puzzled look. So often, lately, I find her watching me. I flushed the aspirins down the toilet along with the mushed saltines and the green bile and I went out to the porch.

"What are you wearing to the bridal shower?" I asked my mother.

Mommy looked at me and patted the seat on the glider next to her. I sat down and put my head on her shoulder. She took my hand.

"I'm going to wear the blue dress I wore to Easter dinner," my mother said. "What are you wearing, honey?"

My mind ran through my closet, mentally putting together skirts and tops, shoes and bags, stopping for a moment at the white tulle formal that would never go to college now. "I'll wear the brown suit that I wore to Uncle Pat's wake last year."

My mother sat up abruptly. "You certainly will not, Maureen Malloy. We are going out tonight to Denby's to find you a pretty, flowery dress to wear to your own bridal shower."

I took a deep breath and, somehow, I smiled and I leaned forward to kiss my mother. "Thank you, Mommy," I said and I put my head on her shoulder again. I thought, we Malloys were putting our best foot forward, no matter what.

Clare

"Will you keep a list of the gifts, Anna?" I asked my sister-in-law as I looked around Bridey's living room, crowded with shower guests all trying to pretend this sudden wedding was just a normal turn of events.

Mo had just opened a toaster oven from Richard

O'Connor's sister, Francine.

"Oh, that is the nicest gift!" Mrs. O'Connor, Mo's soon to be mother-in-law, said and clapped her hands together.

I thought of my own daughter calling Mrs. O'Connor "Mother" and my lower lip began to quiver. Maybe Ruth Markovitch had been right. Maybe this baby would ruin Mo's life.

I watched Mo, lovely in the new, lavender-flowered dress we'd bought for the shower, open a set of pink towels.

"Thank you, Aunt Meg. Richard and I can always use towels," she said.

I knew she was trying hard to be cheerful. I remembered our fruitless attempt at aborting this child. God forgive me, I actually thought we could go through with it. I drove Mo to the place in Rensselaer, near South Albany, after Ruth had arranged it.

Driving there, I tried not to think of that tiny, living thing inside Mo. I thought only of Mo's many scholarships and how proud Mike and I had been on graduation day. I thought of her future. She would be the first of the Malloy grandchildren to go on to a four-year college. As we drove in silence, I thought of her having a career. Maybe she'd be a doctor or a lawyer or even a college professor, not just a teacher or nurse, like the women of my time.

It was too hot that day. Too hot to do anything strenuous, too hot to be going anyplace but the lake for a swim. Too hot even to talk.

The Markovitches had arranged this and offered to pay for the whole thing. Mo and I had not told Mike. An abortion—that would be something Mike couldn't bear. He would consider it murder. He would consider it against everything we ever believed in. Last year, I would have agreed, but this was now and Mo was my child and she was in trouble. That's how I felt that day.

We pulled up to a block of row houses baking in the noonday sun. There were no trees, just hot sidewalks and paved streets smelling of melting tar. The houses were near the river. Everything is, in Rensselaer. Everything had that musty, river smell, like old things are in the muddy water. Old decaying things.

"Wait in the car, Mo," I told my daughter. "I'm going to check this place out before I let you go in." I knocked on the door and an old woman in a faded housedress answered. I asked for Doctor Mariano.

"Do you have an appointment?" the old woman asked.

I looked her over. She can't be his nurse, I thought. Was her faded dress and tattered apron part of a ruse to throw off suspicion from an illegal abortion clinic? Was there a spotless operating room in the back of this shabby house?

"Do you have an appointment?" the woman repeated.

I nodded my head yes. "Ruth Markovitch set up an appointment," I said.

"Ah yes," the woman smiled. "Just let me check the doctor's appointment book." She left me standing at the door and walked back to a table in the vestibule of the house. She picked up a small, black plastic day book.

She scanned the pages with her finger and I noticed a line of black grime beneath her fingernail.

"Yes, here it is." Her finger stopped moving and she pointed at a spot on the page. "You must be Maureen," she said, looking up at me.

Before I had a chance to explain, she grabbed my hand and pulled me into the room, closing the door behind me. "Can't be too careful, my dear. The doctor helps out women, you know, but if he were found out . . ." She stopped talking and stared at me, leaving me to contemplate what would happen if the doctor were found performing illegal abortions.

"Julian," she called out. "Your patient is here."

I heard some rustling in the back of the house and a man walked through the doorway, parting old curtains that hung there. This was certainly unlike any doctor's office I'd ever been in. I thought of Dr. Moriarty and his leather chairs and his spotless examining room, the stainless steel shining.

The old man looked at me. "I expected a younger patient."

I explained that I was Maureen's mother and she was waiting in the car.

"For God's sake, woman, bring the girl in. We can't have her sitting out in the car with all the neighbors watching."

I turned to leave the room, to get my daughter, to

offer her up to this old man.

As if to reassure me, he said, "Mrs. Markovitch has arranged everything. This is not the same girl, I presume."

Jesus Christ, the same girl? Ruth had done this before, for another of David's girlfriends? Inadvertently, I thought of Laurie Glassman, the girl who didn't get to go to the prom.

I stopped. "I'd like to see the facilities," I said.

"The facilities?"

"Yes, the operating room, the sterilization procedures, you know."

The doctor answered matter-of-factly. For the first time, I noticed he had a slight accent. I also noticed his hands shook as he talked.

"There is no operating room, my dear. I perform the abortion on a table in the back. Of course we boil all the instruments." He pointed to the woman with the dirty fingernails. "My wife, Marie, sees to that."

Ruth Markovitch had no daughters. She would never understand. She was protecting her son, I understood that. But goddamn it. My daughter wasn't going to be touched by this old hack.

"We won't be using your services," I said.

"But what about the payment? My time is valuable," the old man protested.

"Talk to Mrs. Markovitch," I said, and slammed the door in his face.

My daughter's voice brought me back to the present. "Isn't it pretty, Mommy?" Mo was holding up a light blue peignoir set. "Aunt Anna gave it to me."

"Oh, Anna, you shouldn't have," I said, knowing how much such an expensive gown and robe cost, knowing how limited Anna's income is with Johnny gone.

"But I wanted to, Clare." Anna smiled, looking at Mo. "I love Maureen."

Anna's sweet words and lovely gesture brought tears to my eyes. I pictured my beautiful daughter in the blue silk peignoir. I hoped that Richard O'Connor appreciated the woman he had won by default. I hoped he, too, would love Maureen.

Mike

We met at Bridey's house. It was just Clare, Bridey, and me. I hoped that Bridey wouldn't bring up the whole public school/Catholic school thing again. Bridey could be depended upon to be insensitive, but that issue would only infuriate Clare now. One crack about how Mo would never have met "that boy" at Catholic Central and they'd be at each other's throats.

"As I see it, there are two options for Mo," Bridey said. "She can go away and have the baby and give it up for adoption to some Catholic family. Or she can marry."

We were having this meeting with my sister because Bridey knew all about St. Cecilia's Home for Unwed Mothers. Annie Carey, from the Careys over on First Street, had spent nine months there last year. People weren't supposed to know, but they did. Especially Bridey; she made it her business.

"It's expensive, Mike, but we can all chip in if that's what Mo wants," my sister said.

What Mo wants, I thought. What does Mo want? Probably just to be herself again. To not be two people, one a teenager with an uncertain future, the other a wee thing no bigger than my thumb, but making its presence felt in so many ways. If Mo decided to keep this baby, could we ever love this child?

"Don't be silly, Bridey," my wife's voice was sharp. "We can afford to take care of Mo."

"To the tune of five thousand dollars, Clare?" Bridey asked. "St. Cecilia's isn't cheap. They have to pay the doctors and then the lawyers for the adoption, and provide room and board for the length of the pregnancy."

"Pregnancy"! I wished they'd stop using that word. It was so hard to think of Mo as pregnant. To me, she was still my little girl. I pictured myself throwing her up into the air, her red curls bouncing, her laugh, high-pitched with danger and delight. I pictured her wearing a white pinafore, her legs short and chubby, freckles dancing across her nose. The tall, thin, beautiful woman with the child growing inside her, how could she be my Mo?

"Well," Clare said, "marriage is out of the question."

Bridey and I stared at my wife. Her voice was so flat and emotionless I was afraid she was regressing to the state she was in following our boy's death.

"What do you mean, Clare?" Bridey asked.

"David will not marry Mo. His family feels it's out of the question."

"Well, what are they suggestin'?" Bridey asked.

"They suggested an abortion."

"Jesus, Mary, and Joseph," I said and Bridey blessed herself.

As if to prevent any further discussion, Clare said, "Mo will not have one."

"Well, of course she won't," Bridey agreed.

As for me, I have to admit it never crossed my mind. No one in the Malloy family had ever done that. At least, I never heard of it, if they did.

Out of the blue, Bridey announced, "Richard O'Connor will marry Maureen."

Clare and I both stared at my sister.

"I know, I know, he's much older, but his mother is lookin' for a wife for him. He's just been reclassified 1-A. That means he's bound for Vietnam unless he can get a deferment. A married man with a child on the way would never be sent. Richard O'Connor would be happy for a wife like Maureen, beautiful and smart, even if she is damaged goods. Maureen could do worse."

I looked at Clare to see how she took the "damaged goods" part. I thought she would slap Bridey, but she was just staring. Staring and thinking.

Bridey was right. Maureen could do worse. Richard O'Connor is a decent young man. He respects his family, takes good care of his widowed mother, has a good job working for the state, and owns his own house in South Troy. He'd even been to a few years at Siena College night school. We know his family from way back.

"What makes you think Mo would marry him?" Clare asked Bridey and I thought her tone was insulting.

"Maureen is caught now between a rock and a hard spot, she doesn't have that many choices, Clare," Bridey said. "Besides, she made her bed, let her lie in it."

My sister's words hurt, but they were true. Mo had made choices, the wrong ones for sure, and now she was being made to pay for them. Only Mo had to pay, it seemed. Mo had won all the scholarships, but David was going off to college. It was all so unfair to my girl. I knew if I ever saw David Markovitch again, I would have to punch in his handsome face. I wanted to hurt him. I thought of me offering cocktails to Ruth and Max that happy prom night with everyone smiling into the camera. I'd watched them beaming at their son that night and understood how they felt proud of such a boy. I wondered, were they proud now? I thought about him making love to my daughter, outside the sanction of Holy Matrimony, and, God forgive me my unchristian thought, I prayed he'd have a terrible life. I pictured that tiny baby growing daily inside my daughter and I wondered if she would give it up or give it a name. That would be her choice, too.

THE IRISH PRINCESS

Margie

My sister's bridal shower at my Aunt Bridey's house made me certain that I never want to get married. Instead of the usual presents, like books and records and bracelets and things that you get when you have a birthday, or on Christmas, Mo got toasters and ironing boards. I know she was trying to be gracious, and I suppose she can use waffle irons now that she's really getting married, but cripes, does she have to act excited about them?

We started to plan the wedding all of a sudden. It was a big shock to me because I was looking forward to how I was going to spread my things out onto her side of our room, when Mo moved out for Syracuse. Now, Mo is moving out forever, and I don't want her to go. She's the only sister I've got and after losing our baby last year, I don't think I'll have a chance at getting another.

Mommy came in our room one night and said, "Mo has something to ask you, Margie."

Sure, I thought, ask away. She probably wants to take my rhinestone bracelet to college with her. I had already decided that I'd let her.

Mo came into the room behind Mommy. She was acting sort of weird, I thought. She sat down on my bed and smoothed down the wrinkles in the chenille spread. I watched her hands, pushing down the nubby white balls, making the patterns disappear.

"Will you be in my wedding, Margie? Will you be my maid of honor?"

"What?" I asked. "Are you marrying David before you go to college?" In a way, I hoped that was true. I liked David so much. He's fun and so handsome and I could tell he just loved Mo.

"No, Marg . . . I'm going to marry a really nice man, Richard O'Connor."

"Man," did she say? A "man"? She was going to marry a man! I looked at my mother, but she was staring away at the picture of the Sacred Heart on our bedroom wall. She didn't look at me.

"I'm going to marry Richard O'Connor. You remember him, Marg. We saw him at the Democrat picnic last year. He was that tall guy with the red hair and glasses. He told us all those funny jokes."

"Mo," I gasped. "He's old!"

"No he's not, Margie," my mother said. "He's only twenty-five."

Twenty-five might be young to my mother, but it's pretty old to me and I'm sure it's old to Mo. She just turned eighteen!

"But you don't know Richard O'Connor," I protested.

"Of course I do," Mo said. "I've known him all my life and so have you, Margie."

"But you don't really know him. You haven't even

gone out. How can you say you know him?" I persisted.

"We have too gone out," my sister said and her voice sounded angry. "That just shows what you don't know, Little Miss Know-It-All."

"Well, I've never heard of you going out. And what about David, all that crying until Daddy let you go out with him again after graduation? What about David Markovitch? You said you loved him!"

"I don't love David Markovitch. I'm marrying Richard! And that's final!"

Mo stormed out of my room and I looked again to my mother.

"We'll be going to look for gowns tomorrow, Margie. The wedding is September twenty-first."

"But what about Syracuse?" I asked. "Mo's supposed to go to college on September eighteenth." I had seen those papers on Mo's desk. I knew what was planned. What was wrong with these people? What about Mo's scholarships and her working so hard to get good grades at Troy High? I don't like it when grownups don't make sense. And Mo I counted with the grown-ups now. What was wrong with my beautiful, exciting sister with the big IQ?

And now, here she was after her own bridal shower, twirling an umbrella made of crepe-paper streamers around her head, wearing a new, flowery dress, pretending to like ironing. Just when I thought I had things figured out, everything changes. I hadn't expected my sister to be a full-fledged grown-up so soon. But anyone who chooses waffle irons over college has left the rank of kids forever, that's for sure!

16

Wedding Bells

September

❧

Mo

My wedding gown didn't come from Baronson's, though that's where most of the girls in Troy buy their wedding dresses. Mommy wouldn't go back there and I know why. How could we explain to nosy Mrs. Baronson that I was now buying a dress to be married in, only four months after we'd talked about my prom gown going off to college with me? Instead we went to Albany, where no one knows us, to a store called Lucinda's Bridal Shoppe.

Lucinda was no Mrs. Baronson. She came out chewing gum and she had a strange accent, barking out her *r*'s like she was growling or something. She made me nervous, more nervous than I already was.

"You must be from western New York State," my mother said to her, trying to make conversation. I think she was trying to make us both feel more comfortable.

"Rochester," Lucinda said, barking her *r*'s again. "How'd ya guess that?" she asked.

"I had an aunt from Rochester. She had the same accent," my mother said.

I remembered my crazy Great-aunt Lizzie and the day of the Last Will and Testament. It seemed so long ago. Then I remembered what happened to her baby, how he had starved to death. I thought about my own baby. I was sure he'd be a boy, too. I thought about that other baby, dead from starvation fifty years ago and I shivered.

"Mo, honey, you're shivering," my mother said. "I hope you're not catching a cold." Automatically, she felt my forehead. "You're as cool as a cucumber," she said.

"I guess I'm just feeling a little tired," I answered and I sat down in one of the rose-colored, crushed-velvet chairs that were scattered about the shop. Tired was pretty much a way of life for me lately.

My mother sat down next to me and patted my hand. She gave me a tight, little smile and then said to the gum-chewing Lucinda, "We're looking for wedding gowns."

"Congratulations, dear, I'm sure we must have just what you're looking for. Tell me, what is the time schedule we're looking at? Christmas? Spring?"

"The wedding is September twenty-first," my mother said flatly.

"Well now, that's not very much time, dear. We can't possibly order anything and have it arrive in two weeks." Lucinda stopped for a moment, put her finger to her lips, and squinted her eyes. This must be the

Lucinda "thinking" position, I thought.

"We have several ready-to-wear gowns. What that means is we keep them in stock for people who need gowns in a hurry, I, uh . . . mean, people who can't wait for six months delivery. I mean . . ."

Lucinda was not handling this well, I thought. My mother cut her off. "We'd like to see some of those dresses. Maureen has just found out that her fiancé will be coming home from Vietnam on a sudden leave. He's a Green Beret," my mother lied. Behind Lucinda's back, my mother winked at me.

I wanted to laugh out loud. If there was one thing my fiancé was not, it was Green Beret material.

"Oh, am I relieved. I thought maybe your daughter was in the family way and I was embarrassing you," Lucinda said as she pulled long, clear plastic bags filled with fluffy, white wedding gowns from the rack.

"If you'll please show us some gowns," my mother interrupted, cutting Lucinda short.

"Of course," Lucinda said, snapping her gum more vigorously and pulling out a creamy-looking dress from one of the plastic bags. "With your lovely color, dear, ivory would be perfect. Especially for an early fall wedding."

I tried on the ivory silk, tent-style dress, thinking that the no-waist design might have an added advantage by September 21.

"It makes you look too fat, Mo. I don't like it."

My mother surprised me with her opposition to the

dress for the very reasons that I thought it would be practical.

"Let's try that gown with the Empire waistline," my mother suggested, pointing to a dress that hung from a nearby display rack.

"Empire waistline"? I thought. Since when does my mother know fashion terms? I marveled at her ability to pick out just the right design for a slightly pregnant bride. I slipped the gown over my shoulders.

"Oh my, it looks just too lovely on you, dear," Lucinda said, her flattery reminding me of Mrs. Baronson's compliments on the white prom gown last May. I thought of that wonderful prom night and of David going off to college in a few weeks and suddenly I felt drained of all energy, as if my shoulders couldn't bear the weight of the heavy wedding dress for one minute longer.

"The alencon lace sleeves are the perfect touch and the chapel train is exquisite," Lucinda babbled. "It is the perfect dress for the perfect day!"

"Mo, are you all right?" my mother asked.

"If I can just sit down for a moment," I said. I felt hot all over and I didn't think I could remain standing much longer.

"Oh my dear, let's just get that pretty dress off you," Lucinda said.

I could tell she was more worried about me wrinkling the gown than she was about me fainting.

"Sit down, Mo," my mother commanded and I plopped down, chapel train and all, into one of the crushed-velvet chairs. "Could you please get her some water?" she asked Lucinda.

Lucinda scurried toward the back of the shop and my mother said, "She acts like a chicken with its head cut off."

My mother's old-country description of Lucinda's babbling and bustling and eagerness to complete the sale was so accurate that I laughed out loud.

My mother looked relieved and laughed, too. "Feeling better now?" she asked.

"I'm okay, Mom. I just felt a little faint for a few minutes. Can we get this dress and just get out of here?" I asked.

My mother put her arm around my shoulder and patted my back, as if I were a little child. "It will be all right, Mo."

I knew my mother was trying to make me feel better, to reassure me in my decision to go through with this wedding and this pregnancy, but there was something in her voice that made me uneasy. Some holding back that made me think that what she said was just words with no real meaning at all.

Lucinda returned from the back of the store with a glass of cold water. "Feeling perky again, I see. Let me just get my trusty yardstick to mark for alterations and then you two can be on your merry way."

My mother wrote the check for the down payment and Lucinda marked the hem of the wedding dress for alterations. As I watched my mother sign away what would have been my first month's room and board money at Syracuse, I thought about September 21. I thought about being married to Richard O'Connor. He was okay, but would I be able to love him, or even like him? Would I let him touch me in the same way that David did? The way I looked at it, we were doing each other a favor. I was keeping him out of Vietnam and he was going to give my baby, David's baby, a name. David's baby, David's baby. I had wanted an abortion at first, when abortion was just a word to me. Then when it was time to do it and I rode to Rensselaer with my mother, I was relieved when she came running out of that tumbledown old house. "No way is that disgusting old hack going to touch you, Mo," she'd said and then, "damn that Ruth Markovitch!" I could have gone to St. Cecilia's, too, like Annie Carey did last year. That sounded like a good plan at first. Then I saw myself handing over my child, David's child, to someone else. Giving up my claim forever.

I watched Lucinda snapping her gum as she drew blue, chalky lines on the white satin material. "The seamstress will have this back to us in just a few days," she said. "You'll see, the alterations will make it just perfect!"

That's what we're doing, too, I thought. Alterations, in my life. They wouldn't make it perfect, I knew that. But I'd make the best of it. On September 21, I'd smile and look beautiful. I wouldn't think of David Markovitch. As my Aunt Bridey said, I'd "made my own bed." Now, I'd lie down in it.

Clare

I prayed for a hurricane for September 21, or a tornado, or even an earthquake, God forgive me. I prayed for any natural disaster the Lord could rain down on us. Anything that would stop this wedding, which I knew was the wrong thing for Mo. The night before the wedding, after the rehearsal dinner, I begged her to reconsider, to go to St. Cecilia's and have the baby, to give it up for adoption and then go to college, but she would hear none of it.

"Mo, you can still change your mind, even with all the plans set. You don't have to go through with this wedding tomorrow," I said.

"You don't understand, Mommy. I can't give up this baby."

"Why, why, Mo?" I asked. "Why must you marry Richard O'Connor, why can't you let this child go? There'll be other children for you someday."

"There'll be no more babies for David and me," Mo answered.

"Damn it, Maureen. We could place this child in a good Catholic home. You're entitled to a life, too."

"I don't want someone else to raise my baby, Mom. This baby is part of me, too."

I thought of that tiny life growing daily inside my daughter's uterus. I thought of the cells dividing and making fingers and toes and maybe green eyes like Maureen's, or blue eyes like mine, or maybe deep brown eyes and black hair like David Markovitch. I thought of my own dead baby, Michael, and how at first I hadn't wanted him, but then how I grew to love him. Perhaps Mo felt the same. Perhaps she loved this baby as much as I loved Michael. No natural disaster would stop her from going ahead with this marriage, if that was the case. I knew my daughter and she had made a choice. She would bear David Markovitch's child.

Then I thought of myself. I'd be this child's grand-mother. Could I ever bring myself to love this baby that had ruined Mo's life? And what about Max and Ruth Markovitch? They'd be grandparents, too, even though they'd denied it. This child, without the Markovitch name, would be as much their flesh and blood as mine.

I made myself a cup of tea and sat down at the kitchen table. I pulled my daughter into the seat next to mine and held her hands. "I think I understand, Mo."

Mo smiled at me and squeezed my hand. "You know, Mom, when I first discovered I was going to have a baby . . . I hated it . . . him, I mean."

"Who? David?" I asked, thinking of how Mo must feel with David going off to college as carefree as a lark, while she stays here in Troy, a woman with a husband, tomorrow, and soon a child.

"No, not David. I could never hate him, you know." She looked to me for understanding. I nodded, pretending sympathy, only pretending for her sake. I hated David Markovitch for what he'd done, leaving like that to start a new life. I supposed I'd hate him till the day I died.

"I meant the baby," she continued. "I hated him . . . it's a boy, you know, I'm certain of that."

She pulled her hand away from mine and placed it on her stomach, still flat and girl-like, showing no signs of the life growing there.

"I hated him for just being here. I knew if I didn't get rid of him, there'd be no chance for me ever to get out of Troy. Remember that day down in Rensselaer when we tried to get an abortion?"

I nodded my head yes and closed my eyes. I still wish we could have gone through with it, for Mo's sake.

She grabbed my hand again, and as if she knew what I was thinking, she said, "I'm glad we didn't go through with it. We've had too much death around us."

Oh Mo, I thought, and I could have wept on the spot. Are you doing this for all the wrong reasons? I wondered.

Once again, my daughter seemed to read my mind. "Mom, this is life," she said, holding her hand to her stomach. "And I love this baby. I do. I can't explain it, how it happened, going from hating to loving. But it happened. That's why I'm not going to St. Cecilia's. That's why I'm keeping the baby."

"That's why you're marrying Richard O'Connor," I added, reminding Mo of the other half of the bargain. Her decision to raise the baby also brings her a husband that she doesn't love.

"It will be all right, Mom. I just know it will. I'll make it all right."

Such courage in the face of calamity. Such foolishness, I thought. God forgive me, I didn't have the heart to tell her it might not be all right. She might be trapped in a loveless marriage with a child she could grow to resent.

Mo stood up. "Let's clean up, Mommy," she said, pointing to the scraps of rolls and leftover cold cuts and half-eaten pickles on the plates, debris from the rehearsal dinner. "We have to get to bed early. We've got a big day tomorrow."

As we washed and dried the dishes, we listened to the radio, hoping for a weather report.

"This is the WTRY Weather Watch for September twenty-first. Another nice one coming up, folks. High cirrus clouds will give way to sunny skies and low humidity tomorrow. A perfect day, temperatures coming in at around seventy-five degrees Fahrenheit, barometer rising."

Maureen smiled at me as she put away the crystal wine glasses, the only things I'd allowed myself to take from my Aunt Lizzie's house after the reading of the will. "Looks like we'll have a nice day, Mommy."

It looked like no natural disasters were brewing to save my daughter from herself.

Mike

"Don't be nervous, Daddy," Mo said to me and she patted my arm with her left hand as she slipped her right hand into mine. "Everything will be all right."

I looked down at my daughter dressed in white lace and satin and remembered her other white dress, the simple, cotton eyelet dress that she had worn the day of graduation—the day she charmed me into letting her see David Markovitch again. I could feel myself getting hot under the collar just thinking of the boy and the things that he and Mo had done and the way he'd just walked out on my daughter and gone off to college, not a care in the world. Calm down, Mike, calm down, I told myself. Just get through this day.

The organ was playing "Ave Maria" and I opened the heavy oak doors a crack and peeked into the church. It was packed, with Malloys on the left side of the church and O'Connors filling the pews on the right. Father Mullen stood on the altar at the end of the aisle and to his left was Richard O'Connor. They were surrounded by flowers, bouquets of white gladiolas that had cost me a small fortune.

Jesus Christ, Richard O'Connor, I thought. I suppose I should be grateful he was wanting to marry my daughter, but Jesus, he looked like an old man standing there, waiting for my girl at the altar. Tall and gawky, with that bright, wiry, red hair that some Irish people have. I tried to remember him as a younger man, someone Mo's age, but I couldn't. I pictured him carrying a load of heavy books, going off to Siena College, wearing thick glasses, his face all broken out with pink pimples. I know it wasn't fair to him, but I swear looking down the aisle and seeing him, so thin and spindly, wearing contact lenses now, waiting patiently at the front of the church like a well-behaved child, waiting for me to hand over my beautiful daughter like she was the prize in a Cracker Jack box, just made me think of him like that, a real pantywaist. My daughter, who was beautiful enough to be marrying a Cary Grant or an Errol Flynn.

"It's all right, Daddy, everything's going to be all right," Mo said again as she looked up at me through the white veil that covered her face. The white veil that played out the pretend game that my lovely daughter was still virginal and chaste and protected from prying eyes by white lace.

No, Mo, I thought, it's not all right. Run away from here, run away from this arranged marriage, I wanted to say, but instead I nodded my head and smiled to reassure her and we started down the aisle.

I watched the faces of my family as Mo and I passed through the pews. My brothers looked solemn, reminded that their own time to give away their children would soon be coming. My sister, Bridey, looked, God forgive me for thinking this, smug. She'd been right, of course, to her way of thinking, and she *had* helped us arrange this whole thing. But should we be thanking her for it? Only time could tell.

All these things I thought of as we walked down the center aisle of St. Jude's Church. When we got to the altar, I looked up at the cross and said a quick silent prayer as I handed my girl over to Richard O'Connor. Please look after her, Lord. Look after her. I kissed Mo, turned, and walked back to the first row where Clare sat alone. I genuflected and entered the pew. Clare reached up with her white lace hanky and brushed my cheeks.

"What're you doin', darlin'?" I whispered.

"Brushing away the tears, Mike. You were crying as you walked down the aisle."

Jesus, Mary, and Joseph. I walked the length of that aisle, that aisle that seemed longer than a football field, crying like a baby and I didn't even know it.

Clare took my hand and whispered in my ear, "Everything's going to be all right, Mike."

First Mo reassuring me and now Clare. Why were they so damn convinced that everything was going to be all right now? I sure as hell wasn't. I focused on the words the priest was saying. It was the Epistle to the Ephesians: "Husbands, love your wives, just as Christ also loved the Church, and delivered Himself up for her, that He might sanctify her, cleansing her in the bath of water by means of the word; in order that He might present to Himself the Church in all her glory, not having spot or wrinkle or any such thing, but that she might be holy and without blemish." The priest droned on and I closed my eyes. "Without blemish"? I thought. Well, not exactly. Mo was standing there receiving the sacrament of Holy Matrimony with one man and carrying another man's child.

Margie

I sure don't think I'm ever going to get married, but if I do, I'm going to climb out my bedroom window and run away to do it instead of having a big, fancy, church wedding. I never want to be a bridesmaid again, either. I had to stay in that long, lacy dress with all those bone stays poking me in the ribs for the whole day. From nine o'clock in the morning till six o'clock at night. And the worst part, the very worst part, was that I was the one who had to make a toast to the bride and groom after the best man did, because I was the maid of honor.

"I hope Mo and Richard have a nice life," I said, but it must have been too low, because my cousins yelled, "Say it louder, Margie," and I had to say it again. Everyone clapped and clinked their spoons to their glasses after I said my toast and that meant that Mo and Richard had to kiss, but I noticed it wasn't a romantic kiss they did, like in the movies. My sister kissed Richard O'Connor on the side of his face, the exact same way she kisses my Uncle Jim or my Uncle Danny. It didn't seem like a very romantic thing to do. I remember walking in on her and David Markovitch one night last summer when Mommy and Daddy had gone out for ice cream. They were sitting on the couch in the living room, with their arms and legs all wrapped around one another and they weren't kissing each other on the cheek. Their mouths were wide open and they were kissing the heck out of each other. Now that was romantic kissing. I tried to imagine Richard O'Connor kissing like that.

All the aunts and uncles danced with each other at the reception. Even Uncle Danny and Aunt Hildy danced. That made me happy. It made me think that I might get to be friends with Gretchen again. When the band played "Daddy's Little Girl," Daddy came over to the head table and asked Mo to dance. Richard O'Connor looked at Mo's empty seat and slid over next to me.

"I guess I have a new little sister now," he said. "You know, all my sisters are much older than me." He pointed over to the O'Connor side of Hibernian Hall. There was a table of chubby, older women. They were all red-haired and red-faced and they all wore lacy dresses in blues and purples. I wondered if they'd planned to look like a spring garden full of overripe hyacinths just asking to be picked. That's just what they reminded me of.

"It might be fun having a kid sister. I've always been the baby of the family, you know." Richard smiled at me.

"I know what that's like," I said and then I remembered how I almost wasn't the baby in our family and

I felt a shiver of sadness. I looked down into my champagne glass. I had been allowed a sip of champagne for the bridal toast, but *phew,* was that stuff disgusting. I swirled the leftover champagne around, wishing it were ginger ale, and said, "My little brother died last year." Richard O'Connor took my hand.

"I'd heard that," he said. "I think you would have made a grand big sister."

"You do?" I said, pulling my hand away.

"I sure do. You could have taught your little brother lots of things. I heard you are a pretty fair softball player and that your lay-up shots are pretty good, too."

"Do you like basketball?" I asked him.

"I'm a Knicks nut!" he said and he grinned at me.

"All right!" I said and slapped him five, and I thought maybe Richard O'Connor wasn't all that stuffy after all and I began to like him a little.

Daddy brought Mo back and reached for my hand to dance.

"May I have this dance, Princess?" Daddy said.

I didn't really want to dance out in front of all those people clapping and cheering, but Daddy pulled me up to the dance floor. The band was playing "My Wild Irish Rose" and Richard and Mo danced alongside Daddy and me.

"Ah, Margie, darlin'," Daddy said. "This tune always brings a tear to my eye."

He reached into his pocket for his fancy silk hanky and wiped his eyes. When he did that, I remembered how he had cried as he walked Mo down the aisle and how my mother had wiped his face with her lace hanky. I thought about the other times that I'd seen my father cry. First at Uncle Pat's wake, then at my Uncle Johnny's hospital bed, and then when they put that tiny white casket into the ground at my brother's funeral. He bawled like a baby then.

That got me to thinking. If weddings are supposed to be such happy occasions, with handshakes and kisses and congratulations all around, then why was my father acting so teary, like he wasn't really happy at all?

17

Baby Boy

March 1966

❧

Mike

Mo's baby was born on March 21, six months to the day after her marriage to Richard O'Connor. I got the call from Mo at 10:00 P.M.

"Daddy, Richard's at his taxation and accounting course at the Adult Ed. and I . . . I think I'm having the baby." Mo's voice sounded so young and really scared that it reminded me of Clare, the night we had Mo, when we'd even forced a taxi off the road in our rush to the hospital.

"Hold on, darlin'," I said, "your mother and I will be right there."

Clare, who was listening by my side, grabbed my sleeve and shook my arm for attention.

"Ask her if she's called Dr. Moriarty yet," she demanded.

"Have you called the doctor yet, darlin'?" I asked, trying to make my voice sound calm.

"No, I was scared and I called you first. I'll call him

right now. Daddy, is Mommy there?"

"Yes, she's standin' right here," I answered.

"Can you put her on. . . . Please?"

Mo sounded like she was about to cry. I gladly handed the phone to Clare. Clare held the receiver close to her ear. "I know, honey, I know it really hurts. The pains are close?" she asked. "We'll be right there, Mo. We'll be right there. We're leaving right now. Okay," she added in response to some question that Mo had asked. "Ten minutes," she said, banging the receiver down.

Clare and I threw on our coats and ran out to the car. We even forgot to tell Margie where we were going and when we'd be back. We just left her sleeping in her room, not knowing.

It was frigid outside and a light snow was falling. We had a fifteen-minute drive to Richard O'Connor's house and then a twenty-minute drive to St. Mary's. It was a night just like this, also in March, that Pat froze to death, I thought, and I said a prayer that the roads wouldn't be too slick.

"Slow down, Mike. We'll be in a fine kettle of fish if we have an accident," Clare said, gripping the dashboard with her hands.

I took my foot off the accelerator and let the speedometer drop to thirty miles per hour.

"Besides," Clare added, "this is her first baby. She has a lot of time yet." She reached over and touched my arm and smiled. "Don't you remember the night that Mo was born, how we rushed to the hospital, only to wait in the labor room for seven hours while my pains started and stopped, started and stopped?"

Actually, I was remembering another wintry night, a little over a year ago, when we'd rushed to the hospital in a snowstorm just like this. The night our son was born. The only night he lived. I was glad Clare was remembering Mo's birth and not Michael's. I didn't want her to be slipping into sadness on me tonight. "How could I ever forget that, darlin'?" I asked and I pressed my foot again to the gas pedal, remembering how scared we had been with that first baby coming. I knew how Mo must feel right now. And she was alone.

When we got to Second Street, I decided to double-park because there weren't any spaces close to Richard O'Connor's house. I could see Mo watching for us out the window through those old, lace curtains. It gave me a bad feeling, seeing her like that, watching the street like an old lady. I don't know why, it just gave me the chills.

Clare dashed into the house, while I waited in the car. Before you could say "Jackie Robinson," she was back. "Her water just broke, Mike," she said as she helped Mo into the backseat of the car. "I think you better drive as fast as you can. She's much further along than I expected." Clare climbed into the back, too, and wrapped her arm around Mo's shoulders, stroking Mo's cheek with her free hand. "Everything's going to be fine, honey," she whispered to Mo.

"Mommy," Mo wailed, "it hurts so much. I feel like I'm being torn apart."

"SPEED!" my wife commanded.

In all our married years, Clare has never asked me to speed. Just her yelling that one word at me got me real nervous. I pictured Clare and me delivering our first grandchild in the back of my old Dodge, with snow falling down all around us, and I stepped on the gas.

I was watching the speedometer climb to sixty miles per hour when I noticed the red lights flashing behind us.

"Christ! There's a cop in back of us," I said.

"Thank the good Lord! Tell him we've got to get this girl to the hospital! Oh," Clare added, "and tell him you're Jim's brother."

After I mentioned Jim's name and pointed to the backseat, those cops couldn't have been nicer. They sped in front of us, clearing the road, their sirens screeching. They called ahead to the hospital to have the doctors waiting for us, and they even called Jim at the station so he could pass the word to the rest of the family: the first Malloy grandchild was about to be born!

When we got to St. Mary's and Mo had been rolled away on a gurney, with Clare right beside her, holding her hand, I thanked the officers and excused myself to go to the john. My bowels were feeling weak, like maybe I had a touch of diarrhea. Nerves, I suppose. After I'd used the toilet, I went to the sink and splashed water all over my face. Better wake up, I thought, it's going to be a long night. I dried my face with those rough brown paper towels that come out of the dispensers and I looked in the mirror.

Christ, I thought, I look a hundred years old. Too damn old to be doing this sort of thing. Damn that Richard O'Connor and his tax course. Damn him for not being there. I picked up my hat and coat and went to look for a phone to let him know that his wife was having *her* baby.

Mo

They wheeled me away on that cold gurney bed. I could hear the wheels turning and squeaking and I told myself, listen to the wheels, Mo. Concentrate on the squeaks. Don't think about the pain. It worked for a little while, until the next really bad pain came. I screamed and Mommy squeezed my hand really tight.

"It's okay, baby, it's normal. It'll be over soon," she whispered in my ear. Then I heard her yell at the nurse. "God damn it, get her some relief. Where the hell is the anesthesiologist?"

Hearing my mother losing it like that didn't do much to comfort me and I had this thought: no one can help me through this. Not Mommy, not Daddy, not Richard, and certainly not David. I'm in this alone.

I guess I got a little delirious then, for as the pains came quicker and the sweet air started to work, I could picture David Markovitch studying at Cornell. I saw him in his dorm room, running his hands through his curly black hair, studying equations. I saw him so clearly

I could read the formulas on the paper before him and I thought if I could speak to him, he would hear me. Later, after Mikey was born, I wondered if I ever saw David again, would I ask what he was doing on the night of March 21, 1966? Was he studying in a room filled with bookshelves and dirty laundry, hunched over a thick textbook, wearing an old red sweater with holes in the elbows?

When Richard finally got to the hospital, I was already back in my room, holding my son.

"What do you think of him, Richard?" I asked.

Richard stood there in the doorway, just watching me, turning his hat in his hands. He didn't smile. He didn't talk. He just watched me.

"Well?" I asked again.

"He has so much hair," Richard said.

And it's so dark, I thought, knowing what Richard must be thinking. What other people would be thinking. How did two fair-skinned redheads get such a dark boy?

I tried to make Richard feel better. "He looks like Daddy, don't you think?"

Richard bent over and squinted at the baby. "Well . . . sort of . . . ," he said. He took my hand and held it for a while. "I'm sorry I wasn't here with you, Maureen. I promise the next time, I'll be here."

"The next time"! I wondered if there'd be a next time. Richard just doesn't seem to want to do it all that often and even when we do, I don't feel like anything happens. It's like there's no magic, no spark that would start life. I know from Mrs. Hencke's biology class that if the sperm meets the egg, a baby will be born, but somehow I just don't picture that happening with Richard and me. I looked down at my baby and wondered if he'd be the only child I'd ever have.

I was so tired, I just wanted to sleep. I closed my eyes for a moment and I started to drift off, but then I saw a terrible thing. I saw myself, sitting in my mother's car in front of those run-down buildings in Rensselaer, waiting for an abortion. I could feel the heat of the day and even smell the tar, and suddenly I felt like I was going to throw up.

"Richard," I gagged, "take the baby."

He looked at me and didn't move.

"For God's sake, get me a nurse then." I knew I couldn't hold down the burning vomit in my throat much longer.

Richard bolted from the room.

I swallowed the bile rising from my stomach so that I wouldn't throw up on my child. Thank God, a nurse ran into the room.

"Don't worry, honey. It's just the aftereffects of the anesthesia. Happens all the time. Nothing to worry about at all." She held my baby in the crook of her left arm and with her right hand she held my head over the cold metal pan by the side of my bed. I was thankful for the cool touch of her hand. When I finished throwing up, I lay back on the stiff hospital sheets. They smelled good, clean and full of starch. I wanted to close my eyes and sleep.

"Let's take this little guy back to the nursery and let you get some sleep, hon," the nurse said. I liked her. I liked the easy way she talked. I liked feeling that I was safe. I nodded, for I was too tired to talk. Before I closed my eyes, I looked around for Richard, but he was gone.

Clare

Mo named the baby Michael. Michael Richard O'Connor. His first name in honor of Mike, his second for Richard O'Connor. Considering Richard's disappearing act on the night the baby was born, I kept my feelings about his middle name to myself.

I'm glad they call him Mikey, because it doesn't remind me so much of my own Michael, who'd be a toddler now if he'd lived. How weird, I thought. If my son had lived, he'd be a playmate to my grandchild. If . . . who knows . . . if Michael had lived, maybe Mo would have been at home babysitting the night that her child was conceived. Maybe this child would have never been born. Maybe we'd be at Parents' Weekend at Syracuse instead of getting ready to baptize our grandson. Who's to know?

The christening was held on April 1. I wondered what the Markovitches would have thought of that. Us christening their grandchild on April Fools' Day. It seemed ironic somehow. Us baptizing their grandchild in St. Joseph's Church with all the Malloys and

O'Connors present. Well, it had been their choice. It was not for me to worry about.

Mikey was a cherub all through the beginning of the ceremony until we came to the time when the priest poured the water on his head. It's good luck if the baby cries when the priest pours the holy water on his forehead and Mikey howled like a banshee. All of the mothers breathed a sigh of relief. We wanted no bad luck for this little one.

After the christening Mo held a big party in her house in South Troy. All the Malloys and most of the O'Connors were there. Mo had outdone herself in cooking and cleaning for the day. I could only hope that she hadn't done too much. After all, it was less than two weeks since the baby's birth, and she looked so thin and pale. In some ways, she didn't even look pretty anymore.

"Mo," I said, "you should have let us help you. We could have had the food catered from Longo's like we did at your graduation." The minute I said that I knew I shouldn't have, because I could tell that it got Mo thinking of that day last June when everything had seemed so perfect and everything was before her.

Mo gave me a peculiar look. "Richard wanted me to do all the cooking, Mom," she said.

"But darling, aren't you tired out from all those nighttime feedings and getting up before the crack of dawn?"

Mo sighed. "Yes, I'm tired, Mom, but he's worth it, isn't he?" She leaned into the bassinet where our baby lay sleeping on his stomach, his little hands balled up into tight fists. Every so often, he'd make a contented little purr.

"Have you ever seen a more beautiful baby, Mom?" Mo asked me and it was more of a rhetorical question. One that I needn't answer, one that we both affirmed. Michael Richard O'Connor had a perfectly shaped brow, a full head of dark hair, a beautiful mouth, large dark eyes, and lovely hands. He was a perfect baby. I felt sorry for Ruth and Max Markovitch. They would never know or take pleasure in this beautiful child. I bent over and kissed the top of his head. He smelled so good, a little like baby powder, a little like warm milk. And he smelled so new. I was glad that he was our baby.

"C'mon, Mom." Mo beckoned me into the dining room. "We're going to cut the cake now."

We don't ever have a Malloy party without a big cake from Nelligan's Bakery. This one had a mound of blue-and-white buttercream roses. In the middle was written "God Bless Michael on this Holy Day."

"Richard didn't insist that you bake this, too?" I whispered to Mo, teasing her, for we all know a Nelligan's cake when we see one. Mo looked at me so strangely, for a minute I thought she'd lost her sense of humor.

"Mom, Richard is okay," she chastised me.

"Of course he is, honey. I was just teasing." I wanted to explain myself further. I wanted to tell Mo that I thought her husband meant well, that I thought he was a good man, that I was happy if she was happy, when we heard a commotion in the kitchen.

"What's going on out there?" Mo asked. "Honestly, they're getting so noisy, they'll wake the baby."

Margie appeared at the doorway of the long, dark hallway that led from the dining room to the kitchen. Mo's house is one of those "railroad" flats, where all the rooms are situated off of a long, narrow hall. "Mommy, you'd better come get Daddy," she said and her voice sounded scared. I heard a glass break and a table scrape across the floor. I knew the christening party was about to break up.

Margie

My father will tell you that he was the first person to "go to bat" for Mikey. That's how he explains the fist-fight that almost ruined all those beautiful plates and glasses that Mo got for her wedding. That's how he explains Marty O'Connor's black eye.

Not that Marty O'Connor—he's Richard's cousin—didn't have it coming. He'd been asking for it all day at the christening party. Mommy said it was because they had a keg and Marty was the one in charge of getting it from Fitzpatrick's Brewery, so he set it up and had been drinking from it all day, even when the rest of us were in church getting the baby baptized. At first, Marty was funny and was telling jokes that made everyone laugh, but then he started to slur his words and started saying swears and that's something that my father thinks is way out of line. I mean, my father doesn't care if men swear around men, but if there are women or kids there, he really gets mad if people use foul language. The *F* word particularly gets to him.

"Fuck you," Marty said. "You can fuckin' pour your own fuckin' beer, Your Honor," he said to my Uncle Danny. "I ain't no fuckin' slave to the fuckin' Malloy family. Think they're such hot shits, anyway, havin' a mayor and a police captain and an honor student who's so fuckin' smart she can have a nine-month baby in six months."

"Margie," my father said, "they're cuttin' the cake in the dining room. Be a darlin' and go get me a piece. One with a lot of roses, if you will." My father did not want me hearing this language, I knew that. So I left the kitchen, but I didn't make it to the dining room. I just hung around in the long hallway. I wanted to hear what they were saying, I wanted to hear more about this six-month/nine-month thing.

"I'll thank you not to be talkin' like that in front of my girl, Martin." My father was talking in his no-nonsense voice, a voice that Marty O'Connor should have paid more attention to, for sure.

"Don't be braggin' on your girls, Mike. 'Fuckin' ' seems to be their favorite word."

That was the last bit of talking I heard before the chairs started tipping over and the glasses started breaking. I ran down the hallway to get my mother. I could hear a fist landing on a chin in the kitchen. I was wondering if Marty O'Connor was on the receiving end of my father's punches. I know he deserved it, but in a way I felt sorry for him, because my father had been an amateur boxer when he was a kid. He'd even won the Golden Gloves. When I was little I used to wear the tiny gold charm on a necklace. One of the few times my father was ever really mad at me was when I told him I'd lost those little Golden Gloves. I think they meant a lot to him.

Well, anyways, soon a lot of my uncles and O'Connor relatives were in the kitchen pulling my father away from Marty O'Connor and Marty didn't look too good. He had a lot of blood on his face, mostly coming from his nose, and his right eye was all swollen up.

"You're gonna have a nasty shiner in the mornin', pal" was all that my Uncle Jim said. I thought he'd arrest that lousy Marty for making all the trouble. Then, as if he could hear me thinking, he said to Richard O'Connor, "Get this troublemaker outta here, Richard, before I have him arrested for drunken and disorderly conduct."

Richard didn't say "boo" to my Uncle Jim. He just got up and walked his cousin to the back porch and arranged for one of the other O'Connors to drive him over to his house on Jackson Street.

Mommy and Mo and the rest of the aunts were trying to sweep up the broken glass and straighten out the kitchen. People were starting to talk again and some people, both O'Connors and Malloys, were even laughing. "It's not a *real* Irish party unless there's one good fight," my Uncle Danny announced.

"He's not really a bad egg, Mike. Just shoots his mouth off is all," one of Richard's uncles explained to my father.

"Well, he just shot his mouth off in the wrong direction, insultin' my girls and my new grandson. There was no call for that."

Everyone agreed with my father, there was no call for that, and then the party broke up. The funny thing was, Mikey slept through the whole fight.

On the way home my father was trying to explain his behavior to my mother.

"You just don't understand, Clare. I couldn't help myself. He was insultin' our daughters and he called our grandson a 'fuckin' class-A deferment.'"

"Michael!" my mother said. I knew she didn't approve of my father using swears with me in the backseat.

"I'm only quoting what that no-good Marty said, Clare."

"Not in front of Margie," my mother said, silencing him with a look.

"Sorry, darlin'," my father said, reaching over into the backseat and patting me on the knee. "Never take to usin' such foul language as you heard tonight. It's very unbecomin'."

"Well, I guess Mikey should have cried a little louder at his christening," my mother said.

"Why's that, darlin'?" Daddy asked.

"It's not such good luck to have your christening

party broken up with a fistfight," my mother explained.

I don't know about that, I thought. My father is pretty special, defending his daughters and sticking up for his new grandson. My mom says it was foolhardy, getting into a fight like that, but in a way, I think it was kind of brave, because Marty O'Connor is about twenty years younger than my father and about twice as big. And since no one in the O'Connor family was about to stop that big jerk from running off at the mouth, somebody in the Malloy family had to. And that somebody was my dad, former Golden Gloves Champion of the Troy Boys Club. I was proud of my father for taking a stand, for "going to bat" for Mikey, as he calls it.

18

Birthday Boy

March 1970

❧

Clare

The morning the letter arrived, we'd had a teacher's conference, so I'd had a chance to take a break and go home for lunch. I stopped by Mary's Grocery and Deli and picked up a roast beef sandwich and a Coke. I don't often buy lunch out, but I felt like treating myself before going back for the afternoon session. I wanted to kick off my high heels and put up my feet for a few minutes. I love teaching kids, but those teacher's conferences, where they have a speaker from the State Education Department tell us about the new mandates, could bore you to tears.

I checked the mailbox because Mike was expecting an early refund check from his income tax and we were hoping it'd be enough to help Richard and Mo rent the cabin next to us at the lake this summer. Actually, it was Mike's idea. What he won't do for that little boy!

"Just think, Clare," he'd said. "I can teach him to fish and we can work on his swimming, and do you think he's old enough to dive from the boat dock yet?"

"Are you sure you won't be stepping on Richard's toes, teaching him all those things, Mike?" I teased my husband. You would think Mikey was his own son, the way he loves him.

"Hell, no," Mike answered me, not even realizing I'd been joking. "Hell, no," he repeated, "Richard can come, too."

"Oh, that's big of you, Michael," I teased. "You're going to let Richard go fishing with his own son."

We both laughed.

"You know, Clare, the boy is like a son to me. Sometimes I think it's God's way of paying us back for taking our own boy so soon."

Mike has a naive kind of faith: you're good, God rewards you, either here or in the hereafter; you're bad, you get punished. Mikey was a good-thing payback for us.

I sometimes wish I could have that simple, trusting belief. There's so much I don't hold with in the Church. So much I just don't believe in since my own child died five years ago. But I've learned to take what I like and throw away the rest. "Putting the dogma out with the dog," Mike says and he teases me about it. He can't really understand, I don't think he gives the Faith that much thought. He just accepts. Occasionally, we've disagreed and he's called me on it, like on Sundays when I miss mass for no good reason. "It's a Church law, Clare," he'll complain to me. "Don't be bothering me about it, Michael," I'll say. "What works for me, works for me." Usually, he just shrugs his shoulders and leaves me be. Our marriage is good that way.

"It will be fun to have Mo and Richard and Mikey with us at the lake," I said, not endorsing his payback idea.

The tax refund check was there and a pile of other things, mostly junk mail, and a letter in a lavender, scented envelope. It was from Florida and I thought it must be from my sister Nora, who was spending March down in Lake Worth this year. I ripped it open, expecting to see Nora's fine, spidery handwriting. She'd won all the penmanship awards at Granville Elementary when we were kids.

"Dear Mrs. Malloy," the letter began. I didn't recognize the handwriting. "Forgive the temerity of this request, but when you hear the circumstances that I'm writing under, I am sure you will be able to understand."

I sat down at the kitchen table and continued to read. When I'd finished reading, I put my head down on the table. I was so tired. I thought, if I could only sleep for a while. I forgot about my lunch, I forgot about going back to the teacher's conference. I thought about how I would tell my daughter what was in the letter.

I tried to remember Ruth Markovitch from prom night. In her handsome brown linen suit and brown-and-white spectators. I tried to remember Max, attractive in an overweight, florid way, slapping Mike on the back, congratulating him on his "excellent Manhattan." I tried to remember the conversation I'd had with Ruth when she was trying to arrange the abortion. The abortion, God forgive me, that had turned out to be Mikey. I tried to remember all those things, but what I kept coming back to was the empty feeling I'd had on the day I buried my own son. I knew what Ruth was feeling.

Mo

Richard and Daddy were in the kitchen, starting to clear the dinner dishes so we could have the cake. Margie had taken Mikey outside. Even though it is only March and we usually have cold, wintry weather in March, cold enough for an uncle to freeze, today had been beautiful. A gift from God or Mother Nature for Mikey's birthday, so balmy that my daffodils had poked their heads up in the backyard. So mild, Mikey didn't even need his winter coat. Margie was outside with him, helping him with his new bike with the training wheels that Richard had surprised us with.

"My God, Richard, I've never seen a two-wheeler so small," I said when my husband had helped Mikey unwrap the huge carton. "I don't know. Is he old enough to ride it? Will it be safe?" I looked at Richard, but in my mind I could picture Mikey riding under the wheels of a big delivery truck. A four-year-old boy had been killed just that way over on First Street last summer.

"Mikey can only ride this in the park or on the sidewalks, AND only with your permission," Richard said sternly for Mikey's benefit, but then he turned and tousled our boy's dark curls. "Understand, big fella?"

Mikey shook his head solemnly to show he understood the importance of Richard's rule and ran his hand along the shiny, new chrome of the Grand Prix Flyer, fingering the red, white, and blue streamers that fell from the handlebars. Then he looked up at Richard and gave him that wonderful smile that he only reserves for very special people. "I love you, Daddy!" he said, wrapping his arms around Richard's neck and giving him a hug.

"I love you too, sport. Happy birthday!" Richard said as he looked around at the mess of leftover spaghetti on the plates. Mikey had chosen his favorite food for his birthday dinner. "Let's get these dishes cleaned up so we can have that big cake that's waiting out in the kitchen. Margie, will you help Mikey get the bike outside?"

"Sure," Margie answered. She'll do anything to escape helping with the dishes. "C'mon, Mikey. Let's get this thing in gear."

Mikey jumped up from the table and grabbed my sister's hand. "Can we take it over in back of the school, in the big parking lot, Aunt Margie?"

Margie grabbed Mikey and lifted him up and swung him around. "Anything you say, birthday boy!"

I watched as they twirled around the dining room.

267

I thought, what a lucky boy my son is, to be loved by so many fine people.

Richard smiled, too, watching them, and then he said to me, "Maureen, sit a while." Cleaning away dishes hasn't always been Richard's forte, but he's changed so much since Mikey's birth, it didn't surprise me at all when he recruited my father to help in the kitchen. "What do you say, Mike? Let's give these ladies a little rest. You and I will start the dishes and get the cake ready."

I watched the two men leave the dining room and thought how unlikely it was that they had grown to be friends, cemented together by their mutual love for my son. They carried the plates and the platters from the dinner down the narrow hallway. My mother looked at me and smiled as we watched the men balance the dishes on their arms. "Be careful with that blue-flowered serving platter, Richard," I yelled after them. "That's the one your mother gave us for our third anniversary."

We had lost Richard's mother last year and I was more saddened by her death than I ever would have thought possible. Sure, she had encouraged Richard to marry me for her own reasons, but once we were married, especially after the baby had been born, she made me feel welcome in the O'Connor family. Sure, it used to aggravate me when she'd sidle up to me and put her pudgy hand against my face and say, "We're waitin' on more grandchildren, Maura, darlin.' " She never called me anything but Maura, and I grew to like that name, and now that she's gone no one ever calls me it any-more. I'm sorry she didn't live to see any O'Connor grandchildren. It would have made her so happy.

"Don't worry, Maureen. Richard and I can handle these dishes," my father yelled back. Like I said before, he's grown to like Richard and I'm thankful for that. We've all grown to like Richard's steady ways. Well, all of us except Margie. I think she just tolerates him. I write it off to her teenage years.

While the two men were in the kitchen starting the dishes, we could hear snatches of their conversation. "Boston's got it all over New York, no question." My father had been a basketball player in high school and in the army for his battalion. He'd even been offered a college scholarship, but he couldn't go because he had to help support his mother. It was still his favorite sport, and he was a Celtics fan. Richard loved the Knicks and I could hear him starting to get argumentative. If there's one thing that Richard does have a strong opinion on, it's Knicks basketball. "But do they have anyone like Willis, I ask you? Just think about it, Mike, how can they win without someone like Willis?"

My mother smiled at me from across the table and I thought, she's awfully quiet tonight. She slid into the seat right next to mine and reached for my hand.

"Cream and sugar, honey?" she asked me as she poured me a cup of tea. She dumped two spoons of sugar in, not waiting for me to tell her I'm trying to diet. I'm trying to get my girlish figure back. "Mo, I have something serious I need to talk over with you," she said in a low voice. She looked toward the kitchen. I knew it was something she didn't want the men to hear.

Sweet Jesus, I thought. I hope it's not something with her health or Daddy's. "What is it, Ma?"

"I've been putting this off for a few days. Telling you. I don't want to spoil the party, but it can't wait any longer. They'll be coming up to Troy at the end of the week."

"They"? I watched her reach into the pocket of the yellow cardigan that she'd laid over the back of her chair. She handed me a letter. It was addressed to her and postmarked Palm Beach, Florida.

"I don't know anyone in Palm Beach," I said.

"Open it, honey." My mother's voice was low and tired-sounding.

I pulled the lavender sheets out of the envelope and started to read. When I'd finished both sides, I laid them on the table and told my mother, "No." Then, very politely, I said, "Mom, you'll have to excuse me for a minute."

I managed to stand and walk out of the room. I was trying to stay in control, but I could feel my legs trembling as I walked slowly down the hallway toward my bedroom. I could feel my mother watching me. When I turned the corner, out of her sight, I ran. I ran into my room and then into the closet. I closed the door behind me and dropped to the floor. My head lay on my shoes; I could smell the leather. I covered my mouth with my fists so that no one at the party could hear the moans. I could feel hot wetness on my face, but at the time I didn't realize it was tears. "No, no, no, no, no," I said over and over as I rocked back and forth.

I remembered the last time I had seen him, the night that Mikey was born. No, I just *thought* I had seen him, studying in his dorm, running his fingers through his black curls, the same black curls his son has. Then I remembered seeing him standing at my back door, looking at me through the Venetian blinds and me just pulling the string to shut out his face. "No, no, no . . ." I tried to picture his face, the curves. I tried to remember the feel of my hand on his cheek, the little stubble that was always there.

I don't really know what I was thinking, not that he'd ride up on some white horse, or in his father's white Cadillac convertible. Not that he'd ever come back for Mikey and me. I didn't even want that. I'd grown to love Richard in my own way and I could never hurt him like that. And Richard had grown to love my son, love him so hard, it scared me sometimes. I don't know what I was thinking or dreaming as I lay on my hard closet floor, smelling the leather of my shoes. I only knew that I'd never see him again and that made me feel like an old woman, an old woman who'd fallen down into a black pit and couldn't get out, the sides all slippery and slimy. Sadness, hard and heavy, like the concrete blocks we're using to shore up our back porch, hit me with such power, I felt paralyzed. I couldn't move my arms and legs. I could only lay there with my knees tucked into my belly and my fists in my mouth. I could only moan and feel the hot water on my face.

When my mother found me, she sat with me for what seemed a long time, her body hugged close to mine. I felt her hand rubbing my back and then stroking my forehead like she used to do when I was a child and had a fever. Then I began to come out of it.

"I'm sorry, Mo. But I didn't want you to find out from them," she apologized. "I wanted to prepare you." She paused. "You have to let him go now."

I shook my head in denial. I kept shaking it till Mommy reached over with her two hands and held my cheeks firmly. "Stop this!" she said. "Nothing can be done. There's no good to this."

I understood what she meant.

I took a deep breath and held it and then I took another. I calmed myself. Finally, I felt steady enough to stand. "I'll be all right now, Mom," I said.

My mother put her arms around me and pulled me to her. We stood there wrapped together in my closet, surrounded by Richard's wool suits and my skirts and blouses. She held me like that till my breathing became slow and regular. "Come now, Maureen," she said, leading me out of the closet, "we've got to serve Mikey's birthday cake."

We walked hand in hand down the narrow hallway. It was dark, because Richard had turned off the lights so that the candles would shine even brighter. I was glad. I didn't want my family to see my teary face. Mikey sat at the head of the table, Richard's usual place.

Richard had placed the blue-and-white birthday cake before him. It had five blue candles, one for each year and one to grow on. Richard stood behind my son and put his big hands on Mikey's skinny shoulders. "C'mon, Daddy's big boy. Show Grandpop how strong you are. Blow out all those candles." I looked at my husband and then my child, our child.

"No," I whispered to my mother. "That's final. Don't ask me again."

Margie

The Saturday after Mikey's birthday party, an old couple came to our door. My father wasn't home and later I realized maybe it was planned that way. My mother was in the kitchen mending socks, which is something in all my eighteen years I have never seen her do. I watched her pull the needle back and forth, back and forth, until what was a hole became a tiny bump of thread. I began to wonder about Daddy walking his route with that bump.

"Ma," I said, "that's going to give Daddy a blister." How unlike my mother, who's always lecturing me on plucking hairs or popping pimples, to forget about black socks and blisters!

"Would you like to do this, Miss Know-it-all?" she crabbed at me.

"No way," I teased back, "I think I'll go practice

my jump shot instead," and I left to look for my basketball in the trunk on the back porch.

I was digging through the trunk containing old baseball mitts and softballs that Daisy, our new dog, had mangled, when I heard the front doorbell ring. We always know it's our front doorbell because it makes the most annoying noise. It's one of those old Victorian keys that you turn and it grates out a sound. Anyways, there was no mistaking it. Someone was at the front door.

"Margie! Get that!" my mother commanded.

No "please," no "Margie, would you?" Just "Get that," barked at me like a drill sergeant.

Geesh, I thought, what's bothering her?

I pulled myself out of the trunk and walked through the house to the front foyer, which we only use on special occasions. I looked out through the shirred white curtains stretched across the front door window. An old couple stood there waiting. I didn't recognize them. I unlocked the door and opened it. "Yes?" I said.

"Is Mrs. Malloy home?" the woman asked.

"Just a minute," I answered and then turned and yelled, "Mom, it's for you."

My mother was right in back of me in the foyer, almost like she'd been waiting there, expecting company.

"Oh, hello," she said. "Please come in."

Her voice was weird, like she was trying to be cheery but really wasn't. "Margie, you remember Mr. and Mrs. Markovitch, don't you?"

"Mr. and Mrs. Markovitch"? David Markovitch's parents? I tried not to act too surprised.

"Yes." I smiled politely and held out my hand like I'd been taught. I remembered them all right, but not this old couple.

"Well," the old man said, "she certainly turned out pretty, just like her sister."

He smiled at me when he said that. But it was a weak smile, like he was just trying to make polite conversation, like he was really thinking of something else. He looked around the foyer. I wondered if he was remembering the last time he was here, the only time he was here, on prom night. Because I sure was. I was trying to place these old people as the same lively couple that arrived in the white Cadillac the night that Mo was queen.

That lady had shiny, blond hair and carefully applied makeup. You could tell it was makeup, but it looked so nice you thought she was pretty. And she had on a really stylish suit with a very short skirt and matching shoes and lots of gold jewelry. I remember thinking she was very elegant and I wished that my mother would dress like that. My mother, in her white blouse and navy blue skirt and white high heels, had looked so plain next to Ruth Markovitch. And the man. The man I remembered had been big, with a red face and lots of reddish-brown hair. He'd given my father a cigar. He'd slapped my father on the back saying, "Pretty fair Manhattan, Mike." He seemed like he was a lot of fun. This old man was skinny, almost weak-looking. His hair was almost gone. He looked like he'd been in a bad car accident.

"Come sit down in the living room," my mother said as she ushered them out of the foyer toward our living room with the new wall-to-wall, green carpet and sectional couch. I wondered if they'd notice how different it looked from the last time they were here.

"Margie, if you'll excuse us," my mother said to me, and behind their backs she shooed me away with her hand.

"Nice seeing you again," I said and gave a little wave at the old man and woman. I turned, pretending to go toward my room, but planning to stand in the kitchen hallway, where I could hear what they were saying. There was no way I was going to miss *this* conversation.

"I have some pictures," my mother said, and I could hear her walking across the living room to the desk where we keep our albums. I heard her return to the couch and sink down onto the springs, then there was no sound for a while. It was so quiet I wanted to peek around the corner of the hallway to see what they were doing.

Finally, Mrs. Markovitch said something.

"Oh, Max," she said in such a low voice I could hardly hear her, "look, his dimples, the very same, and the curls. It takes me back, it takes me . . ." She stopped mid-sentence and it sounded like she was choking. I realized she must be crying. All of a sudden I got a chill, as if I finally knew why these people were here. They were looking at Daddy's album of Mikey. Then it all dawned on me who Mikey really looked like and why he had such dark skin and black curls, and it wasn't because the Spanish Armada crashed off the coast of Ireland in 1588, like Daddy's always telling people. I realized what I'd never been told, but what, I guess, I'd always known.

I crept closer down the hall toward the living room, for they were all talking now and their voices were so low I could barely make them out.

"And then we had to go to Washington for the ceremony," Mr. Markovitch was saying. "My boy was a hero. They say he did it to save his squad. My boy was a hero."

"Was"! David Markovitch *was* a hero! David Markovitch was dead? It hit me like a ton of bricks. Handsome David Markovitch who Mo had loved so much, and me, too, I guess. Handsome David Markovitch who was Mikey's real father. He was dead.

"Why, why . . . why?" I heard Mrs. Markovitch moan. "Why would he do that, to throw himself on a grenade? What about his family? What about this boy he'd never seen?"

"Ruth, Ruth," I heard Mr. Markovitch trying to console his wife. When she seemed to calm down a little, he continued: "Our congressman gave us the medal, the Medal of Honor, the highest award. We'd heard about the boy, of course, and we just thought . . . we thought . . . someday, maybe his mother would like to have it for him. Maybe he'd want to know about his real father someday, that he'd been a hero."

Max Markovitch's voice was shaking now, and I realized that he, too, was crying. They were all crying, even my mother.

I walked into the room. I didn't care if they saw me. I walked almost like I was in a dream or sleep-walking. Mr. Markovitch sat on our new couch with his head cradled in his hands. My mother stood with both her arms around Ruth Markovitch, patting her back as gently as you would burp a baby. My mother's face was wet and her eyes were closed, but Mrs. Markovitch stared across the room at nothing. She didn't even see me. It scared me and I didn't want to be there anymore. I left quickly, but I was so quiet. I didn't want to make any loud noises. I felt like the ground was made of eggshells and if I made too much noise the bottom would fall right out. When I got to the back porch, I ran.

I got my old three-speed out of the garage and took off down the hill. I rode for a long time before I even knew where I was or where I was going. I rode out toward West Sand Lake on Route 66. I don't know what I was thinking, but I wasn't paying attention to cars or any of those mean farm dogs that live out that way. When I think back now, I guess I'm lucky that I wasn't killed. I rode feeling the wind cut out all the other noises in my head. I didn't want to hear Max Markovitch telling about the grenade, I didn't want to hear Ruth Markovitch moaning. I rode till the muscles in the top of my legs were burning. They hurt so much

THE IRISH PRINCESS

I wondered how my legs kept spinning round and round. When I finally had to stop because of the pain and my not being able to breathe anymore, I lay down on the side of the road and then I just cried. I cried for a long time. When I stopped, I thought to myself, I have to see Mo.

I got back on my bike and tried to find out where I was. I saw a sign that said "Averill Park—2 miles," so I went the other way. I have a pretty good sense of direction and I was right. Soon I found myself back in Wynantskill. From there I could get to Mo's house in South Troy in about twenty-five minutes, and lucky for me it was mostly downhill, because even though I'm a sixteen-hundred-meter relayer and the starting center on Troy High's Girls' Basketball, my legs had had it.

When I finally got to Mo's house, I leaned my three-speed against the wrought-iron railing of the front stoop, rang the bell, and dropped down on the top step. My legs were cramping so bad by then they wouldn't even hold me up, and I must have looked as white as a ghost, for when Richard O'Connor opened the door, he sat right down by my side.

"Margie, what's wrong?" he asked in such a voice that I knew I must be scaring him.

"Is Mo here?" I squeaked out. I could feel I was on the verge of tears again and Richard must have known that, too, for he jumped up like I had leprosy.

"I'll get her," he said and he yelled back into the house. "She's here, Maureen."

The way he said it made me think that they'd all

probably been looking for me. My sister came out the door.

"God, Margie. Where the hell have you been? Mom saw you take off down the hill and she's been calling everybody. Daddy's been driving all over Troy looking for you." Mo looked at her watch. "You've been gone for over four hours."

"Mo, can I talk to you?"

My sister's face suddenly softened and I remembered a day, a long time ago, when I wet my bed at Aunt Bridey's when we were sleeping over. I'd gone to Mo for help in cleaning it up so Aunt Bridey wouldn't be too mad. She'd given me that same look then. Like she had to protect me . . . from something. I knew I'd be able to talk to her about all this. She took my hands and helped me up from the stoop.

"Richard," she called out. "Could you take Mikey to the playground for a little bit? Margie and I want to talk."

Like magic, Richard appeared in the doorway with Mikey's spring jacket.

"Okay, sport," he said, "zipper up, we're getting kicked out. They're *making* us go to the playground."

Suddenly, I liked Richard a whole lot more than I ever had and I could see why Mo liked him, too. He was good to Mikey. As good as any real father would ever be. I guess he was a real father.

When they were gone, my sister sat me down at her kitchen table and shoved a cup of hot cocoa in my hands. I didn't know where to start, so I studied the pink-flowered design of the faded tablecloth, something Mo had inherited from Richard's mother's house after she died.

"You've been out on a bike for four hours in just a T-shirt?" Mo asked. She didn't wait for me to answer. "You're going to catch your death, Margaret Ann Malloy," she scolded and she sounded so much like my own mother I had to blink to make sure Mommy wasn't standing there talking.

"Margie, are you 'in trouble'?" she asked.

"In trouble"? I thought. Like "in trouble" like she'd been? In trouble enough to marry a man she had to learn to love? Just then, I felt what it must have been like for her. To be pregnant and to give up college, to have your boyfriend leave. I felt the panic. I shook my head. I didn't bother to tell her I hadn't started that kind of stuff yet. That I'd liked a few boys, but there was no one special. No one like David Markovitch had been for her. I just shook my head.

"Then what's gotten into you? Why did you just take off like that, scaring Mom and Dad? What is the matter?"

"What's the matter"? I thought. Mom hadn't told her about the Markovitches' visit yet? It was going to be up to me?

I couldn't hold it in any longer, what I'd learned today. Suddenly, it all came spilling out. How when I was younger, I'd thought David Markovitch was wonderful. I had wished he'd be my boyfriend someday. How I remembered his laugh and how he teased me, making me blush. How I remembered him and Mo kissing and necking and how I snuck in to watch them and began to feel something stirring in me down lower than my stomach. How I remembered him picking me up and twirling me around at the Malloy picnic and saying, "Watch out, Mo, she's going to be even prettier than you are someday."

And then I told her about how he threw himself on a grenade and why would he do that because now he was probably in a million pieces just like Glenn and why was it all those wonderful people had to be dead? Why couldn't they have come back from the war like our cousin Peter? He'd been a hero, too, but he'd lived to tell about it and now he was going to college and said he'd be a lawyer someday and Uncle Danny was telling everybody maybe Peter'd be the next mayor of Troy. Why couldn't Glenn and David have come back like Peter?

And then I told her about Max and Ruth Markovitch and how old and sad they were and how, when I left, Mommy had been holding Ruth, patting her like a baby and Max had been crying.

When I got done with all the talking, my sister watched me for a while. She didn't say anything, but gave me such a strange look, like she was peeking into my brain and seeing me think. Like she was seeing me for the first time.

I was so tired I put my head down on the table and closed my eyes. In my mind, I could see Mikey smiling at me from the playground and his face turning into

David's face. My sister got up from her chair and stood behind me. She put her hands on my shoulders and massaged my neck and my back. It felt so good.

"You should let them see him, Mo," I said. "At least once."

"Maybe," my sister said in a voice that was surprisingly sweet and calm. "Maybe I will."

I was glad to hear my sister say that. Her voice had no meanness or anger to it. I rested my head back against her stomach and she pushed my hair to the side, out of my eyes. My sister was listening to me. I may be only eighteen, I thought, but there are some things I've learned from living in this family. I know about losing people and I know about forgiving, but most of all, I know about loving. And letting Max and Ruth Markovitch see Mikey, letting them touch his black curls, hear his laugh and the *vrooming* noises he makes with his Matchbox cars, letting them imagine his face someday growing into David's face, is an act of love. As sure as God's in heaven, it's an act of love.

Epilogue: Washington

November 1982

❦

Mo

I went to the wall and though it was past midnight, I could clearly see the snapshots laying there and the wilted flowers and the women standing alone—wives, mothers, sisters. I wanted to touch it, to feel the cold stone. There were so many names, I didn't know where to start looking. A soldier in battle fatigues stood next to me. He had tears on his cheeks. His friend told me there was a list in a book, alphabetical by name. And on the wall, by year.

1970. . . . The year my son was four. The wall was so high that year. I scanned the names, my eyes drifting from letter to letter. Bartle, O'Leary, Smith, Wadlowski, Cohen, Kelley, Collier, Jones, DuBois, DiMassio, Jackson, Lopez. I scanned the list of Americans and then I saw it and I felt my heart skip. Just one name, two words, about two feet from the bottom: DAVID MARKOVITCH.

I stooped down to touch it, to run my fingers over it and feel the indentations, the shape of the name that used to mean so much to me. As if feeling the letters would be proof that he was really dead, that the only place he existed now was in our memories, young forever, like the night he was king of the prom.

Margie knelt down beside me and she put her arms around me. She had made me come here. I really didn't want to. I didn't think I could, but she convinced me and she was right. As I laid down the flowers—the roses, the daisies, and the bachelor buttons—I could feel my eyes welling up with tears. Margie grabbed my hand and squeezed it hard.

"Someday, Mikey will come here," she said, her voice low and reverent as if she knew we were in a holy place.

Margie

"Del Monico Teacher of the Year" . . . I had come to the D.C. convention as a regular delegate from my school. But my sister . . . my sister was there to be honored. Winning all the prizes again! Some things never change.

We had both gotten our teaching degrees. Mo had

gone nights for eight years to Russell Sage in Troy and I had gone four years to State. We graduated the same year. Mom and Dad tried to convince me that it was harder to be summa cum laude at State than at Sage. "There's more competition at State," they said. But I knew better.

We both teach in the same district. I like teaching, but I have to admit I'm just doing it till I make enough money to pay for my tuition at N.Y.U.'s graduate program. It's taken me a while, but I'm going next fall. Mo's different. She's in teaching for the love. As Daddy says, "The apple doesn't fall far from the tree," and Mo, like Mom, is a natural teacher. That's why she's here getting trophies and I'm just here.

When we got back to our hotel room after the ceremony, there were two bouquets of flowers for Mo.

"Look, Marg, someone sent flowers," my sister said. "I wonder who?" She winked at me. We both knew.

"Congratulations, Irish Princess!" the first card, attached to the daisies, read. Mo smiled at me. "Will he ever stop calling us that?" she asked. She picked up the card attached to the roses, "To the most wonderful Wife and Mother, and Best Teacher in the World! Love, Mikey and Richard."

"I feel just like a celebrity," Mo said, sticking her nose into the roses. I watched her and I remembered the night of her senior prom, how she'd stuck her face right into the flowers that David Markovitch had sent.

THE IRISH PRINCESS

The night she was prom queen. My sister was born to be a celebrity.

"Mo! Let's order some champagne from room service to celebrate."

"We can't afford that, Margie," she chastised. Sometimes she can be so annoyingly practical.

"Well, maybe you can't, but I can," I announced. "I'm paying! This is my treat to you. My way of sending flowers." I went to the desk and picked up the room service menu. Fifty dollars! I tried not to gasp, but there was no backing out now. I had opened my big mouth and stuck my big foot right in. I called down the order.

The waiter came up with the ice bucket and two long-stemmed glasses. I even tipped him ten dollars. Hey, I thought, when you go for broke, go all the way.

We sat around in our nightgowns, sipping the champagne and getting a little silly, talking about our childhood memories, as we often do, retelling the funny stories of our family.

"Remember the day Mom took us to the Grove instead of church?" Mo asked and we both fell to giggling as we remembered the Easter-dinner brouhaha.

"Remember Aunt Bridey's hairdo?" I added, and we both howled with laughter, falling back on the bed, holding our sides, picturing our aunt's perfect beehive hairdo, so lacquered in place that it never moved. It just seemed so funny.

"Margie, remember the poem I wrote on water lilies for Mrs. Corcoran in sixth grade? And she thought it was so terrific she sent it to *The Weekly Reader* and I won that book on haiku?"

" 'Haiku'!" I screamed with laughter.

"I never opened it," Mo confessed.

"And now we're both English teachers," I added. Our sides hurt from laughing. Everything struck us as hilarious.

Not really thinking about what I was saying, I added, "Remember the poem I wrote on the day that Binky died? The one Mom said was a masterpiece?"

Mo stopped smiling and I could have smacked myself, for I knew what she was remembering then. The day that Binky died was the day she found out for sure that she was going to have a baby.

We looked at each other. The champagne, which had initially made us so happy, now pushed us into sadness. The room was so quiet I could hear my heartbeat. I needed to break the silence.

"Mo? Are you sorry the way things turned out?" I dared to ask.

"No, never. I'm never sorry," she said immediately, and I knew she was thinking of Mikey. "I mean, I'm not sorry I had Mikey or had to marry Richard. Not at all."

My sister bit her lip, and I knew from years of watching that meant there were things yet unsaid.

"But?" I encouraged gently.

"But," she added, "I wish David hadn't died. I wish he'd had a chance at life, too." Mo was looking down at the rings on her left hand. "Not for me, not for

Mikey, just for him. Such a waste of a beautiful person."

My sister let her head drop to her chest. I'd never seen her show such a physical display of defeat or grief. She's always been so determined and strong, I didn't think she had it in her, that kind of sorrow. I couldn't stand seeing her like that.

"Mo, get dressed," I commanded. I jumped up from the bed and pulled on my jeans and sweatshirt right over my nightgown. "We're going for a walk."

She looked at her watch. "It's after midnight," she said.

"I don't care," I answered. "We're going to the wall."

My sister sat there on the bed just looking at me. She didn't move a muscle. "I don't know if I can," she said.

Again, her reaction surprised me. I'd never seen such a lack of nerve on her part. Only bullying would work, I thought. "Get dressed, Mo. We're going," I ordered. "And let's bring the flowers. We're going back on the plane tomorrow. We can't take them with us," I reasoned. "We'll lay them there for David and our other friends."

The idea of the flowers won her over. I think it was the physical act of laying down the flowers, the act she could picture herself doing, that got her moving. She slipped on her skirt and her flats and looked at herself in the mirror. She pulled a brush through her long red hair and then pinned it back in a barrette. Her cheeks were flushed from the champagne. She looked so pretty standing there that I just admired her, the way she looked, the way she was.

She grabbed her tan raincoat and the flowers. "I'm ready," she said.

It was dark, but the path along the wall was lit. Even though it was after midnight, there were many people there. A soldier told us where to look for names. We found his name under 1970, the year he died. Mo and I knelt down and she touched the wall. I grabbed her hand and I could feel her shake, just a little. She was crying. I was, too. Everybody does in that place.

"Someday, Mikey can come here," I whispered.

Mo nodded and laid the flowers down. "Good-bye, David," she said and then she stood up and pulled me up, too.

It was over then. We had laid to rest the man who gave us Mikey. Just as we had done for so many others—our uncles, our little brother. We were done with grieving for a while.

"Let's go home," Mo said to me. At first I thought she meant back to the hotel, but as we walked I thought about what she said and I understood.

"Let's go home," I said.